'T... ...fully ...ustr... ... and
elegantl... ...novel' *Daily Telegraph*

'This clever, complex and emotionally rich novel is written in
simple but dense prose that is always readable'
Times Literary Supplement

'Martin . . . once again proves herself adept at blending
precise characterisation with shrewd plot twists' *Sunday Times*

'Valerie Martin writes beautifully and this novel is often
moving and heartfelt' *Sunday Telegraph*

'Valerie Martin's talent for showing how the meanderings
of day-to-day thoughts shape lives is at once authentic and
powerfully ironic' *Waterstone's Books Quarterly*

'Melancholy seeps into this novel – a thoughtful, outstanding
and sometimes hopeful story of love, regret and uncertainty.
Trespass is a very worthy follower to *Property*' *Herald*

'Valerie Martin elegantly combines the menace of physical,
emotional and ethical trespass in this penetrating novel,
whose serene echoes of Ian McEwan's *Saturday* are punctured
by visceral dispatches from the Balkans war' *Financial Times*

'Martin's writing is crisp and delicate' *Metro*

'Among the recent novels that tackle contemporary events,
Trepass is one of the best. The novel's gradual, teasing revelations will make you want to read it in one sitting' *Big Issue*

'Strung with measured menace' *Good Housekeeping*

'An absorbing family story' *Dublin Evening Herald*

Valerie Martin is the author of three collections of short fiction, most recently *The Unfinished Novel and Other Stories*, and seven novels, including the 2003 Orange Prize-winning *Property*, *Italian Fever*, *The Great Divorce* and *Mary Reilly*, the Dr Jekyll and Mr Hyde story told from the viewpoint of a housemaid, which was filmed with Julia Roberts and John Malkovich. She is also the author of a non-fiction work about St Francis of Assisi: *Salvation: Scenes from the Life of St Francis*. She lives in upstate New York.

Trespass

A Novel

VALERIE MARTIN

PHOENIX

A PHOENIX PAPERBACK

First published in Great Britain in 2007
by Weidenfeld & Nicolson
This paperback edition published in 2008
by Phoenix,
an imprint of Orion Books Ltd,
Orion House, 5 Upper St Martin's Lane,
London WC2H 9EA

An Hachette Livre UK company

1 3 5 7 9 10 8 6 4 2

A CIP catalogue record for this book
is available from the British Library.

ISBN 978-0-7538-2403-0

Printed and bound in Great Britain by
Clays Ltd, St Ives plc

The Orion Publishing Group's policy is to use papers that
are natural, renewable and recyclable products and
made from wood grown in sustainable forests. The logging
and manufacturing processes are expected to conform to
the environmental regulations of the country of origin.

www.orionbooks.co.uk

*For Christine Wiltz, who drove me down the river
to find the Oyster King*

I cannot tell you everything that we know. But what I can share with you, when combined with what all of us have learned over the years, is deeply troubling. What you will see is an accumulation of facts and disturbing patterns of behavior.

—COLIN POWELL at the United Nations
New York, February 6, 2003

PART ONE

Dark hair and lots of it, heavy brows, sharp features, dark eyes, dark circles under the eyes, dark looks about the room, at the maître d', the waitress, the trolley laden with rich, tempting desserts, and finally, as Toby guides her to the table, at Chloe, who holds out her hand and says pleasantly, though she is experiencing the first tentative pricks of the panic that will consume her nights and disrupt her days for some time to come, "Salome, how good to meet you."

The hand she grasps is lifeless and she releases it almost at once. Toby pulls a chair out, meeting his mother's eyes over the truncated handshake with a look she characterizes as defiant. "My mother, Chloe Dale," he says.

"Hello," the young woman says, sinking into the chair. Toby lays his fingers upon her shoulder, just for a moment, very much the proprietor, and Salome sends him a weak smile.

On the phone Toby said, "You'll like her. She's different. She's very serious."

Which meant this one was not an airhead like Belinda, who had ruined an entire summer the year before. On hearing Toby's description, Brendan warned, "Brace up. Young men go for extremes."

"That's true," Chloe agreed. "You certainly did." She recollected Brendan's mad poet and the bout with the anorexic alcoholic, but she herself had not been a model of probity—the misunderstood artist who read too much William Blake and spent a semester poring over accounts of the Manson murders in preparation for a series of lithographs depicting dismembered female bodies.

The waitress approaches, brandishing heavy, leather-backed menus. Toby reaches for one, so does Chloe. Salome keeps her hands in her lap, forcing the waitress to stretch across the table and slip it in place between the knife and fork. "Can I get you something to drink?" she inquires.

"Let's have a bottle of mineral water for the table," Chloe says, "and I'll have a glass of the white Bordeaux."

"That sounds good," Toby agrees. "I'll have the same."

Salome's eyes come up from the menu and rest on Toby's mouth. "Coffee," she says.

She doesn't drink. Is that a good sign?

"She lives on coffee," Toby chides indulgently, as if he's letting his mother in on some charming secret. Chloe studies the young woman, who has lowered her eyes to the menu again, a faint smile playing about her lips.

She's confident, Chloe thinks. "So, how did you meet?" she asks.

"We're in the same poli-sci class," Toby says. "It's a big lecture. I spotted Salome, but we didn't actually talk until we both showed up at a meeting to organize a campus antiwar group."

"That's good," Chloe says. "You won't have to go through boring arguments about politics."

"What kind of arguments?" Salome asks offhandedly, still studying the menu.

"About politics," Chloe replies. "You're already in agreement." The drinks arrive and the conversation is suspended while the waitress pours out the water, arranges wineglasses and Salome's coffee, which comes in a silver pot with a smaller silver pitcher of cream. "Shall I give you a few minutes to decide on your orders?" she asks.

"I think so?" Chloe says to her son, who replies, "Yes. I'm not ready yet." All three fall silent, concentrating on elaborate descriptions of food. "What are you having?" Chloe asks Toby.

"I'm not sure," he says. "Maybe the salmon."

Salome pushes the menu aside, nearly upsetting her water glass, but her reflexes are quick and she steadies it with a firm hand laid across the base. Her fingernails, Chloe notes, are short, filed straight across. For a moment all three are fascinated by this decisive movement—no, the glass is not going to tumble—then, for the first time, Salome directs upon Chloe the full force of her regard. It's unsettling, like seeing a spider darting out crazily from some black recess in the basement. "Why would an argument about politics necessarily be boring?" Salome asks, her voice carefully modulated, free of accusation, as if she's inquiring into some purely scientific matter—why does gravity hold everything down, why does light penetrate glass but not wood.

Toby is right. There is nothing ordinary about this young person. "Well, not necessarily," she concedes. "But sometimes when people disagree strongly on principle, and there's no reconciliation possible, it can get pretty dull, pretty . . ." she pauses, looking for the noninflammatory word . . . "unproductive."

"Salome loves to argue about politics," Toby observes, temporizing, as is his way.

Lives on coffee, loves to argue. Could there be a connection?

"I don't actually love it," Salome corrects him. "But when it's necessary, I never find it boring."

Fast work. Chloe now stands accused of calling Toby's new love interest boring.

She takes a sip of her wine, casting her eyes about the room in search of the waitress. It's an attractive, tastefully appointed room, richly paneled, with dark, solid furnishings, damask cloths, strategic flower arrangements, and the glint of glass and copper. The food is excellent, though, of course, absurdly expensive. She chose Mignon's because she knows Toby likes it, and it's close to the university. She took the train, an hour and a half to Grand Central, and then another twenty minutes on the subway, which put her four crosstown blocks from Mignon's. It's twelve forty-five, she has an appointment midtown with her editor at three thirty, plenty of time for a leisurely lunch with her son and his new girlfriend. It's intended as a treat for them; they're students who eat grim cafeteria food or the cheap and nourishing fare served in Ukrainian restaurants on the Lower East Side. Her eyes settle on Toby, who looks anxious, pretending interest in the menu. She turns to Salome, who is ladling sugar into her black coffee, two full teaspoons.

She feels a stab of pity for the young woman, so clearly out of her element and on the defensive. Meeting the boyfriend's mother is never fun; for one thing, one gets to see one's lover transformed into some older woman's son. But it could be so much worse, she wants to tell Salome. You should have seen my mother-in-law, a true harridan, and the worst part was that Brendan thought his mother was fascinating and acted like a giddy puppy in her presence, falling all over himself in his effort to please her. Whereas Chloe is charming, everyone says so, and her relations with her son are genial. These self-congratulatory musings relax her, and when Salome raises her cup to her lips, darting a quick, nervous glance at Chloe over the rim, she sends the girl a sympathetic smile. "You're right," she says. "Politics is serious. Especially in these dismal times."

"Can you believe the arrogance of this clown!" Toby exclaims. "Now we don't need the United Nations. The rest of the world is just irrelevant."

"He's a puppet," Salome says. "The dangerous ones are standing right behind him."

The waitress appears, ready to take their orders. Chloe feels a quiver of interest in Salome's choice; doubtless she is a vegetarian. Toby orders the salmon; Chloe her usual duck salad. The waitress, a bright-eyed redhead—why couldn't Toby fall for someone like her?—looks attentively at Salome, her pen poised above her pad.

"I'll have the Caesar salad, no anchovies," Salome says.

Very pure, Chloe will tell Brendan. No alcohol, no meat, no fish.

The waitress retreats. Toby takes a roll from the bread basket and begins slathering it with butter. "There's going to be an antiwar rally in the park on the fifteenth," he says. "We've got about eighty people signed up already."

"Excellent," Chloe says. "I'll tell your father. He's so enraged, he needs an outlet."

Toby nods, stuffing half the roll into his mouth. He is always hungry. He developed an appetite when he was fifteen, it's never let up, and he still doesn't have an ounce of fat on him. Chloe takes up the basket and offers it to Salome, who chooses a wheat roll and places it carefully on Chloe's bread plate. If she takes no bread herself, Chloe reasons, the girl will never know her mistake. "Are you majoring in political science too?" she asks, setting the basket close to her son.

"No," Salome replies. "International relations, with an emphasis on the Balkans."

"How unusual."

"She's a Croat," Toby announces.

Chloe takes this information in quietly, uncertain how to respond. Does it explain the passion for politics? Are Croats Muslims? "But you don't have an accent," she says.

"I grew up in Louisiana," Salome says.

Croats in Louisiana? Chloe thinks.

"Her father is the Oyster King," Toby says.

Chloe takes another sip of her wine, thinking of the Tenniel illustration of the Walrus and the Carpenter inviting an attentive clutch of unwary oysters *for a pleasant walk, a pleasant talk, along the briny beach.* "What made you decide to come to New York?" she asks.

"I got a scholarship."

"She's very smart," Toby adds needlessly.

"It must be quite a change for you," Chloe observes. "Do you like it here?"

For a moment Salome's eyes meet Chloe's, but distantly, disengaging at once in favor of a leisurely survey of the room, as if her answer depended upon the framed photographs of Parisian street scenes arranged along the far wall, the quality of the table linens, the low hum of chatter from the other diners, the neat white blouse of the waitress, who, Chloe notices with relief, is approaching their table, skillfully balancing three plates, on one of which she recognizes her duck salad. For God's sake, she thinks, impatience constricting her throat around a jumble of words that must not be said, I wasn't asking for your opinion of this restaurant. Toby sits back in his chair, his eyebrows lifted in anticipation, waiting, now they are both waiting, for the verdict of this odd, dark creature he has extracted, it now appears, from some refugee swamp and set down before his mother in a perfectly respectable corner of New York. Salome's eyes pass over his attentive face and settle upon her coffee cup, which is empty. She lifts the silver pot and pours a ribbon of black liquid into the porcelain cup. "Not much," she says.

"You see," Toby chides Salome when they are on the sidewalk watching his mother disappear into the ceaseless flow of pedestrians. "That wasn't so bad."

"I don't think she liked me," Salome says.

"She likes who I like," Toby assures her, though this is not, strictly speaking, true. He knows his mother won't criticize any friend of his to his face, but that doesn't mean she has no feelings in the matter. He hadn't expected Salome to charm his mother, but he'd assumed they would find some obscure common ground of femaleness to ease the inevitable tension. That hadn't happened, and not, he admits, for lack of trying on his mother's part. Salome leans into him so that he feels the soft give of her breast against his arm. She is embarrassed that she acquitted herself poorly, he concludes, and anxious that he might be displeased.

"It doesn't matter," she says. As they turn south, toward the university, she slips her hand into his. At the light she reaches up to touch his cheek, and, when he looks down, rises up on her toes to brush his lips with her own. He accepts the kiss, bringing his hand to her chin to hold her lips to his a moment longer. They have two hours before his roommate will return from his job, and they will spend them sprawled on the futon that takes up most of the space allotted to Toby. It is a perfect fall day, cool and dry; the leaves on the stunted trees plugged into squares of colorless, vitrified dirt along the sidewalk have already turned an anemic yellow. Toby wants to sprint the few blocks to the apartment just to have a few more minutes of being in bed with Salome. He passes his arm around her back, urging her to a speedier pace. The fineness of the bones beneath her skin, the slenderness of her waist, send a shiver of excitement from his stomach to his groin. She is right; it doesn't matter what his mother thinks of her, or his father, or anyone else for that matter. That they will feel strongly, one way or the other, is inevitable, because Salome is so entirely different from any woman he has ever known. Compared to the officious graduates of expensive prep schools who are made anxious by her opinions, the city denizens with their tongue studs and tattoos, the scholarship girls from the Midwest who greet one another with shouts and hugs after an hour apart, Salome is a jaguar among nervous chickens. "Pretty exotic, Toby," his roommate observed upon meeting her. "Are you sure you've got the energy for that?"

He doesn't deny that she's difficult. She has few friends, only her roommates, two theater majors she dismisses with a wave of the hand. Her room, formerly a walk-in closet, is hung with embroidered pictures. There's a shelf crammed with statues of her favorite saints and votive candles, which she lights to solicit favors. On Sundays she wraps her hair in a lace shawl and goes off to Mass at the Croatian church on 51st Street, after which she receives her weekly call from her father, the Oyster King. While she talks, Toby stretches out on her narrow mattress, baffled by her harsh, impenetrable language. Her voice rises to a shout, she sounds furious—he can't imagine what it would feel like to address either of his parents with so much force—then abruptly she is calm and affectionate. The conversation invariably ends with what he takes to be cooing endearments.

When she waits for him in the coffee shop, she passes the time crocheting lace squares which she will give out to the professors who earn her admiration. Those who displease her must put up with such serious and close questioning that they blanch when they see her hand shoot up in the midst of her somnolent peers.

She brings the same energy and essential forthrightness to the minimalist bedroom where they will soon pounce on each other with feline exuberance, tussling for the fun of it. She will start throwing off her clothes as soon as they are inside the door, pulling Toby toward the bed with an impatience that delights him. Her hair falling over his face smells of cloves, the perfume of her skin is complex, warm, spicy. When she wraps her arms and legs around his back, she holds him so tightly he can feel the taut vibration of her muscles, and her breath in his ear is quick and even to the end.

As they turn the last corner to the apartment, his mother is the farthest thing from his mind, so it surprises him when Salome says, "What I don't understand is why your mother volunteered your father for the rally. Why doesn't she come herself? Is she afraid she'll get arrested?"

"No, no," he assures her. "She'll come. That's a given."

"Why? So she can find it boring?"

They have arrived at the doorway, two concrete steps to a barricade of bars and steel plate. Toby digs in his pocket for the keys, releasing Salome, who perches on the step behind him, glowering at the poor scrap of blighted grass enclosed by a ragged bit of chain-link fence. "Jesus," Toby says, jamming the first of the keys into the lock. "Why did you jump all over her about that? She was just trying to make conversation."

"I didn't jump all over her," she replies. "I just asked her what the hell she meant."

The first bolt clicks; Toby yanks the gate open, dislodging Salome from her step. "It's obvious what she meant," he retorts. The scene replays in his memory at such a volume that the whole restaurant has stopped dead, bearing witness to the outrage against his mother. "She meant it was nice that you and I agree about politics, that we don't argue about politics. It was a perfectly innocent observation, Salome. She didn't say politics was boring, or that you were boring. She said arguing was boring, and she's right about that." Locks two and three give way before the force of this reasoning, and Toby shoves the heavy door open with a grunt.

"It was a condescending thing to say," Salome insists to his back. He charges into the foyer, making straight for the steps without looking back, leaving her to close the gate, the door, and follow. "It was condescending," she repeats, trudging up the stairs behind him. "She wanted to make sure I understood she doesn't care about what I care about."

Toby takes the next flight two steps at a time, a final key gripped in his fist. At the door he slides it into the lock, looking down at Salome in the dim light of the stairwell. Her head is lowered; her white hand grips the rail as she climbs toward him. A sensation of pity mixed with consternation assails him, dampening the desire he felt on the sidewalk as thoroughly as a hand laid flat across a vibrating string. "Look, Salome," he says. "It was very thoughtful of my mother to invite us to lunch. Mignon's is a good restaurant and not cheap, and she did it because she wanted to show us a nice time. She's a nice woman. She likes to make people comfortable, she doesn't have ulterior motives."

"If she wanted to make us comfortable, why didn't she choose someplace where a normal person would be comfortable?" Salome arrives at the landing, where she pauses to push her hair back from her eyes. "What's comforting about paying twenty dollars for a salad?"

"You didn't have to pay for it," he snaps, blocking the doorway so that she is forced to look up at him. "She paid for it; she can afford it; it was a gift. She took us there because she knows I like it. I'm a normal person, and I like it."

"So you take her side," Salome says calmly.

"There's no side to take," he exclaims. She pushes past him into the dimly lit space that comprises the sitting room and kitchen and goes straight to the sink, where she takes a glass from the dish rack and fills it with water.

Toby pauses in the open doorway, precisely representing the state of his emotions: he could go in or out, he could pursue this argument, their first, or close it down, he could take the glass of water from her hand, set it in the sink, and lead her to his room, or he could dash the water into her face. Each option has a certain appeal. She swallows half the glass, watching him indifferently as he stands there in an agony of indecision. Then, still frowning, she brings her free hand to her collar and begins unbuttoning her blouse. In the next moment Toby observes that she is wearing the black lace bra that fastens at the front. He steps into the room and closes the door behind him, facing it only long enough to shoot the bolt into the lock.

"How did it go?" Brendan inquires, examining the return addresses on the four envelopes Chloe lays, one by one, before him. "Nothing but bills," he adds.

"Good," she says. "He loves the novel and doesn't know much about engraving. I think he'll let me have my way. I keep thinking the whole thing should have the feel of thorns and rough bark."

"That might be hard on the reader," Brendan observes. He angles his cheek to receive the brief kiss she offers him. "But I meant the lunch, the new girlfriend."

"Not promising," she says. "Very weird actually. She's a Croat; does that mean she's a Muslim?"

"A Croat? No. Croats are mostly Catholics. Where is she from?"

"Louisiana," Chloe says, making for the door. She doesn't want to talk about Toby's girlfriend one minute more than is absolutely necessary.

"Well, then she's not a Croat, darling. She's an American of Croatian descent."

"Toby said she was a Croat and she didn't object," Chloe says. "Her father is the 'Oyster King.' "

"This gets better and better."

"Probably a vegetarian, rabid about politics, drank four cups of coffee with lunch, majoring in international relations, emphasis on the Balkans, definitely sleeping with Toby."

"Emphasis on the Balkans?"

"I knew that part would get your attention."

"Whereas the sleeping with Toby part got yours." Brendan smiles at her maternal jitters.

"She's very abrupt," Chloe says.

"Was she rude to you?"

"Not exactly. She just made me feel . . ."

Brendan swivels his desk chair to face her. As he waits for the word that will describe how Toby's new girlfriend made Chloe feel, he stretches his long legs out across the carpet.

"I don't know," Chloe concludes. "Creepy."

"Creepy," he repeats, without emphasis.

Chloe tries again. "Uncomfortable."

"What's her name again?" he asks. "Something heartless and biblical, isn't it? Delilah? Lilith?"

"Salome," Chloe says and Brendan nods. "Salome Drago."

"That's got to be shortened from something. It's probably Dragonovich, something like that."

"Which would mean what?"

"Ovich is son of," he speculates.

"Son of a dragon?"

Brendan shrugs.

Chloe shifts her canvas bag from one shoulder to the other.

"Son of a dragon and daughter of the Oyster King," Brendan says. "I can't wait to meet her."

"It won't last," Chloe predicts.

"No," Brendan agrees. "Seems unlikely, doesn't it?" His eyes wander away, back to the clutter of pads and books on his desk.

"How's the crusade?" Chloe asks, hoping the answer will be brief.

Brendan takes up his glasses. "Frederick's about to cut a deal with the Sultan al-Kamil for the city of Jerusalem."

"That can't last either," she says.

"It'll last eight years, which is better than we'll see again anytime soon."

Jerusalem, Chloe thinks. If only God would send down a new tablet telling which set of outraged refugees are the "real" chosen people.

"I'm going to work for a bit," she says. Brendan raises his fingers over his page, something between a dismissal and a farewell wave, his attention already absorbed by his companion of choice, Frederick of Hohenstaufen, the thirteenth-century emperor whose puissance and cunning so confounded his contemporaries that they called him *Stupor Mundi*, the wonder of the world.

As Chloe comes into the clearing, she spooks a doe, which eyes her for scarcely a moment before crashing off into the underbrush. She crosses to the narrow deck, strewn with crimson and yellow leaves, and lets herself in at the glass door. Autumn is a contradictory season, she thinks, dropping her bag on the worktable, setting the kettle to boil on the hot plate. The explosion of colors, the ionized, energizing air; it feels like a promise of something, but autumn bodes ill for all living creatures. The days are already shortening; it is only five thirty and the room is gloomy. She will have to turn on the light. She takes her mug from the sideboard, glancing about the cluttered room as she opens the tea packet. Now is the time to clear everything out from the last project, the wretched children's cookbook she took on because the money was good and the art director an old friend. She had little pleasure in the job. The dummy came to her with the illustrations specified. She has an ersatz child in her repertoire, a serenely smiling, genderless creature who can be made to look mischievous or serious with an adjustment of the eyebrows. There were five of these children in the cookbook, one brown, of course, one vaguely Asiatic with straight black hair, all mixing things in bowls, running blenders, flipping pancakes, and, in the final spread, gorging themselves on brownies.

Good riddance, Chloe thinks, and now banish all color. She opens the canvas bag and reaches inside, feeling a curious, almost cinematic thrill as her fingers discover, lodged between the drawing pad and the wallet, the paperback novel she picked up at the bookshop in the train station. A legend floats up on an imaginary screen—*With tremulous fingers the artist undertakes the definitive project.* She extracts the novel and examines the cover. The windblown tree stretching menacing branches over the figure of a woman struggling against the force of the blast is, she discovers, a detail from a painting by Corot, *The Gust of Wind*, which, by some process, doubtless involving theft and war, is currently in the possession of the Pushkin Museum in Moscow.

It's a cheap paperback, with minimal apparatus, and the virtue of being small. It will be in her pocket every day for the next six months, to be perused in every spare moment, marked with yellow and blue highlighters, indexed with sticky tabs, its spine broken, its pages stained with coffee and ink. Brendan calls her method "billeting the book," not a bad description, as she is not seeking to memorize or critique the text, but to inhabit it. It is to become, for the duration, the terrain of her imagination.

The kettle shrieks. Obediently she lifts it from the burner and pours the boiling water into the mug. Her eyes rest on the framed watercolor over the counter, a prequel to the pinecones that served as endpapers for the children's *Walden*, the poorly paid, entirely absorbing job she believes has led her to this one. "Thank you, Henry David," she whispers. Her *Walden* didn't win any prizes, but it was a finalist for three of them and sold well. It is an elegantly made book; Chloe controlled every detail of it, and Professor Warnick, the scholar who excerpted the original text, told her he thought it a pity it was relegated to the children's section. She had immersed herself in the life of the great eccentric, read two weighty biographies, twice driven down to Princeton for long conversations with Professor Warnick, and then, armed with his letter of introduction, driven up to Harvard and Concord to examine the surviving papers.

The jacket and binding of the book are sap green, but inside all is sepia. She had done a hundred drawings and a dozen watercolor sketches in preparation for the twenty engravings; it took her the better part of a year. It is a small book, modest in scope, spare in design, suitable for the dictums of an ascetic who saw no point in having more than two chairs in his sitting room. She had achieved a Buddhistic detachment as she worked, an elemental restraint and serenity she hopes to call up again in the work ahead.

Taking her mug and the novel, she settles into the reading chair next to the cold woodstove. On the train she read the introduction, with its summary of the criticism over the years, including a bibliography worth investigating. Then there was the "biographical notice," a self-serving and cowardly piece of work, in Chloe's view, such as one might expect from an unimaginative parent, but not from the author's sister, who was a novelist herself and should have known better. At least the author, having lived only long enough to see the force of her imagination reviled in the pages of the London press, had been spared the humiliation of reading her sister's lame defense.

Even so, Emily Brontë had been more successful than poor Thoreau, who furnished his bookshelves with most of the first printing of *Walden*. Another glance at the biographical note informs Chloe of a surprising fact: Emily Brontë was born just a year after Thoreau, and likewise in a backwater, though the wind-lashed parsonage at Haworth was more removed from the world of commerce than Concord. Could two more disparate sensibilities ever have occupied the planet at the same time? Thoreau, all patient observation, ironic, obstreperous, oddly genial; Brontë, rebellious, passionate, chilly, imperious, raised on fantastic tales in a house with a graveyard at the front door. Yet both could not bear being housed, both felt more at ease in a windstorm than by the fireside, both were unemployable, constitutionally solitary. Even with the time difference, there must have been many hours of many days when the youthful Henry and Emily were both out walking in bad weather, Henry occasionally accompanied by a friend, Emily by a dog.

A walk with Henry and Emily. Chloe closes the book and gazes out past the deck at the woodland path, overarched by maples, horse chestnut, and beech, all weeping particolored leaves. They would have hated each other. She would have thought him dry and lifeless, and he would have dismissed her as self-absorbed and irrational.

The sharp report of a rifle, very close, jolts Chloe from this critical speculation. A pause tempers the air, followed by three more shots in rapid succession. "Bastard," Chloe exclaims, leaping to her feet. In her haste to rush across the deck, she bangs her shin cruelly against the hob of the woodstove. "Damn," she says.

❖❖

Mike stalks purposefully along the drive, shoulders low, head lifted at an angle to accommodate the struggles of the doomed creature clamped in his merciless jaws. Murder, Brendan thinks, turning from the window. What is it? A vole, a chipmunk? Mike is relentless, the terror of the world beneath his paws. If Chloe saw him, she would wrest the wounded creature from him, fighting nature, tooth and claw. If the animal died, she would spend a few hours sketching the furry or feathered corpse, then take out the shovel and bury it. This, in Brendan's view, is a gruesome, unnecessary routine, though he understands that for artists the dead subject is desirable, as it is unlikely to move. Chloe has a whole book of sketches she did in the hospital when her mother was dying; the last, she confessed to Brendan, completed in the two or three minutes between the moment when she knew her subject had departed this life and the moment when she got up and went out to notify the night nurse.

At the coffee urn, Brendan refills his cup, idly stirs in a spoon of sugar, keeping his back to the world of death outside. Even the slanting golden light, the shimmering shower of leaves, which is continuous now, heralds the cruel, frigid darkness to come. It is fine weather for walking, but he is condemned to his study, trying, not unlike Chloe, to wrest from the world of the dead the image of a living, breathing potentate.

In the hall, he experiences a moment of professional angst. Though it passes quickly—he is not given to brooding—it is as suffocating as a mouthful of ash. What is the point of dredging about in the past? What difference does it make to anyone living if he disagrees with Bowker about the cause of Frederick's delay in entering the Fifth Crusade? It doesn't matter to Bowker, who is as dead as Frederick. Nor is there any sense in which Brendan's opinion can be said to rely upon solid evidence; he can't prove that Frederick's fascination with the East and distaste for the cynical machinations of the papacy made him reluctant to set out for Jerusalem or that the pope ultimately excommunicated the emperor because he had proved too soft on Islam.

And even if he could prove it, who would care?

He drops into his chair, sloshing the coffee on the page of scrawl he's been working over all morning. Dabbing at it with his handkerchief, which will now be stained and unsightly, he gives himself up to gloom. There's a photograph of Toby on the desk, clowning at his high-school graduation, his mortarboard at a slant, his smile goofy and winning. It is a picture that usually cheers Brendan, but now it only reminds him of the president's bragging to the assembly of students and faculty at his Ivy League college that he had not studied much in school, not even gone to class. Chloe read the article to him, then crumpled the newspaper and threw it on the floor. "Crass, insulting, stupid, empty-headed prick!" she cried.

This recollection is comforting, Brendan admits, folding the damp handkerchief and jamming it back into his pocket. His wife's outrage is a source of solace to him, though it sometimes exasperates Toby, who believes in the possibility of change in the world.

Toby, Brendan thinks confidently, and then, with less assurance, Chloe.

The likelihood that Chloe will be dissatisfied with any girl Toby cares for is so strong as to be something of a joke between them. It's natural enough, Brendan supposes. Toby is an only child, Chloe an indulgent mother, but her distrust of his judgment augurs a dismal future. In high school there were three girlfriends: a Japanese pianist, something of a prodigy; a powerful redhead who rode horses; and a feisty blonde who intended to become a great actress. Brendan was impressed by the range of his son's taste; in Chloe's view each girl presented insurmountable difficulties. The Japanese, a hypochondriac, was always sick, the equestrian not very bright, and the actress fatally self-absorbed. Though his mother was unfailingly polite to each of these young women, Toby had perhaps caught on. In his first year at the university, he hadn't brought a single girlfriend home to visit. His classes were large, his subjects varied, and the burning question in his mind was where to settle. He was good at many things; he had his father's aptitude for languages, his mother's draftsman's eye. Architecture appealed to him briefly, then philosophy. In his sophomore year he took a course in political science that ignited his imagination, and he began to see himself as someone who might change the world. At least, he declared, he did not want to hide from it. Brendan thought this assertion contained a reproach to his parents, the artist and the academic, who passed their lives buried in books and ink, absorbed in the past, timorous in the present, indifferent to the future. But the many summers the family spent abroad, Brendan in pursuit of dead kings, Chloe of light, have, after all, made an impression on their son: Toby contemplates a future in international law.

Belinda Stanford appeared just after Christmas of Toby's sophomore year and lasted into the summer. Chloe loathed her on sight; Brendan gave her the benefit of steadily mounting doubt. She was rich, bossy, and wholly false. She insisted that the Dales spend their summer in her family's cabin in Maine, making the offer irresistible by arranging, through her connections,

a job for Toby at a posh hotel. When Chloe showed little interest in the offer, Toby arrived home on the weekend with a
package of photographs of a log cabin on a lake with a wide
porch and steps down to a secluded boat landing. Each picture
was labeled in Belinda's careful print: *the kitchen, the bedroom, the
stone steps.*

After dinner, Toby, clearly persuaded of the virtues of this
scheme, presented the photos one by one to Chloe, who
passed them on to Brendan. He knows his mother, Brendan
thought as he examined the undeniably attractive screened
porch. Money was tight, tuition was high, and Toby's job, which
would pay enough to cover his rent for the fall term, would
provide much needed relief. All three would feel the financial
benefit of Toby's plan and now he had come up with a further
benefit that would allow them to pass a pleasant summer together at small expense. "Maine is lovely," Chloe said, turning
over the photograph of *the view.*

Brendan, pouring out a thimbleful of the Calvados they had
brought back from Normandy the year before, nodded at his
son. I hardly know him, he thought. He's making himself up
on his own now.

The Maine adventure was a fiasco, which Toby referred to
wryly as a "learning experience." It rained continually and
when the sun did find an opportunity to appear, it was fierce.
The lake was shrouded with a steam of mosquitoes. There
were holes in the screens, holes in the boat; the cabin was air-
less and damp. Belinda demanded that the Dales join her family daily for lunch at their "regular" restaurant, a noisome eatery
where one paid a lot of money for small portions of very bad
food. At Toby's hotel the guests were all in foul humor because

of the rain, and the staff, minimal at best, was increasingly overworked and hysterical. Toby's essential competence and stolidity endeared him to his employers, though not sufficiently to raise his minimum wage. He worked ten hours a day, six days a week, and fell into the narrow cot at the dormitory provided by the management too exhausted to move. But Belinda was intensely conscious of every hour in the twenty-four allotted to a day and determined that a summer in Maine meant play; and play meant arduous hikes in the rain up and down the rocky trails, or furious sets of tennis on the indoor court at her family's club. Gradually it became clear that the Dales, though adequate lunch company and tennis partners, were not up to the standard that resulted in an invitation to the cool sanctum of the Stanfords' "cottage." Chloe and Brendan were driven past it on several occasions, or rather past the iron gates through which they could make out, at the end of a tree-shaded drive, ivy-covered stone walls and the glitter of the ocean. They were informed by the always informative Belinda that the house was simply "packed with Mommy's friends."

They lasted a week. On Sunday, Brendan and Chloe arrived at the cabin, weary from hiking, to find their son idly batting mosquitoes on the screened porch. It was the first time the three had been unsupervised since their arrival and they greeted one another almost shyly. "Mom, Dad," Toby said as they sloughed off their sneakers and sank into the damp cushions of the wicker chairs, "this place is hell. Go home."

"What about Belinda's parents?" Chloe asked cautiously.

Toby grimaced. "Have you ever met worse people!" he exclaimed. "They're like caricatures of people."

"Oh, thank heaven." Chloe sighed.

"What about Belinda?" Brendan asked.

For answer Toby covered his eyes with his hand and groaned.

"Will you come with us?" Chloe asked.

"No. I'm making too much money to quit. I think I'll just take off the last week and go to the cape with David."

David was Toby's cousin, the closest thing he had to a brother, and the cape was a ramshackle beach house in Truro, where the boys had spent the last week before school since they were children. Relief was palpable on the screened porch. Toby had returned to the fold and, as if to announce the accord of nature, the clouds parted and a shaft of bright sunlight swept across the placid water of the lake to the rickety boat dock below.

On the long drive home, Chloe was triumphant. She entertained Brendan with various scenarios in which Toby was corrupted and abducted by the Stanfords, never to be seen again. He agreed that they were a banal, acquisitive, and manipulative family, also patronizing and smug, but he thought their rudeness might be as much the result of a determination to rid their family of Toby as an effort to spirit him into their familial malaise. Another possibility was that the Stanfords were actually what they seemed, free of calculation, possessed only by an impenetrable indifference to the world around them. That they were intent on anything struck Brendan as unlikely. He advanced this proposition over the lunch table in Portsmouth as Chloe skillfully dismantled another lobster, but she was having none of it. "Those people are monsters," she concluded, and Brendan felt a shiver of anxious sympathy. Who was it for? For Toby? For Chloe? Or was it for himself?

To her credit, Chloe doesn't allow her son access to the

darker precincts of her maternal fantasies; it's a policy of hers. If Toby invites this new girl, Salome is it? to visit his family, he won't suspect that his mother's heart is already set against her.

Brendan gazes down at the ceaselessly rotating neon pixels on the computer screen and past it to the window, where another bright leaf flutters to its death. He looks over the scratchy page he had abandoned in hopes that a shot of caffeine would enliven his style. Deadening stuff, though it shouldn't be. The Fifth Crusade was coming to a close. When Frederick arrived in Jerusalem, he stayed up all night to hear the muezzins call to prayer. But the Sultan al-Kamil, out of respect for his Christian guest, had ordered the muezzins to keep silent. When Frederick learned of this, he was furious; he made a public scene. The sultan in turn was deeply offended. A classic misunderstanding, the details of which had survived seven hundred years. Brendan takes up his pen and scratches out the last sentence. He rubs his chin, gazing out the window. Another leaf.

The shots, plosive and sharp, echo out concentrically, as water eludes a sudden stone. Pow. A pause. Then three more. Pow. Pow. Pow.

"For God's sake," Brendan says.

Toby and Salome clasp hands at the edge of the sidewalk, waiting for the light to change. Around them their fellow students engage in casual banter, good-natured shoving. They have spent the last four hours drinking coffee amid stacks of books, grilling one another on dates, places, names, and arcane religious distinctions. Every one of them knows the difference between a Shia and a Druse. Now they are going to drink quantities of beer and talk about themselves. The air is crisp; their spirits are high, not one among them has buttoned a coat or wrapped a scarf against the chill air. "Why are the Christians called Phalangists?" a tall blonde asks her neighbors, only to be shouted down by cries of "No more Lebanon!" and "Because they have fingers" as the light changes to green and they sweep into the street.

Salome shifts her hand to the inside of Toby's arm, drawing close to him as they walk. He smiles down upon the top of her head. What is she thinking? He has no idea, yet feels no anxiety. Like the blonde, he is still engaged by the recent and savage history they have been drumming into one another.

The group achieves the opposite curb, the traffic filling in behind them, intense yet orderly. An elderly woman walking a chow pauses, unfolding a page of newsprint as the animal squats on the pavement. Not long ago, passing a similarly preoccupied gentleman, expensively coiffed and stylishly attired, distinguished in features and bearing, crouched over a stinking pile of feces while his impatient poodle danced at the end of his leash, Toby observed to his mother, "If New Yorkers can be persuaded to pick up after their dogs, there's hope for the world."

The vanguard of students arrives at the bar, surging through the opaque glass door. Behind Toby there is laughter; Salome's hand on his arm urges him forward. His stomach growls, he is light-headed, the result of too much coffee. This place serves cheap pseudo-Mexican food, lots of beans, cheese, and avocados. It can't hurt, he reasons.

Salome releases him and goes ahead through the door, saying something to Bruce Macalister, the excitable Marxist. Then
they are all inside, swarming around the tables, pulling out
chairs, calling out to the indifferent waitress who idles before
the barman as he fills the first of many pitchers of beer. Toby
falls into the nearest chair; Salome takes the one next to him.
She is still talking to Macalister, who leans toward her, his expression animated, as it so often is, by an earnestness Toby
finds irritating. It can't be denied that Macalister is sincere and
energetic. He has organized this study group, he is forever
sending out e-mails to keep the antiwar group apprised of the
latest events, on weekends he works in a soup kitchen. A med-
dler, in Toby's opinion, full of enthusiasms and unrealistic
ideals, contentious and dangerous, something rodentic about
him, relentlessly gnawing and scurrying, carping about dialect-
ical materialism, praxis, and the evils of capitalism. He sees the
implosion of Lebanon entirely in terms of class struggle,
which strikes Toby as reductive. For one thing, the shifts of al-
legiances in Lebanon during the sixties and seventies were so
confusing the study group resorted to making a chart to figure
it out. Christians allied with Jews against Muslims, nothing unusual in that, but the Shia split. The older ulamas sought pro-
tection from the Christian Phalangists and got it. Then every
man was armed, each had a sacred loyalty to a militia or sect,
and all hell broke loose.

Beirut was the fulcrum; the struggle for the country was for
Beirut. Whenever one group captured a block or two, they
chased everyone out, looted, and then leveled the buildings.
Women were constantly running from place to place, screaming, weeping, clutching children. A riot broke out in a church

when a Sunni militia attacked Shia squatters, who refused to run because they had no place else to hide. In the mayhem, the church was destroyed. One account described a battle that went on for days between two militias attempting to secure a wide avenue to the sea. Finally, after heavy losses on both sides, the victors arrived at the water's edge, where they celebrated by taking a swim.

Beirut was their city, ancient and proud, the "pearl of the Middle East," and they demolished it utterly, but all Macalister noticed was that, as the streets turned to wreckage and ash and the citizens dodged bullets to buy a loaf of bread, the rich retreated to their summer houses in the mountains.

Toby fills his glass from one of the pitchers lined up along the table and takes a long swallow as he contemplates the Marxist, now spinning out his shopworn dialectics to his fellows. Revolution is inevitable throughout the world, he announces. Toby leans close to Salome and whispers, "What an ass this guy is." The glance she gives him is an icy dart; she is not amused. The Marxist warms to his theme.

Does she take this Macalister seriously? Does she admire him? Across the table Susan Davies, the tall blonde, attends to the Marxist with a shy smile. Cities, Macalister maintains, intensify the iniquities of capitalism; all over the world cities are the tinderboxes smoldering to ignite the coming conflagration. Next to Susan, Brent—Toby doesn't know his last name, but he's a Southerner, possibly a Virginian—laughs his genial Southern laugh and says, "Revolution in Manhattan?"

Toby catches Brent's eye, gives him a conspiratorial nod. This should quash the Marxist, but it only encourages him. "Why not?" he replies. "Why not here? Aren't there enough poor immigrants crowded into miserable, rat-infested, over-priced rooms who fall asleep from exhaustion every night thinking, 'I risked my life to live in this hell?' Aren't there mad-men enough, armed and dangerous, enough guns and ammu-nition and religious fanatics, all ready and eager to exterminate the other fanatics down the block? The suffering is here, the anger is here. What's missing is a cadre of professional revolu-tionaries to serve as the vanguard of the working class."

"Civil war in Manhattan," Brent suggests to general amuse-ment. "The Village laid waste by a battalion from Soho."

"Night skirmishes in Central Park between the squadrons from the Upper East and West Side," Toby puts in.

Salome takes up her glass and sucks at the foam on the top. He can't see her face, but he doesn't think she's laughing. Mac-alister, to his credit, takes the ribbing with good grace. "The East Village could use a buffer zone," he says. "You can't deny that."

Someone observes that the battle in the East Village would be between the junkies and the rats, and the conversation shifts to tales of break-ins and drug-addicted supers; even the Marx-ist has a story to tell. Groups of two or three break off, their complaints unintelligible in the general din as the plates of soft tortillas filled with beans and cheese appear between the pitch-ers. Toby leans into Salome, pulling off a section and laying it on a paper plate. "Do you want a slice?"

"Sure," she says, setting down her glass. Toby slides the plate in front of her. Purposefully he bends over the table so that he can look into her face. Her expression is solemn, her eyes low-ered. "Everything OK?" he asks. In the same moment the Marxist brings his mouth close to her ear and whispers some-thing Toby can't hear. Her eyes come up, a sly, complicit smile spreads across her lips. She rests her hand upon the Marxist's forearm and whispers to him, turning her back on her lover's friendly question.

Toby sinks in his chair. He has half a mind to get up and walk out, but that would be too dramatic a gesture. He chews his tortilla, which tastes like a wad of resignation. She has no concept of manners; it's as if she was raised by hyenas. Is he to bear her rudeness without complaint? Will that forestall another argument? Which does he dislike more, rude treatment or pointless arguments?

In the first weeks of their affair, such dispiriting choices didn't present themselves; there was only the shock of recognition, the novelty of being swept along without the necessity for resistance by an attraction both powerful and mutual. He recognized that she was inadequately socialized, that she unsettled the placid scene around her, but this amused him; he was no great fan of the proprieties. He considers Susan Davies, who is laughing at some remark of Brent's. Her blonde angularity is certainly appealing, coltish and hesitant, the laugh nasal, comical, showing her even white teeth. Not a thing wrong with her, but she leaves Toby cold. She's a good girl of a good family; he doesn't have to see her bedroom at home to know what's in it. Her future is equally predictable, and he wants none of it.

Salome concludes her confab with the Marxist and takes up the limp segment of quesadilla. As she bites into it, she turns to Toby, but he doesn't look at her. Something is turning in him, in his head and in his stomach, but he doesn't think it has anything to do with the food, the coffee, or the beer. What if Salome prefers the Marxist? Is there anything to keep her from making a choice, right now, next week, years from now, and simply walking away? She can go home with Macalister this very evening if she likes, and Toby will have little to say about it. She can kiss him on the street as she kissed Toby that first night they spent together, her hand resting at the base of his skull, her eyes dreamy and half-closed. Macalister has a good deal of wiry black hair; she might run her fingers through it, pulling gently, teasing him. She might like that.

He has not, thus far, been rejected by a woman. Either his interest waned or the disillusion was mutual and the parting amicable, without so much as a harsh word. The thought of Meg, or Michiko, or, oh please, Belinda Stanford in the arms of another caused him not one moment of anxiety. He hasn't felt this tightness in his throat, this heat in his face, this pulsing in his ears. Bitterness floods his mouth; what is it? He reaches for his beer and takes a long, cooling draught, but it only adds a sloshing, gulping soundtrack to the racket in his head. Salome's hand moves near his, taking up her glass. Cautiously he allows his eyes to follow the glass until it arrives at her face, where he finds her looking back at him over the rim. She swallows; he watches the contraction of the muscles in her throat. How white that throat is, how slender. She sets the glass down, wiping her lips with the back of her hand. "The communists looted my country for thirty years," she says calmly. "If my father were here, he would pound Macalister into the floor."

❖❖

He was one of them. They had been steadily pushing into our town for months and there wasn't much to be done about it. No one liked them, but we didn't go out of our way to let them know our feelings. Children, of course, can be cruel, and there were squabbles among them, but some friendships grew up as well. His family came in the spring; the river was swollen from the melting snows. I remember seeing their decrepit truck with all their possessions, including a wizened old woman, piled in the back, rattling down the lane by the church. I was on my way to the market. The truck window was open and he was driving, smoking a cigarette. A worn-out-looking woman holding a baby against her shoulder sat slumped next to him; beyond her several children squirmed like piglets. The street was so narrow that when he reached down to flick off the cigarette ash it blew against the edge of my basket. He flashed me a grin; he had very good teeth, they all do, and said, "So sorry, madam. I didn't see you there." I ignored him and he drove on. That was the first time I saw him.

That night my husband said, "There's a new family of them. They've got Tereza's old house, don't ask me how. He's a bricklayer. There are eight of them in that little place."

"I saw them," I said. "They had an old woman stacked on top of the mattresses like a piece of furniture."

"That's the wife's mother," he said. "She's from Ogulin."

"You know a lot about them," I teased him.

"It's important to know about them," he said. He gave me a sharp look. I was not sufficiently serious about the threat they constituted to our town; that was his view of the matter. Later, after the children were in bed, he told his parents that I'd seen the new family and they sat at the kitchen table cursing about how the town was going to hell. I put on my wool sweater and went out to the garden to gaze at the stars. The stakes for the tomato plants gleamed like cemetery markers. It bored me, this hatred they were so bent upon cultivating. Better to tend the tomatoes. I thought about the man in the truck, our new neighbor, and his smile came back to me, his dark eyes so full of amusement, his deep voice, slightly mocking, calling me "madam." It pleased me to think of him. I felt myself smiling back

at him and I knew that the next time I saw him, if he spoke to me, if he smiled like that, I would smile back. It was cold and I began to shiver, but I didn't want to go back inside.

So you'd already made your choice.

Yes. I must have. When I think of myself shivering there in the garden under the cold stars, I must have already made up my mind to destroy my family.

❧❧

Chloe bolts from the porch, her shin smarting, straight toward the sound of gunfire. The reports fade, replaced by a dull clapping sound that puzzles her. She follows this sound, pushing through the waist-high milkweed, the faded goldenrod, ducking low tree branches, stumbling amid the tough creepers that crisscross the ground like veins, until she sees the dog, nose to ground, zigzagging in the low grass. A bell fastened to his collar clanks with every step. He is beaglish, but with something bigger, more sluggish, in the mix. Chloe crouches down, calling out to him, "Here boy, come over here." He lifts his muzzle without alarm, takes one last sniff of the fascinating patch near the trunk of an ailing hickory, and trots up to see what Chloe smells like.

He isn't attractive. His head is large, he has an overbite that makes him look obstinate; two shiny, gray, blood-gorged ticks are nestled in the thin fur near one ear. He is bandy-legged, barrel-chested, not fat but beefy. Not young. Chloe pats his head and shoulders, looking past him at the field where she does not doubt his master stalks with his rifle at the ready. A gruff voice calls out a word she identifies only as not English.

Carefully she slips her fingers beneath the dog's collar and holds him. Indeed, he shows no inclination to heed his master's call. Chloe is excited, curious, unafraid. She is about to put a face upon the trespasser she and Brendan refer to indignantly as the "poacher," who has punctuated their lives with gunfire every fall for the last two years.

The tall weeds before her part and he steps into view. He is not an impressive figure. No camouflage suit, no high-powered rifle, no hunter's cap or heavy boots. He has a canvas bag slung over one shoulder and at his side, its barrel shifting loosely in his grip, a rifle. A small man, dressed as if he's going out for the paper: a short-sleeved black polo shirt, shabby black pants, scuffed brown loafers, no socks. His hair is thick and black, his skin weathered, gray, unhealthy. His shirt clings damply to his concave chest. He sees her and knows at once that he will have to speak to her to get his dog. His eyes shift, looking for options. Chloe isn't accustomed to eliciting the flight response in a man, though she has experienced it often enough in herself to recognize it. His evident discomfort strikes her as pitiable. She releases the dog and stands up. "Is this your dog?" she inquires pleasantly.

It's an idiotic question; they both know it. The dog, wandering nearer his master, cuts off into the weeds purposefully, nose to ground. The man looks after him. Chloe has time to examine the rifle, but she knows nothing of firearms. Her father owned a shotgun, long ago, she saw it once or twice; it could have been the same. The poacher watches his dog, his body turning slowly away from her. She has the impression that he is about to walk away.

"What are you hunting?" she asks, again pleasantly, as if she might want to join him.

He turns and gives her a quick, impassive look. "Rabbits," he says. He pronounces it incorrectly, stressing the first syllable, dragging the second, turning the *s* into a *z*. "Rah-beetz."

"I'm sorry," she says, "but you can't hunt here. This land is posted."

He looks down at his shoes, moves one foot forward. "I diden know," he says.

Chloe glances past him at the sign nailed to a tree not twenty feet away, but she decides not to push it. "You're too close to the house." She waves vaguely in the direction she came from. "We have a cat. We don't want him to get killed."

Without raising his head, he shifts his eyes to take her in sidelong. His mouth is set in a grim line; his dark eyes appraise her carefully. His look is cold but not dead, more wolf than shark. She doesn't feel afraid, though she senses it has just occurred to both of them that he could murder her. The sexual component of the look is minimal, but it's there.

"Sorry," he says at last. "I go." At this grudging acknowledgment of the legitimacy of her claim, a warm flush of self-righteousness suffuses Chloe's chest. It is her land, after all, and he's on it. He doesn't say, though he could, "But there are many rah-beetz here. I eat them. You do not." She raises her hand again, pointing to the crumbling stone wall at the back of the property. "There's plenty of land on the other side you can hunt on. Up the hill there. I don't think it's posted."

He nods, not bothering even to look in the direction she indicates. The dog comes back into sight, veers off, heading for the wall in question. "OK," he says, turning to follow the dog. Chloe watches him until he disappears behind a bramble bush.

Her legs tremble as she walks back to the studio, and she

tries to calm herself by attending to the world around her. The light is clear, the air fresh and dry, the fragrance of vegetation more delicate and sweet than it is in the spring, when there's a heady, bitter, competitive edge to it. The rugosa is covered with hips; the milkweed has burst its silk-lined pods and stands in tattered ranks, admitting defeat. There have been two light freezes in the last week, enough to turn the nasturtiums and basil in the garden to mush, but as yet no killing frost. Crows are racketing in the distance; nearer she hears the delicate throb of a dove. She is following a deer path, dodging the oily black clumps of scat. As the roof of the studio comes into view, a rabbit, crashing through the underbrush, streaks across her path. She watches it until it disappears from sight, a small creature, light brown fur, a rust patch at the nape and powerful back legs: an Eastern cottontail. Once she saw a European hare, twice the size of this one, almost as big as Mike, who, like the poacher, is a relentless hunter of rabbits.

She is thinking of Mike, the murderer she loves, as she comes to the open field. Amid the weeds stand three tall junipers, one split nearly in half, the broken portion spilling over onto the ground, the result of a spring storm three years ago. Something romantic about it, something brutal and ruined. She will do a drawing of this blasted tree.

Were there junipers in Yorkshire? Did Emily Brontë pass among junipers, imagining her fantastical scheme, two generations of two families destroyed by the vengeful fury of a foundling in their midst?

Chloe stands still, listening, breathing deeply the delicious air, raising her eyes to the treetops and beyond them to the pale blue sky. The sun warms her neck and forehead. Is it Indian summer or global warming? Will these unusual warm spells result in the explosion of some ravenous insect population, some beetle or termite that can lay waste the forest for miles around, as she read was recently the fate of four million acres of trees in Alaska? She tries to imagine four million acres of dead trees.

High up in an aged horse chestnut she spots a chittering squirrel. A hawk sails lazily overhead. Then, from the direction of the stream, she hears two rapid gunshots.

Once they step off the train, Toby and Salome have to walk along the platform to the steps at the end, then back on the paved walkway to the parking lot where Brendan sits in his car watching their progress. Chloe is right, he thinks. They are definitely sleeping together. How does he know this? It's in the air between them, the ease of their young bodies, side by side, not looking at each other, not actually touching, but inclined, in tune, somehow. Toby is carrying a shoulder bag and Salome, wrapped in a thick brown woolen sweater that comes to her knees, clutches an overstuffed backpack to her chest. She is talking, as they walk, her face lifted toward Toby, who listens attentively, his chin lowered. She is smaller than Brendan anticipated, though her mass of black curls adds an inch or so. It's hard to tell much about her body, because of the sweater, or her face, because of the hair. As they draw closer, she scans the waiting cars; there are only three, and Brendan sees that her brows are thick, her complexion fair. She has a sharp little chin; her face narrows abruptly below the mouth to accommodate it. A sly, vulpine face, very wily and determined, elusive too. Toby points out the car, and her eyes find Brendan's. Something in her look makes him conscious that he is slumped in his seat. He straightens his spine, presses the button to open the trunk, turns to watch Toby swing down his own bag, then her backpack, slamming the flimsy door with a thud.

There is no question of their being roomed together; Toby surely knows that and has informed Salome. She will have Toby's old room; Toby will sleep on the daybed in Chloe's sewing room at the end of the hall. Toby and Brendan will share the downstairs bath, the women the larger bath upstairs.

"He says they want to talk to us about something," Chloe said, pressing her lips so tightly together that they darkened to purple.

"Did he sound cheerful? Or was it ominous?"

"Cheerful," she said.

They look cheerful. Toby introduces Salome through the car window. Should Brendan get out? Yes, he decides, but as he feels about for the handle, Toby opens the back door and Salome slips in. Brendan turns to the other side, addressing her between the seats. "How was the trip?" he asks.

She looks puzzled. "Fine," she says. "It was fine." The "trip" is an hour and a half on a commuter train; how good or bad could it be? Brendan's question is obviously a stupid one, which suggests that he must be nervous. But why? Toby opens the passenger door and drops into the seat next to his father. "So Dad," he says, patting Brendan's shoulder amiably. "How's it going?"

Brendan catches Salome's sharp eyes in the rearview mirror, glancing from father to son and back again. He shifts into reverse and backs out slowly. "Good," he says. "Everything is good."

The conversation on the drive home is largely about Toby:

his classes, his teachers, his enthusiasm for the antiwar group and the plans for the coming rally in Central Park. Salome says little, perhaps she can't hear very well, though Toby occasionally turns in his seat to include her. She murmurs agreement. They pass out of the town and into the gently rolling countryside, the fields dotted with cows and framed by the dark evergreen slopes of the Catskills, a landscape Brendan prizes and no one fails to admire. He repeatedly scans the rearview mirror, in which he can see Salome's profile, gazing out the window without comment.

Is she shy? As he turns into the quiet tree-shaded road leading to the house, he resolves to draw her out with interest, with kindness. She's a scholarship girl, he reminds himself; her father is a fisherman and an immigrant. The car climbs the hill past a few tract houses, and then, on one side, the bucolic stretch of the neighbor's farm appears, his cornfield ragged now, but the grassed area still green, and at the very top his venerable farmhouse, bigger than most, built for a gentleman farmer just after the Revolutionary War. On the other side a stretch of untended woods ends abruptly at a well-trimmed lawn and the short drive that leads to the Dales' house. It's not a grand place, but Brendan knows that guests are often impressed by the first view of it. The setting is pleasing: the shady drive, the lawn that slopes down to a stream, Chloe's garden that runs across the screened porch, all gold and russet now. The rambling structure of the house itself, built in increments over a hundred years, the last being more than a century ago, is charming, welcoming. "Here we are," he says, pulling in next to Chloe's car at the end of the drive. Toby jumps out at once, heading for the trunk, which Brendan pops open. He turns off the engine, opens the door, steps out onto the drive. Salome's door is open; first her feet, clad in neat black boots that come to the ankle, black tights over the shapely calves, then the rest of her comes up beside him, but she hardly seems to notice him. She is looking at the house. From the chimneys to the flagstone terrace, she takes it in, appraising it with a pert smile that surprises Brendan. So she is not humorless. Chloe appears at the mudroom door, wearing, bless her, a quilted apron over her sweater and corduroys. "Do you need help?" she cries out.

Salome turns from her house inspection to offer Brendan a complicit lift of the eyebrows. Here we go, she seems to say, or is that it? Without thinking, he smiles back, thereby taking, he senses, her side. Against what?

She joins Toby at the trunk, takes up her backpack, and follows him toward the house.

A cunning little vixen, Brendan thinks, and then it strikes him almost painfully—he would be embarrassed to own the thought—that Chloe, hovering there in her apron, clucking welcoming endearments, encouraging her son and his guest into the warm domesticity of her kitchen, looks very like a foolish, fluttery, and entirely defenseless mother hen.

Toby takes Salome on a tour of the house, including the attic, for the view it affords of the property. She spies the roof of the studio nestled in its clearing. What is that? she wants to know. Toby explains that his mother is an artist.

He probably didn't use the word "artist," Chloe muses as she walks out ahead of them on the narrow path. He probably said "illustrator," or "children's book illustrator." She feels wounded and defensive. But, after all, why would Toby have mentioned his mother's profession? Does Chloe imagine that young lovers talk about their parents, that after that uncomfortable lunch in the city Salome turned to Toby and said, "Your mother's fantastic. What does she do?"

Yet Chloe had been informed before the entrée arrived that Salome's father, that noble immigrant, though insufficiently royal to pay for his clever daughter's college education, was the Oyster King. And she didn't doubt that Salome knew what Brendan did for a living, a college professor, an historian, a man who knew where Zagreb was; now there was something to write home to the Oyster King about.

At dinner, Chloe resolves, she will ask about Salome's mother. Active in the church group, was she? An indefatigable teller of beads?

A squirrel, busy with an important nut, scurries up the trunk of an ash, interrupting Chloe's bitter musings with a righteous rebuke of his own. They have come to the plank that runs across the stream, which is only a trickle now, clotted with bright yellow leaves. All along the bed the rugosa runs wild, snagging bits of fur or flesh from whatever passes by. "Watch out for the thorns here," Chloe warns, turning back to her son and his companion. They are holding hands, gazing up at the angry squirrel with matching expressions of amusement. How young and fresh they look, how innocent their pleasure in this forest scold. Chloe forgives Toby, subdues her resentment of Salome, who is wagging her finger at the squirrel and pursing her lips in silent mockery. A thin breeze ruffles her hair and she pushes it back, revealing the breadth of her forehead, the sharp widow's peak of her hair-line. She looks intelligent, Chloe admits, not a classic beauty, but lovely and compelling nonetheless. For a moment she sees what Toby must see in her.

They cross the stream single file and follow the path until it opens into the clearing. There is the studio, the smoke curling up dreamily from the stovepipe, the many windows glittering in the sun. At once Chloe notices something—could it be an animal?—on the deck, pressed against the casement door. She goes ahead, up the wooden steps. It is a carcass of some kind; in a reflex of revulsion she takes a step back.

"What is it?" Toby asks, coming up behind her.

"A dead rabbit," she says.

Salome passes them both, bending over the bloody wad of fur and bone. "It's only the head," she observes.

"Ugh," Toby says.

Chloe joins Salome for a closer look. "Mike must have left it," she says. Salome gives her a quizzical glance. "He's the cat," she adds, but even as she says this she is thinking that Mike leaves entrails, not heads. Once she caught him in the garden chewing up a baby rabbit, head first.

Salome turns the severed head over by the ears. "It was a big rabbit," she observes.

Toby, hanging back, says, "Don't touch it."

The frozen brown eye looks up at the two women. The muzzle is damp, the whiskers flattened back from the velvety nose, the lower lip slightly open, revealing a line of pink gum and two worn brownish teeth. "Poor creature," Chloe says. She focuses on the blood-stiffened fur at the base of the head—does it look chewed or chopped?—but she can't tell.

Toby, reading her thought, asks, "Did the poacher leave it?"

"I saw him," Chloe admits. "A week ago. I told him to stay off the land." She looks out past her son in the direction of the clearing. Toby follows her gaze—trees, brush, only the sound of a woodpecker drilling in the distance comes back to them. "I think you should start locking your door," Toby says.

"I don't think he's dangerous," Chloe replies. "And there's nothing here he would want."

"Did he apologize?"

"In a way. His English isn't good. He's a foreigner."

"What is he?"

"I don't know. I had the feeling he was Lebanese."

Toby snorts. "She thinks all Middle Easterners are Lebanese," he informs Salome, who has not ceased her examination of the rabbit head. She stands up, holding it by the ears. "What should I do with this?" she asks. Chloe frowns. She would not have handled it so brusquely. She would have gone inside and found a cloth or even a paper towel to put between her flesh and the dead fur. Why? "Just throw it in the brush," she says. "The coyotes will get it." Salome marches out across the clearing, the head dangling from her outstretched hand. When she reaches the copse of juniper she swings it out before her. All three watch the gory trophy sail through the air.

"She's not squeamish," Chloe observes.

"She's a country girl," Toby says.

❖❖

In the studio Salome is fascinated by the woodstove, which Chloe tends routinely, opening the damper, stirring the embers, adding a few sticks from the wood box. "How long will it run if you don't put more wood in?" she asks.

"That depends," Chloe says. "In the winter when I'm out here all day, I damp it down when I leave and I've still got embers in the morning, so basically it never goes out."

"It's nice and warm here." Salome bends over to look through the glass at the sputtering flames. "It's warmer than in the house."

"It's actually more stove than I need," Chloe agrees. "But I like it because it means I don't have to wear a sweater when I'm working."

Toby takes the hint. He is standing before a table on which opened books, a tray of charcoal sticks, and several pages of sketches compete for limited space. He takes up the top drawing, holds it out at arm's length. "Is this for the new project?"

"It is," Chloe says. "I'm just getting started. That's Thrushcross Grange."

"It's *Wuthering Heights*, isn't it?"

"Yes." Chloe joins him and pulls out another drawing. "This is the Heights. Or something like this. I can't see it quite yet."

Rubbing her hands, Salome turns from the fire, but she makes no move away from the warm stove. Her eyes wander over the furnishings of the room, the shelves of inks, paints, and brushes, the pile of boxwood and lemon wood discs, the stack of Resingrave blocks, the leather sandbag, the open drawer of burins, the sharpening stone, the computer stand, the reading chair with its shelf of books and magazines, the hot plate and small refrigerator tucked into a corner behind a trestle table laden with oversized folios containing engravings of flora, fauna, architecture, and costumes, the various prints

and drawings, some framed, some tacked up by the four corners, that enliven the walls of the room. She settles on one of
these, a sepia tint engraving of a dandelion dispersing feathery
seeds on an invisible breeze. "I like that one," she says, crossing the narrow space for a closer look.

Chloe lays the sketch down, eager to sct hcr guest at ease.
"That's a study for my last book," she says.

"The Thoreau," Toby says.

Chloe joins Salome at the wall. The bookcase reserved for
finished copies of her own books is near the print, and she
pulls out the slender, autumnal volume, feeling once again a
glow of satisfaction at the look and feel of it. "Thoroughly designed," one reviewer had opined. "Yet the illustrations flow
out of the text as naturally and erratically as leaves fall from a
tree." "This is it," Chloe says, offering the book to Salome, who
takes it willingly and pages through it.

"That one got a lot of attention," Toby says, leaving the
sketches to join the women. "It got nominated for two prizes."

"Three," Chloe corrects him, mildly, modestly, as if his mistake is of no real import.

"Three," Toby says.

Salome stands, turning the pages slowly. There are not so
many and the illustrations are small; it was designed for older
readers, so there is a good deal of text. There are four full-page
plates, but Salome doesn't get to the last, which is the dandelion, before she closes the book and holds it out to Chloe. "It
came out good," she says.

To his mother's chagrin, Toby bends over the shelf and extracts the miserable cookbook. "I haven't seen this one," he
says. Salome looks over his shoulder at the glossy cover, which

features a child, vaguely Asian, on one side flipping a pancake that turns as it rises on the left margin, narrowing to a thin rectangle at the top, then opening in a wider and wider oval down the right, where a second child, blond and blue-eyed, genderless, waits with a second pan to receive it. "That's really cute," Salome says.

Chloe resists the urge to snatch the book from her son's hands. "It's not much," she says. "I did it just for the money."

Toby opens the cover and turns a few pages. "It's the kind of thing that sells," he says. He pauses over a recipe for applesauce, blender on one side of the page, glistening pile of apples on the other. Salome's attention wanders right off the page to Chloe's shabby slippers, which are lined up next to the hassock.

"Actually, it didn't do well at all," Chloe says. Mercifully Toby closes the book and returns it to the shelf.

"Do you ever sleep out here?" Salome asks.

"No," Chloe says. "I should sometime. I'd probably see a lot of wildlife."

"It might be wilder than you bargained for," Toby says.

"How many acres do you have here?"

Chloe gives Salome a sharp look. What business is it of Salome's? She toys with fielding the question with a question: "Why do you want to know?" but Toby saves her from open hostility.

"Ten," he says. He points out the window to the north. "Most of it is wooded, it goes straight back, there's a stone wall at the end." He turns to the east. "That way just to the far side of the stream. There's a pond down there. I used to swim in it when I was a kid."

"I'd like to see it," Salome says, and Toby replies that he'd like to show it to her. Clearly they've had enough of the studio. Chloe escorts them to the door. Off they go, across the clearing and down the path. As they enter the woods, Toby takes Salome's hand in his. She looks up at him, pulling herself in close to touch his jacket sleeve with her lips.

Chloe watches until they are out of sight, her hand clenched at her side. When she turns from the window, back to her crowded workplace in which there really is so much of interest, there are tears standing in her eyes. She tries to calm herself with reasonable observations: it is not uncommon for visitors to inquire into the extent of the property, not entirely inappropriate for Toby to respond to the question as if it was his purview. It is his, to some extent, or will be someday. He grew up here; curious, lively boy that he was, he explored every inch of the place, and it is dearer to him than to his parents because it contains his childhood. It is that childhood that he wants to show now to Salome, his first real love, Chloe admits. And it is not surprising or even insulting that two young people should have scant interest in her work, her life, her preoccupations and opinions. Why should they care that Emily Brontë roamed the harsh Yorkshire moors with a tame hawk perched on her arm, and that Chloe is considering including this fabulous animal in her illustrations, in the background of every scene, flying off in the windswept distance, glowering from a stand in the shadows of the gloomy kitchen, as Lockwood, the busybody tenant of the Grange, enjoys his first interview with his inhospitable new landlord, Heathcliff.

In this way, Chloe releases her son and his troubling friend and arrives at her drawing table, where her sketches of the two houses claim her attention. She pages through the book of photographs, the Yorkshire moors, the town of Gimmerton, the parsonage at Haworth where the Brontë children spent their brief lives, a neighboring estate, perhaps Emily's model for the Grange, the school in which the oldest sister, Maria, died, surely Jane Eyre's Lowood. Poor motherless girls, none of them beauties, passionate, intelligent, doomed, preoccupied, by necessity, with death. Chloe recollects her college professor Dr. Kramer, so many years ago, but she remembers the phrase exactly, as well as the flutter of amusement in the class: "The Brontës died mostly of colds caught at one another's funerals."

One by one, coughing themselves to death, excepting the willful, difficult son, Branwell, who, having failed spectacularly as an artist, a tutor, and a railway clerk, drank himself to death at the age of thirty-one. A ne'er-do-well, yet, in his youth, so promising, so beloved by his sisters, who witnessed his steady decline with incredulity.

His mother, lucky for her, didn't live to see the relentless will to self-destruction that characterized the wasted life of her only son.

Halfway through dinner, Toby, reacting to Salome's description of the antiwar group as "tyrannical anarchists," reaches out to pat her shoulder approvingly, his eyes shining with amusement. Brendan sees Chloe see this spontaneous gesture of affection. He has to admire her self-control; only her eyes widen perceptibly as she concentrates on cutting the vegetable lasagna she has prepared under the mistaken impression that their guest is a vegetarian. Neither a vegetarian nor a teetotaler, as it turns out. Before dinner Salome helped herself to a few slices of the expensive salami Chloe had laid out with olives, cheese, and crackers in the kitchen, and she is now well into her third glass of red wine. She has brightened considerably; her cheeks are flushed, she devours her meal heartily. She eats a lot, Brendan observes, in great contrast to the Japanese pianist, what was her name, who picked at her food as if she suspected it was laced with arsenic. Surely Chloe will admit that Salome is an improvement over her predecessors. It interests Brendan how many different ways there are for young women to be neurotic and difficult. Boys are largely good or bad. Bad boys hate authority of any kind, straight out; no starvation or self-mutilation is necessary to make the case that they don't fit in.

Chloe is passing the salad around when Toby, exchanging a significant look with Salome, announces that "they" have something to discuss. As the plans for the peace rally have already been laid—the four will meet at the train station and take the subway up to the park—Brendan assumes that he is about to hear something unexpected, possibly unpleasant. Chloe sets her fork down across her plate, fixing her attention upon her son with an intensity that strikes Brendan as unnecessary. Salome stuffs an unwieldy forkful of mixed greens into her mouth, evidently unconcerned. She's not pregnant. She couldn't eat like that if she was pregnant.

Toby explains the problem, as he sees it, and the proposed solution. His roommate is failing four of his five classes and has decided, with some fervid encouragement from his parents, to withdraw from the university and return to Pittsburgh. Salome is miserable living in a closet with roommates who play Broadway show tunes and throw drinking parties late into the night. Toby's current landlord wants him out as he is turning the building into condos; he will let him off the last two weeks' rent if he moves by the fifteenth of the month. Toby and Salome have found a better apartment, closer to the university, a fourth-floor walk-up that even has a window looking into a tree, for not much more than Toby is paying now. They have the money for the first and last month's rent, but they are short the deposit and the landlord wants Toby's parents to cosign the lease.

As Toby lays out his plan, Salome finishes her salad, her eyes moving only from her plate to Toby's articulating profile. "So," he concludes, "we think it's a really good apartment for the price and it will mean we can both get a lot more studying done, and we need your help."

During this last bit Salome takes a swallow of her wine. Brendan wonders if she is keeping her mouth occupied in order to avoid a burst of outright laughter at the notion that she and Toby have been driven to share an apartment because they are keen for the increased opportunity to study. As an iceberg of silence slides down over the diners, Salome brings her elbow to the table and rests her chin in her palm. Her eyes meet Brendan's with a frank inquiry that takes him by surprise. Is she insolent or just honest?

Chloe has not relaxed her close scrutiny of her son. "Do Salome's parents know about this?" she asks softly.

"My father doesn't have much money," Salome says. "But he sends me a little every month. I can make up the difference in what Toby is paying now."

Chloe's look is pure wonderment. Really, these two are stretching her credulity. Brendan braces for a retort, but Chloe only asks, "And your mother? What does she think of this scheme?"

Toby looks from his lover to his mother, his brow furrowed, the first evidence of anxiety he has shown all evening. "My mother died when I was nine," Salome says.

Chloe is flustered. "I'm sorry," she says. She presses her hand along the side of her face, glancing nervously at Brendan. "I didn't know."

"It was in Croatia. That's why my father came to this country."

"So you were born in Croatia," Brendan says.

"Yes. In a little town."

"And do you go back to visit?"

"No. Our family is all dead. My father brought us to Louisiana because he had an uncle there."

"And your father never remarried?" Chloe asks.

Salome doesn't answer this question, possibly because she doesn't hear it. That's the charitable interpretation Brendan prefers, but Chloe will see it as effrontery, calculated rudeness. Brendan knows this, he can feel his wife's rising pique even as Salome turns to Toby and says, "Which reminds me, my father will call here tomorrow at eleven. Don't let me forget."

And Toby, innocent, beguiled Toby, informs his parents brightly, "Her father calls every Sunday."

Chloe gets up without comment and begins taking up the salad plates, leaving Brendan to observe that Salome's father must miss her very much. This leads to further revelations, that she has an older brother who works with her father, that she keeps the books for the family business. Chloe disappears into the kitchen, where Brendan imagines her holding on to the sink for a few moments, taking deep breaths. There is some discussion of the location of the nearest Catholic church—just as well Chloe misses this—the likelihood of a Croatian community in the area. The question of the new living arrangements remains unaddressed. When Chloe returns bearing Toby's favorite dessert, lemon meringue pie, the conversation takes a turn toward the safe subject of food.

Later, when Chloe is clearing up in the kitchen, Brendan, Salome, and Toby take their coffee cups into the living room. Brendan thumbs through his CDs, looking for something that will harmonize the atmosphere. Toby and Salome sit together on the couch, close enough so that, as he stretches his arm across the cushions, his fingertips touch her shoulder. "So Dad," he says, "can we count on you for the apartment?"

Brendan makes his choice, Mendelssohn's *Songs Without Words*, Murray Perahia at the keyboard, one of Chloe's favorites. "How much is the deposit?" he inquires.

"It's nine hundred. I can pay you back four next month when I get the money Arnie owes me."

He slips the shiny disc into its bracket, presses PLAY; the easeful notes fill the air. Mendelssohn, the boy wonder, possessed of a famously sunny disposition that beamed through his music, even in his saddest year, when his beloved sister died. Brendan turns to his son, who leans forward to examine a book on the table, one hand resting behind him on Salome's knee. She is looking at a picture on the opposite wall, one of Chloe's engravings, a close-up of Mike seen from below, from what Chloe calls "mouse level." Her eyes flicker away, to the vase of chrysanthemums on the piano, then to her lover's hand resting so casually upon her knee. Toby looks up at his father expectantly, waiting for an answer.

A sensation of tender bewilderment silences Brendan. He regards his son with something close to admiration. So he is going to live with this self-possessed, provocative, unabashedly sensual young woman who will, who can doubt it, take him for a wild ride to parts unknown. There he sits, open, comfortable, his everyday manner in place, confident that his father will understand how entirely necessary it is for him to take this step. He hasn't the slightest idea what it is like to live night and day with a desirable woman and he wants to know, he needs to know. Brendan recalls this condition distantly. Who was she? How long did it last?

Toby closes the book, releasing Salome's knee to take up his coffee cup.

"I'll speak to your mother about it later," Brendan says. "I don't imagine there will be any problem."

"It's not as if we have an option," Chloe says, furiously brushing her hair. "That's what I hate about it."

"He is twenty-one," Brendan observes. He's already in bed, propped up on his pillows with his book, a new British novel. He tries to keep up with fiction by reading it at bedtime.

"I just hope she doesn't get pregnant."

"He's not stupid. I'm sure he's taking precautions."

Chloe puts down the hairbrush and turns from her mirror to take in her placid husband. "Are you?" she says.

Brendan regards her over the top of his reading glasses. It occurs to him that she is physically the exact opposite of the young woman in the bedroom down the hall. "Do you mean have I asked him?" he says. "No. And I'm not going to either."

"Well, I certainly can't."

"And you don't trust him."

"He's thinking only about sex. He's not thinking about the consequences. He's a boy, they never do."

"Then it's her you don't trust."

"She's a Catholic, for God's sake. She's off to Mass tomorrow morning."

"Do you think she would get pregnant just to trap him?"

"Yes." Chloe gets up and takes off her robe. She is wearing her favorite blue-striped pajamas, which, Brendan notes, are worn at the collar and the cuffs. "Don't you?" She climbs into the bed, flopping back on the pillow next to him.

"You always think the worst of people," he says.

"Am I wrong a lot?"

He neglects to answer, giving his attention to his novel. It's about two British boys during the war; one of them suspects that his own mother is a German spy.

"There was a rabbit head on the deck today," Chloe says.

Without much hope of finishing it, Brendan cleaves to the sentence he is reading. "I thought Mike looked stuffed this afternoon," he says.

"Did he?"

"He came in while you were back there with the kids, drank a lot of water, and went straight to sleep on the sofa."

"It was a pretty big rabbit."

Brendan lets the book fall closed against the blanket. "Do you think he didn't leave it?"

"I just don't know. I suppose coyotes could have killed it and he just brought me the head because he didn't want it himself."

"That seems possible."

"But he usually eats the heads."

"Maybe a coyote left it."

"It was up against the door, sort of jammed against the glass. It looked like it was thrown there."

"So you think it was the poacher."

"Why would he do that?"

"Did he seem angry when you spoke to him?"

"He seemed totally indifferent."

A sharp crack startles them both, but it is only Toby, opening his door. They listen quietly as he pads past their bedroom on his way to the bathroom. There is the sound of water running in the pipes, a cough, the door opens, then silence. Chloe lays her hand on Brendan's arm. Is he going to Salome's room now; would he be that bold? Perhaps he is looking back to see if there is light beneath his parents' door. Chloe is wide-eyed, tense. Brendan would be amused if she didn't look so helpless. A floorboard creaks, then another; yes, he is returning to the narrow bed in his mother's sewing room. The door closes; they hear the creaking of the bed springs.

"I hate this," Chloe says, reaching out to switch off her bedside lamp.

⁂

In the morning Chloe finds Salome and Toby at the kitchen table drinking coffee and brooding over the pages of the Sunday *Times*. "Good morning," they chorus cheerfully and Chloe, making for the stove, replies, "Good morning. You're up early."

"Salome has to go to Mass," Toby reminds her, as if she could forget. Has to. Not wants to, or even needs to, but has to. And what if she didn't go to Mass, what would happen then? Chloe fills her cup with coffee, feeling testy. As she adds the milk—they've warmed the pitcher in the microwave, just as she likes it—she counsels herself to be polite. Consciously she softens the lines of her face, creates an interested expression, and turns it upon her son. "Anything newsworthy?" she inquires, lifting her chin to the pages spread before him.

"The usual," he says. "The Democrats are disgusting cowards."

Salome doesn't look up. She's dressed in black, neatly, a buttoned-up cardigan and a cotton skirt that stops just above the tops of her boots. A pale blue lace mantilla is draped across her shoulders, very fine work, Chloe observes. "That's a lovely shawl, Salome," she says.

The girl looks up. One hand strays to her shoulder, adjusting a fold. "It was my mother's," she says.

The dead mother. Chloe ransacks her drowsy brain for a proper response. Is it sad; should she say that's too bad, or is it nice, comforting perhaps? It must be a comfort to you? Nothing seems right. Salome's eyes flicker briefly across Chloe's face, return to the newsprint in front of her. No response necessary, evidently, but in spite of herself Chloe says, "Oh." Too little, too late.

Toby, swallowing the last of his coffee, raises his wrist to consult his watch. "Time to go," he says. They begin folding the papers. Toby takes their cups and puts them in the sink. Chloe leans against the counter watching them. She's still half-asleep, and their aura of efficiency and urgency irritates her.

From upstairs she hears the bellow of water in the pipes; Brendan has reached the bathroom. These two will be gone before he gets to the kitchen. A thwack-thwack sounds from the mudroom; Mike coming in from his night revels. Toby pulls the door open and the cat rushes past Salome, who draws in her foot as if she disdains being touched by an animal. Chloe sets her cup on the counter and bends down to take Mike in her arms, offended on his account. Well, they're leaving; they scarcely notice. Toby snatches the car keys from the table. "I'm stopping at the market while Salome's in church," he says. "Do you need anything?"

So he isn't going in with her. "No," Chloe says, nuzzling the cat. "Thanks."

Salome passes out the door to the terrace, where she stands gazing at the car. Chloe has a sense that this moment alone with her son is the last one she will ever have. Surely this is paranoia. It is only that such moments will constitute the nature of their time together from now on; it will be time snatched from Salome. This gloomy revelation presses upon her. Toby pauses in the doorway, looking back at her, entirely unconscious of any necessity to reassure her, and surely this is as it should be. But Chloe is thinking of how often they have sat together of a Sunday morning, mother and son, perusing the papers, reading out interesting bits to each other, eating toast and drinking coffee until Brendan appears and she gets up to cook eggs, bacon, pancakes, a late breakfast that sometimes runs right into lunch. Is it possible that this banging out the door to drive an intruder halfway across the valley to fulfill her religious obligation is to be the new order?

"We won't be long," Toby says. Is the wan smile he gives her sympathy or regret?

"Drive carefully," she says.

❧ ❧

Brendan is pouring his coffee and Chloe is reading out an article about the overabundance of deer in Putnam County when the phone rings. She stops midsentence as he picks up the receiver. "Hello," he says.

"This is Branko calling." The accent is thick, the voice harsh and confident.

"I'm sorry," Brendan says. He is about to inform the caller that he has the wrong number when it occurs to him that this is Salome's father. "Are you calling for Salome?" he says.

Chloe folds the paper and rests her chin in her hand, all attention.

"I am her father."

"Yes, I thought so," Brendan says. "I'm afraid she's not here. Toby has taken her to church."

"I know this. I am calling to tell her that I cannot call at eleven when she returns because there is a problem with the boat."

"I see," Brendan says. He raises his eyebrows at Chloe to suggest his amusement at the caller. "I'll give her the message."

"I will call her later, at three o'clock."

"I believe they're taking the two-thirty train back to the city. They won't get into town until four."

There is a pause. Brendan forms a mental picture of the man on the other end of the line, a man who has a problem with his boat. He is big, that's in his voice; he is standing on a dock in Louisiana, down at the very end of the land, water all around, perhaps a palm tree or two. It's warm there; he's wearing only a cotton shirt, with the sleeves rolled back over powerful forearms. There's a cigarette pack in the shirt pocket, the voice is rough from smoke. "Then I will call her at five o'clock at her room. You will tell her this for me?"

"I will," Brendan says.

"Thank you very much," he says, and the line goes dead. Brendan hangs up, smiling to himself.

"Well," says Chloe.

"The father," he says.

"What's he sound like? Was he polite?"

"Not exactly."

"Rude?"

"No. Just curt. He's got a thick accent, but his English isn't bad."

"What does he want?"

"He can't call Salome until later. There's a problem with the boat."

"He called to say he can't call?"

"Well, not at the appointed hour."

Chloe turns back to the paper. Brendan stands looking down at her, sipping his coffee. Though the conversation was brief, he has the sense that he could pick Salome's father out of a crowd. "His name is Branko," he says.

Chloe gives a puff of indignation at this information, but

she doesn't look up from the page of newsprint. "Branko," she says, incredulously.

I was young, I was passionate. I couldn't bear the constrictions of ordinary life, my husband's indifference, the casual cruelty of my in-laws. I turned for comfort and, I admit it, in anger, to a stranger. That's all he was then, later he was an enemy, and once he was the enemy, it was only a matter of time before someone betrayed us, his family or mine.

My father was an educated man from the city, from Zagreb, and he couldn't forgive me for marrying a poor farmer from a small town, so I was already an outcast; I was used to it. My husband was a big man, bursting with life. Father was small, frail, bookish, stubborn. He thought of himself as a Westerner. He hated the government, whatever it was. He hated the Ustashe, he hated Tito; he was democratic. He kept strict accounts, nourished his grudges, remembered every slight. He had big plans for my brother; his son was to be his vengeance upon the world. For me he was not so ambitious. He wanted me to marry a doctor or a university professor.

I was twenty when I ran away with my husband. I had completed two terms at university; I had good marks. I met him on a holiday with friends. We were hiking about the countryside, and there he was, on his tractor in a field.

At first we lived in a small town, then we moved to an even smaller one so that we could be closer to his parents because his father was ill. I had three children in five years. In the city we never paid much attention to where people came from, what church they attended, what alphabet their newspaper came in, but in the small towns it was different. Still there were intermarriages, it's an old story. Unlikes attract, is that what you say?

No. It's opposites attract.

Yes. Like magnets.

❧❧

The train is crowded. They take the windowless seat no one ever wants, which is odd, Toby thinks, because this is a commuter train and the passengers, having viewed the passing scenery a thousand times, are largely absorbed in their computer screens. Toby slings the backpack into the overhead rack and drops into the seat next to Salome, who has pressed herself against the wall. She smiles, resting her hand on his knee. "Kiss me," she says. Toby glances at the middle-aged couple occupied in unwrapping sandwiches across the aisle. "You're so prudish," Salome says, bringing her hand to his chin. He bends down to meet her raised lips with his own. The kiss is immediately complicated by her tongue, her fingers dance up his thigh, and he is both aroused and self-conscious. Does she sense his reluctance? Her lips close softly beneath his, her hand glides back to his knee, and she releases him. When he opens his eyes she is slumped back in her seat, her lips pursed, her eyes amused as if she knows some secret about him, as if he is an adorable, mischievous child.

"Dad gave me the check," he says. "We should mail him the lease as soon as we get back."

"What did your mother say?"

"Never mentioned it."

"She's not pleased."

"She'll get over it."

"She thinks I'm stealing you from her." Toby makes no reply; he doesn't want to talk about his mother. "And she's right."

"Do you think I'm a prize to be passed around among women?" he asks.

"I think your mother thinks you're too good for me."

"Right," he says. He pulls his shoulder bag up from the floor and tears open the Velcro flap, which gives a satisfying screech. He has no doubt that his mother thinks he is too good for Salome, and it troubles him that he should have to defend her from this charge. He rummages in the bag for his notebook. They have an exam first thing in the morning, for which he is insufficiently prepared.

"Give me mine too," she says.

Their notebooks are pressed together, but easy to tell apart. His is small, tan, spiral; hers is pink plasticized with a sticker on the top that reads MIR, which means, he knows, peace in Croatian. Let's have some, he thinks as he passes the binder to her and shoves the bag back down between his knees. Yet, as she opens the stiff cover and turns over the first few pages of her notes, he says, "It's not all that unusual for a mother to think well of her son, is it?"

Salome closes the binder, folding her hands across the cover. "But that's just it," she says. "She doesn't think well of you. She thinks you're too stupid to know what's good for you. She thinks I'm this temptress who is going to bring you down, ruin your life, but you can't resist me because you're just too weak and you need to be protected. From the likes of me. If she thought well of you, she would have respect for your ability to make choices in the world, to choose your friends and the people you love. But she doesn't trust you to do that. She has complete contempt for you, actually."

"And your father is going to be totally accepting and trusting, and just thrilled when he meets me," Toby says.

Salome shrugs. "My father doesn't trust anybody. But when he sees that I care for you, then you will be part of our family. He may not always approve of you, and if he doesn't, he'll let you know, but as an equal. He won't talk down to you, or ask you what your father thinks about your plans."

"That's the part that got to you," Toby says.

"What?"

"That she asked if your father approved of our living together."

She presses her lips together and lowers her eyes. "What bullshit," she says softly.

Toby looks down at her, at the set of her jaw and the shadow her hair casts over her eyes, at her small hands crossed on the binder cover. His anger dissipates, replaced by interest. He puts aside the inflammatory question of whether his mother has contempt for him, a notion that has never occurred to him before, and gives himself over to the curiosity Salome arouses in him. What extraordinary self-confidence she has, and how coolly she assesses any opposition to her views. Nothing passive-aggressive about her, no subtle manipulation, no hurt silence or coy innuendo, just a straightforward dismissal: what bullshit.

"It is bullshit," he agrees. "But right now we need the money."

She opens the binder again, turns a page covered with her cramped script. No doodles in the margin, not much scratching out. In class, she takes copious notes from which she creates complex outlines with page references to the texts. It's a method, she has confided to Toby, that she learned from the nuns. She runs a finger down the Roman numerals on the first outline and Toby, assuming the subject of his mother's anxiety is closed, opens his own notebook. Salome may be more highly organized, but his handwriting is easier to read.

"I know we need the money," Salome says, without looking up. "That's what I hate about it."

❖❖

Toby and Macalister struggle with the futon, which is jammed in the staircase at the turning to the fourth floor. Salome stands in the open door above them, looking down.

"We'll have to get under it," Toby says, disappearing beneath the lower end.

"You need to lift it," Salome observes.

"She's thinking every minute," Macalister says. He bends his knees and drives his head and shoulders into the curve of the mattress, hoisting the floppy bulk across his back. "On three," he says to Toby, whose muffled voice calls out, "One, two, three." The mattress bulges until one end slides free of the banister. Toby and Macalister emerge from beneath it, hastily throwing themselves across the top to keep the thing from sliding down into the stairwell. "It's like a dead body," Toby says.

"Dead bodies are stiffer," Macalister says.

"You've got it now," Salome says, turning back into the apartment.

Toby laughs. "I can't be sure," Macalister says, "but I think we've got it now." Together they slide the futon along the banister, past the curve. On the landing they haul it upright and push it against the wall. Salome looks out the doorway. "Great," she says. "You're almost there." The young men grin at each other.

"What's funny?" she says, ready to laugh.

Toby rests his head against the mattress and closes his eyes.

"You're a lucky man," Macalister says.

"I know you think so," Toby replies, his eyes still closed.

"I've got the kettle unpacked," Salome says. "I'll make coffee." She ducks back inside. The young men take their places on either end of the mattress and slide it along the wall to the open door. They have been lugging boxes and furniture down three flights of stairs and up four for several hours, and this futon is the last of it. As they make the turn into the apartment and past Salome, who flattens herself against the kitchen counter, their spirits rise. They pick up speed, gliding swiftly across the front room, through the arch to the back room. Salome follows, directing them to the wall inside the arch. "Put it here," she says, "with the head against the wall."

"It's a futon," Macalister says. "It doesn't have a head."

"Well, the end where our heads will be."

Toby has a vision of their heads, side by side on two pillows. Macalister's head appears between them, looking cheerful. He shifts the mattress abruptly, forcing the Marxist to stumble against the doorframe. "Go easy," Macalister exclaims. When the mattress is flush against the wall, they both release it and back away. For a moment it stays upright, as if deciding which way to fall; then the top peels away from the wall and the mattress flops down across the floor. "Power to the people," the Marxist says. Salome slips her arm around Toby's waist, nuzzling his shoulder. "We did it," Toby says. All three look about the room approvingly. It is freshly painted, the wood floors are gleaming, at the back there is a large window and through the bars the yellowing leaves of an enormous sycamore shimmer in the breeze. "This is a great apartment," Macalister says. "Perfect bourgeois respectability."

"You're jealous," Salome says.

"Of course I am," he admits. From the kitchen a whistle ascends to a shriek, commanding their attention. "The coffee," Salome says, rushing out. Toby watches her retreating back. She has such good posture. Her spine is as straight as a dancer's. "I don't know about you," Macalister says. "But I don't want coffee. What I want is a beer."

It is agreed that Toby will go down, move the rented truck, and pick up the beer at the deli on the corner. He is standing on the sidewalk before it occurs to him that Salome and Macalister are alone in their new apartment. Should he be anxious?

"He's a good friend," Toby said when Macalister volunteered to help with the move.

"Do you think so?" Salome replied.

"Don't you?"

"You're sweet, Toby," she said. "You haven't even noticed that Bruce is in love with me."

"Has he told you that?"

"He doesn't have to tell me," she said. What worries Toby in this conversation is Salome's use of the Marxist's given name;

no one calls Macalister "Bruce." It suggests a certain level of intimacy. But surely she doesn't have time to be carrying on a secret affair. Toby is with her most nights and her school day is tightly scheduled. So when did Macalister become "Bruce"?

And now "Bruce" is alone with her. How easily he managed that. As Toby turns the key in the truck lock, he gazes up at the front of the building in which Salome is entertaining their mutual friend. They wouldn't dare do anything too complex, he reasons, as they have no idea how long it will take him to find a legal parking place for the truck. It could be a few minutes, it could be an hour. He climbs into the driver's seat and starts the engine. It isn't going to take long, he decides. But even if he is lucky, there will be time enough for kissing and fevered plans for their next rendezvous. He rolls the window down and leans out, gauging the traffic behind him. He is being ridiculous, he knows that, but his sense of urgency is keen. He pulls out abruptly, narrowly missing the car in front of him and provoking the driver behind to blare his horn. This city is a madhouse. Everyone is agitated all the time, and for what? For nothing. Toby jerks the truck through its gears and bursts ahead for two blocks, where he is trapped in a knot of traffic stalled behind a garbage truck. He presses his palm against his forehead, sighs, closes his eyes, takes a deep breath.

Salome is wearing an old red cardigan sweater, the top two buttons undone so that the edges fall open, revealing the smooth knobs of her clavicle bones. Toby can see Macalister's blunt fingers pulling at the fabric around the third button. "Bruce," Salome says. "Don't be silly. We don't have time."

And Macalister laughs. "Are you kidding?" he says. "He's

stuck behind a garbage truck on Houston and Lafayette. He won't be back for hours."

❖❖

Wind. That's the vital element, visible only in its effects. In the Fritz Eichenberg illustrations, which so titillated Chloe as a child, the wind is indicated by a wavy line in the ground and by the streaming hair and ruffled clothes of the humans striving against it. The cover design, printed on durable board, shows Heathcliff leaning against a tree, his harsh features lifted to the storm, his hair, his tie, and the tails of his frock coat furling out in front of him. Chloe finds the image problematic. The tree trunk is twice as wide as the man; wouldn't it block at least some of the wind? The clump of grass at his feet is bent, but it's not flat; it's not a gale force wind. The tree menaces, the limbs leafless and stunted, the bark like a coil of snakes. Heathcliff is burly, his chest strains the front of his coat, but his head is too small and the dark features are exaggerated, the stuff of caricature. As she pages through the plates, Chloe finds much that is overworked, heavy-handed. Eichenberg's line is thick throughout. He uses no line at all for light, leaving white patches surrounding a candle or a raised lantern, reflecting off the blade of a knife.

He hasn't made much of the houses. Wuthering Heights itself is a two-story stone building with a mansard roof that could be thatch. Only the entry of the house at the Grange is visible in the background of the plate in which Catherine Earnshaw is attacked by Linton's bulldog. Cathy lies in the foreground, lifted up on her elbows, her head turned to look back at the dog. Heathcliff crouches behind her, one hand on the beast's collar, a rock raised in his free hand, ready for a mighty blow. Above his head the light of the servant's lantern breaks in a nimbus of white.

It's a pleasing composition. Heathcliff's raised arm makes an arc that curves over the servant's shoulder, down to the bat he is carrying, across the dog's bristling back to Cathy's ankle, from there to her raised arm and Heathcliff's braced leg. This fierce ellipse of outrage and struggle is disconnected from the rectangle of the open door in which the dark figure of a woman stands quietly looking on.

Chloe can still recall the pleasurable and curiously erotic charge this picture gave her as a child; it was so brutal, so unexpected. Where did she first see it? Was it in the town library, where she passed many a summer afternoon, or was it among the forbidden books in her parents' bedroom, which she perused furtively when she was left in the care of her indifferent baby-sitter? Before she knew the story, these illustrations intrigued her, offering access to an interdicted world, a world of cruelty, violence, jealousy, death.

And life. Passionate life. That was how these rough scenes differed most meaningfully from the banal confines of her parents' house, which was a dead zone, a cold, lightless pool at the bottom of a well. Her revolt was early and intense. "This is death in life," she cried out, hurtling herself up the carpeted stairs to her bedroom. "This house is a grave," she shouted, slamming the bedroom door upon which she had taped carefully lettered aphorisms from her true gods, the romantic poets. *Those who restrain passion do so because theirs is weak enough to be restrained.* That was certainly one of her credos. Years later, when William Blake was of more interest to her as an engraver than a moral philosopher, she discovered that he had not had the time to live the passionate life he recommended; he was too hard pressed for cash. He took journeyman's work, passionless stuff, whatever he could get to make ends meet. Toward the end of his life, he did 185 engravings of plates for Josiah Wedgwood's china catalog.

Chloe turns to the last engraving: a shepherd boy and his sheep in the foreground. The landscape is peaceful, there is no wind. The sheep wander along, intent on sheep matters. The boy looks over his shoulder at the apparition of Heathcliff and Cathy, executed in light smudges against the hard lines of the swirling ground. A good choice; this is, after all, a ghost story, a haunted world.

A haunted world. The hairs on Chloe's neck stir as if exposed to a chill breeze, but the air is still. She glances through the glass doors at the clearing. It occurs to her that the birds have fallen silent. She closes the volume, lays it aside. Idly her thoughts conjure visions of graveyards, Keats's touching stone in Rome, the field of crosses in Normandy, the mowed grass and orderly plantings of the town cemetery in Connecticut where her parents lie, presumably, at rest. She crosses to the open door, steps out onto the leaf-strewn deck. There is a rustle of grasses at the edge of the clearing. Mike stumbles into view. That explains the birds. "Hello," Chloe says. Mike sits down abruptly; he looks stunned. "Are you OK?" Chloe says. The cat takes a few more steps, but his legs are uncoordinated, impossibly clumsy, and he sits down again. Chloe hurries to him, down the steps, across the patchy grass. He watches her progress, but his eyes are unfocused, and as she reaches him he slides over onto his back. That's when she sees the dark ooze of red in the thick gray fur on his side.

The vet is not convinced Mike was injured by a gunshot. "It's too neat, and there's nothing in it. It looks like something sharp poked him. It's deep, but it didn't graze any organs." He cleans the wound with a swab and shaves the area with an electric razor. Mike doesn't struggle, but he's not happy; he's shedding fur in handfuls. "See," the vet says. "It's perfectly round. Very odd." Brendan and Chloe gather close to look down at the small, neat hole in the cat's side. "I'm not going to stitch it," the vet says. "Just keep it clean and apply hot compresses three times a day. Take a washcloth and soak it in water as hot as you can stand and hold it against the wound for at least five minutes. If it's not closing up in a week, bring him back."

"Could he have been at the end of the rifle's range and the shot fell out?" Chloe suggests.

"I don't think so," the vet says. "It looks like a puncture."

"Maybe he fell on something sharp," Brendan says.

"I think he must have," the vet says. He releases Mike, who bolts into the cat carrier, as far back as he can get. This is amusing because Mike hates the carrier; it takes two people to force him into it, but he has now concluded that it's the quickest exit from the vet's office. He does this every time he visits the vet; the vet has observed that most cats figure this out, but it's still cause for droll comment. "He's ready to go home now," the vet says, and all three smile and nod at the wonderful cleverness of cats.

In the car, Chloe says, "He didn't say it was impossible that he was shot."

"No, he didn't," Brendan says.

"I'm calling Joan Chase when we get home. She heard him on her land last week. She's worried about her dog."

Brendan casts her an appraising glance. "When did you see her?"

"Yesterday. At the post office. She said Joe went out and told him to stay off their land. It was the same guy, same dog with the bell. He woke them up at six A.M. on Sunday. I said, we need to call the police or the game warden and she agreed, but she said Joe thinks there's nothing they can do. They're not going to stake the guy out for us. Joe talked to Fred Ketchum down on Vechey Lane and he said this guy parks his car at the edge of the woods over there and walks in. I told her about the rabbit head and she said she's worried about her dog."

"That little yappy thing," Brendan says.

Chloe laughs. "Fluffy," she says.

"Didn't he bite somebody?"

"The FedEx man. On the ankle."

"Maybe the poacher's the one who should be worried."

Chloe smiles, but ruefully. Mike lets out a yowl from the cat carrier. "Hang on, guy," Chloe says. "We're almost home."

Brendan views the present, as he does the past, through a long lens. He seldom has the sensation that he is actually in it. As yet another actor mounts the makeshift platform in the park, his sense of being disaffected intensifies. The air is fresh, bathed in autumnal light, and the harmonious, carefully maintained landscape circumscribes the crowd in a saucer of green edged in gold. Frederick Law Olmsted, Brendan thinks. Now there was a visionary.

The crowd is, perhaps, twenty thousand. It fills the designated area with a satisfying density, especially at the front near the stage, but everyone knows it is a poor turnout. Toby's turbulent little girlfriend, who stands in front of him, turns now and then to gauge the edges, a sour look on her face. Overhead a helicopter circles aimlessly, languid as a dragonfly, sent at the behest of a news station to confirm the foregone conclusion that this gathering is not news. "You are wonderful," the actor assures the throng. "It's so good to be here with you. We thought we were alone!"

Chloe, who is beside him, offers her water bottle. "What an idiot," she says sotto voce. Toby, poor optimist that he is, looks back at his parents, pointing to the thin stream of humanity passing through the gate from the street. "They're still coming," he says. The actor settles down for a good long harangue, boldly deploring fundamentalism of every stripe. Behind him on the platform, an African-American imam and a rabbi shrink visibly from this sentiment. It will be their task to explain why their religions cannot be held responsible for anything divisive or inflammatory, the proof of this assertion being their presence together on this stage, calling on the faithful to halt the machinery of war.

It is already so lifeless and platitudinous that Brendan feels his outrage at the government diffusing into a generalized disgust at what passes for political discourse in his own historical moment. Now and then he gets aggravated enough to point out to friends that the events of the sacrosanct 9/11 were not new and didn't actually change anything, that rather than entering a new era, a very old one has only come cycling back into view. The widening gyre, the falcon no longer hears the falconer. He looks up into the flat blue sky overhead; Yeats had it right. History is a bum rap; we stand condemned in the dock. It's time to take sides but . . . *the best lack all conviction*. "Can we go soon, do you think?" he says to Chloe, but she doesn't hear him. She's gazing anxiously at Toby, who has his arms wrapped loosely about Salome's waist, so that she leans against him, full length, her chin raised and turned toward him as he nuzzles her throat, speaking to her. Is it an endearment or an observation about the actor? Brendan can imagine the precise spot at which his son's penis presses against the small of Salome's back, or he thinks he can, and it makes him smile. He's accustomed to the sexual displays of youth; his students have not, as he has, grown older as the years drag by. A group carrying a banner that reads WHO WOULD JESUS BOMB? pushes in from the lawn, greeting Toby and Salome with shouts and embraces. The boys pat one another on the shoulders in the manly version of the hugs the girls promiscuously dispense. Salome, he observes, keeps a little distance, pecking her fellow demonstrators on each cheek, European style. How hideously they are dressed, how many tattoos, rolls of flesh, piercings with silver rings and knobs, are in evidence among them. Salome, in her full skirt and embroidered blouse, looks out of place. Not a mark on her, Brendan observes, or at least none that he can see. Toby's style is minimalist: a single gold stud in one ear, his hair made spiky by the application of some product, a black T-shirt, oversized and logo free. He's wearing sandals with socks. He and Salome have the air of nobility mingling with street ruffians, though one young man sporting rimless glasses and a Trotskyite goatee is dancing in unabashed attendance upon Salome. He takes her arm and whispers in her ear; he makes her laugh. Toby looks on benignly. Doesn't he know his friend is in love with Salome?

"We should have made him go to the Sorbonne," Chloe says. "Or Edinburgh. He liked Edinburgh."

"I'm for art," the actor proclaims. "For novels and plays and poetry and music and painting, for beauty and creativity, and for freedom of expression in the face of repression." Toby has drifted back to his parents. "Salome is unhappy about this crowd," he says. "But I think it's not bad. It must be fifty thousand, don't you think?"

"These are the freedoms I value," the actor concludes, "and these are the freedoms this administration hates."

"Nice," Chloe says. "They hate our freedoms." There is a roll of applause, sparse on the edges, which the actor attempts to quell by holding out his hands and pressing down on the air. "This guy is so lame," says Toby.

"Maybe twenty thousand," says Brendan.

"Twenty thousand?" Toby says. "That's not so great."

"So what will the *New York Times* call it?" Chloe asks.

"And on what page?" Brendan adds.

"Several thousand," Toby reads out. "Several thousand people filled the park's East Meadow." He folds and flattens the paper against the table. "It's in the Metro section."

"Good Christ," Chloe exclaims. She's at the stove, turning

pancakes. She hasn't slept well, and her nerves are frayed from twenty-four hours under one roof with her son's lover. It feels good to swear, and the *Times* is always a safe target.

"Bastards," Salome says, refilling her coffee cup, draining the pot, Chloe observes. "That section doesn't leave the East Coast."

"*New York Times* Provokes Wrath of Peaceniks," Brendan reads. Salome gives him a pensive look. She gets his humor, but it worries her.

"Get this," Toby says. "This is their idea of front page news. 'There's nothing political about American literature, Mrs. Bush said in a telephone interview. Everyone can like American literature, no matter what your party.' "

General laughter. "That's rich," Brendan says. "Is it Barbara or Laura?"

"Laura, of course," says Toby. "She's a librarian."

"Pass the sugar," Salome says to Toby.

For a poor girl, she's mighty comfortable being served, Chloe thinks. Do Branko and the brother wait on her in the oyster kitchen? She has yet to bring so much as a dish to the sink. Toby fusses over her, henlike: Is she hungry? Is she tired? Is she cold? Last night he ran upstairs to get her a shawl; on the train he rolled his jacket into a pillow and obliged her to rest with her head in his lap.

After the ineffectual rally, they had taken the subway downtown so that the Dales could see the apartment where Toby and Salome lived in studious felicity. Chloe, arriving breathless from the climb and prepared for a shock, was relieved to find nothing actively frightening in these living arrangements. Books were piled on the floor, posters tacked to the walls, the furnishings, scavenged from friends and from sidewalk sales, leaned and sagged in all directions, but it was clean enough. There was an old-fashioned crocheted curtain on the big window overlooking the tree and a bright striped cloth on the table in the kitchen. "It's great, isn't it?" Toby said. Chloe stepped into the bedroom alcove, confronting the futon on which her son and his girlfriend spent, she did not doubt, a fair proportion of their youthful energies. It was neatly made up, covered with a down quilt Toby had had since high school. "It's charming," Chloe said, turning to find Salome watching her with her moody frown, scrutinizing her, weighing her up in some balance. How poorly I must compare, she mused, to the missing mother, the saintly martyr. "I like that curtain," she said.

"Salome made it," Toby said.

What luck; she had admired the right thing. Chloe crossed to the window to have a closer look, passing her hand behind the heavy lace, lifting it away from the light. It was fine work, as even and tight as a machine might produce. "My grandmother used to crochet," Chloe said. "I remember watching her do it, but I never learned myself. I still have a tablecloth she made. This is beautiful, Salome."

"She's an artist," Toby affirmed.

"They call it 'Bohunk lace' at home," Salome said, still frowning, but not at Chloe.

"Bohunk?" Brendan asked. "Meaning what?"

"Bohemian," said Toby.

"That's what they call us in Louisiana," Salome said. "They don't know what we call them."

"What do you call them?" Brendan asked.

"Ignorant," she said, and they all laughed.

Ignorant what? Chloe wonders as she shifts the kettle onto

a burner. Ignorant Americans? Ignorant Southerners? Were they Cajuns, these know-nothings who thought Croatians were from Bohemia, was that what they were? She delivers the last pancakes to the warm plate in the oven, paddles the pan in the air to cool it down for the eggs, slides the bacon out of and the syrup pitcher into the microwave, brisk with competence. "This is ready," she announces.

Brendan gets up to ferry plates to the table; Toby gathers the papers. Salome sits watching, placid as a frog on a lily pad. As Chloe takes up the coffeepot, it strikes her that the girl has circles under her eyes and looks a little green. She drank a lot of wine last night, and then brandy when they got home. Perhaps she is hungover.

As it turns out, Chloe is right: Salome is not feeling well and there's a simple explanation for her indisposition. Later Chloe will tell Brendan she knew it then, when she brought the pot to the table and sat down across from Salome. "She couldn't look at me," Chloe will say, and it is true, that, as the plates are passed about and piled with food, Salome keeps her eyes resolutely upon the tablecloth. Chloe finds this behavior so peculiar she stares at the girl, willing her to look up, but it's not until Toby, laying down his fork and addressing his parents in his most sententious tone, says "Mom, Dad, we have some very important news," that Salome raises her eyes and levels at Chloe a look teeming with defiance and calculation.

❧❧

"For God's sake," Brendan says. Chloe, wrapped in her flowered flannel robe, her hair disarrayed, blowing her nose into a tissue, hovers in the bathroom doorway. "Stop crying. You're being ridiculous."

"What am I supposed to do?" she says bitterly. "Jump for joy?"

"It's not the end of the world."

"It is for him. He's twenty-one years old and she's trapped him for life. We'll never be free of her now, none of us."

"Calm down. They can hear you." Toby and Salome, now, for obvious reasons, allowed to sleep in the same bed, are in Toby's old room. As he watched the lovers climb the stairs hand in hand, Brendan had amused himself with the maxim about the pointlessness of closing the barn door after the horse has left the barn. Salome's rising rear struck him as a bit rumpish, her coarse hair not unlike a mane.

Somehow they'd gotten through the day without an outright declaration of hostilities, though it hadn't been easy. Brendan was pleased with his own conduct; he'd been up to the mark— supportive, understanding, confident, masking his concern be- neath a veil of goodwill. Chloe hadn't done so well. After the announcement there was a brief silence in which it was clear the next utterance would characterize the conflict to come. Then, with a ponderous sigh, she said, "What are you going to do?"

Toby cast Salome a rallying glance; they had been preparing for this confrontation for days. "What do you think we're go- ing to do, Mom?" he said. "We're going to get married."

"But you're too young," Chloe exclaimed. "You hardly know each other."

"That's somewhat beside the point, isn't it?" Toby replied.

"I don't think so," Chloe said. "Not at all. I think that is the point. It's too soon. I'm assuming this was an accident. There's plenty of time to have children once you've finished school."

"What are you suggesting?" Salome said.

"Chloe," Brendan said.

"Does your father know about this?" Chloe said.

"Not yet," Salome replied.

"We wanted to tell you first," Toby said.

"I'm sure he won't think it's a good idea."

"You don't know anything about my father," Salome said calmly.

"It's not an idea," Toby said. "It's a baby."

Chloe put her hand over her mouth, holding in the dozen or so things they all knew must not be said. She pushed her chair from the table, got up, and went to the stove. "My God," she said.

"Mom," Toby said. "Try to be reasonable." Chloe moved a pot from one burner to another, picked up the egg carton and put it back down. Her hands were shaking, and when she turned to look at her son, her eyes were filled with tears. "How could you do this?" she said.

"Chloe," Brendan said again.

"Excuse me," Chloe said, passing between her empty chair and the door. She went through the mudroom, out across the lawn, walking briskly, not looking back. Brendan watched her from the window. She was going out to her studio for a good cry.

"She'll be all right," Brendan said. "She's just surprised."

"So are you," Toby said. "But you're not in tears."

"She worries about you," Brendan said. "She just wants you to be happy."

"Do I look unhappy?" Toby said.

Salome took up the pitcher, doused her pancakes with syrup, and attacked the stack with her knife and fork.

"Eating for two," Toby observed, smiling at her.

Chloe stayed away until breakfast was over and the three had cleared up the dishes. They were settled on the screened porch, rummaging through the papers, when she appeared with ghostly calm and requested that Toby come and walk with her. She's miffed that no one came after her, Brendan thought, but if he had gone she would have told him she wanted to be alone. She wanted her son to come to her, but Toby had not come, so now she came to him. "Sure, Mom," Toby said, putting aside the magazine. He accompanied his mother across the lawn toward the pond, where there was a secluded bench. Salome looked after them, her chin lifted so that her eyelids were lowered, her jaw firmly set. My daughter-in-law, Brendan thought, admitting to himself that the idea gave him, well, pause. "She's really upset," Salome said.

Which is true, Brendan agrees, faced with his fuming, teary wife. Chloe is making herself sick. She sits on the edge of the bed, wadding a sodden bit of tissue, her face splotchy, like a child in a tantrum. "They were using condoms when they thought of it," Chloe hisses. "But they didn't always think of it. She wanted to get pregnant."

"He told you that?"

"He seems to think it's fine. He's flattered that she trusted him. He's an idiot."

"It wouldn't be better if he was angry about it, you know."

"Of course it would. She'd have an abortion and that would be the end of it."

"She's a Catholic, Chloe."

"Catholics have abortions every day."

"Her mother is dead."

"What's that got to do with it?"

"Well, perhaps since she doesn't have a mother, she wants to be one."

Chloe is silent a moment, considering this proposition. Brendan takes the time to feel gratified by his own powers of observation, though he had not consciously drawn this conclusion until he spoke it.

"So that's your deep psychological analysis of her motivations," Chloe says.

Brendan gets up from the bed, walks away from her. She's poison when she's like this. It's a side of her no one else ever sees. "It doesn't matter what either of us thinks," he says. "You're just going to have to make the best of it." He goes into the hall, closing the door carefully behind him. He'll spend an hour at his desk in the relative peace and quiet of the Nile delta, at the siege of Damietta, which has been going on for a year.

Long ago, about the time of the Fifth Crusade, he likes to say, Brendan had a contract for his book. There was no money involved; he had submitted a proposal and three chapters to a reputable university press and they had offered to undertake the publication. This agreement was the subject of jubilation at home—Chloe had opened a bottle of champagne—and perhaps some envy in his department, where publication was the mirage they all pursued as they wandered through the desert of stultifying departmental meetings and class overloads. There were three categories of nomad: those who had published only articles, those who had book contracts, and those who had published books. Brendan's elevation into the second class had caused those in the first to look upon him with renewed interest. David Bodley, the tribal chieftain, author of seven thick volumes on the Civil War, had dropped by Brendan's office to chat about the various editors he knew at the press. In the spring, Brendan's request for release time was miraculously approved, and when he proposed a course devoted to the Crusades, as he had done every year since his hiring, Bodley came to his defense, pointing to the suitability of the offering in the light of Professor Dale's expertise and forthcoming book on the subject.

"It's who you know," Brendan assured Chloe when a chapter on the sack of Constantinople was accepted by a journal that had been sending him form rejections for years. Buoyed up by the contract and this publication, Brendan had successfully navigated the perilous straits of his tenure review, though admittedly the water beneath him was shallow. "Lucky for you the student evaluations were strong," Bodley assured him. "That pulled you through."

With no fear of imminent unemployment, the goodwill of his colleagues, and a well-earned sabbatical leave, he is free to concentrate all his energies on his book about the rise to power of a thirteenth-century Norman potentate who ruled his vast dominions from Sicily and passed his own spare time writing a lengthy treatise on falconry still considered definitive by practitioners of the art.

Now Brendan sits at his desk looking steadily back, trying to discern through the centuries this particular madman. There are plenty to choose from. Frederick is the redhead on a horse with a falcon perched on his thickly padded arm. Behind him the brightly caparisoned entourage extends over a green hill. At his signal a courtier spurs his horse and overtakes his lord, who leans down to speak, while the falcon unfurls its wings and screeches in protest. "Get me rewrite," says the emperor.

The word goes out all along the trotting, sweating retinue of those in abject attendance—past the noble lords, the cutthroat Saracens, the Jewish and Arab doctors, the swearing carters on their rattling wagons piled high with provisions, linens, tapestries, piles of dried fish, casks of oil and wine, a mountain of books—all the way to the ragged beggar on his weary donkey plugging along at the end of the line: the court historian, with his bundle of foolscap and sealed pots of ink. So familiar, that wrinkled brow, that squinting eye. Brendan chuckles, having found himself, yet again, at the other end of his telescopic lens into the past.

The past: as threatening as the future and about as comprehensible, and its eager chroniclers, who make a living sorting through it, trash collectors, recyclers, at best; the enterprise strikes him as a ludicrous folly. Everything cooked up piecemeal and after the fact to serve the needs of the present, trotted out to the public, painstakingly garnished and always, always with an agenda. Like leftovers. Here is the historian opening the fridge to find containers of unidentified stuff. Is that what's left of the chicken Kiev? Is this thing wrapped in foil a half-eaten, moldy Napoleon?

Brendan gazes moodily at the last sentence he wrote, two nights ago. When Frederick finally arrived in Jerusalem, he had been excommunicated by the pope. The Sultan al-Kamil didn't know it. Frederick wasn't out to convert the infidel, or even to subdue him, he just wanted to make a deal. He was in earnest, but he wasn't an honest broker.

Honest broker. Exactly the phrase. Brendan takes up his pen and writes it in the margin. There, a good night's work. As he switches off the light he becomes aware of a sound; at first he thinks it's something scratching inside the wall. Gradually he determines that it's coming from above, from Toby's room, and then he recognizes it: muffled laughter. While his mother cries herself bitterly to sleep, Toby is there in bed with his pregnant girlfriend, and they are whispering and giggling like naughty children at a sleepover.

When we married my husband was proud to have an educated wife from the city, but his parents were suspicious of me from the start. I enjoyed reading Italian novels and poetry, a useless activity as far as they were concerned, and I didn't wear practical shoes ever. If we went out to one of the miserable cafés in our town—we had two—I put on lipstick: clearly a slut. My mother-in-law was always sewing and cooking and cleaning; she boiled all the linens every week in a big pot and beat them with a flat bat, a true peasant. Nothing on her mind but bending everyone in the house to her will.

Before we went to live with his parents, we got on well. My husband worked hard all day and came home tired. I prepared a simple meal, we ate, drank, made love, went to sleep, started again the next day. While he was gone, I lay about reading poetry and writing to friends from school. I met an English woman at the farm cooperative, she was married to the town administrator, and she agreed to give me English lessons. My husband encouraged me. It was his dream to go to America, where he had an uncle, and become rich.

Then the children began coming and our lives were changed, but still, I wasn't unhappy. I haven't forgotten those days. I wasn't sorry I'd left my family and gone to be a farmer's wife. I liked having my own house, even though it was cramped and the walls were cracked. When the children came, I was proud of how strong and fierce they were, like kittens, tussling on the floor and shouting. My little girl was the last one, as fearless as her brothers. Her father adored her: she was his darling. Whenever he came home he called for her; if she was fussy or sick, he held her in his arms by the hour until she fell asleep. She was born two months before my father-in-law suffered a stroke. He fell over in his wheat field and was carried home on a board, paralyzed from the neck down. We were forced to give up our farm and take over his. My husband planned to build a new house for us, but somehow that never happened, so we were all crammed into his parents' house, seven of us in four rooms, and pretty soon all I could think about was how much I wanted to get away.

You wanted to go back to the city?

I didn't get so far as to picture a new life. I just wanted to escape the one I was in.

Siting a house at the top of a hill is, in Chloe's view, indicative of an arrogant and aggressive stance vis-à-vis one's neighbors. Look up at me, attack me if you dare. This was clearly the prevailing attitude in medieval Italy, hence the steep climb to the *centro storico* from one end of the country to the other. The high position, the gates closed at nightfall, the parapets from which haughty guards glowered down upon the surrounding plain, all presuppose an enemy. Yet, enclosed though they are, Italian hill towns radiate light and heat. Geraniums line the piazzas, flowering vines spill over the ramparts, and the citizens grow tomatoes on their roof gardens, where the laundry dries in an hour. The breezes are desultory, lifting a napkin from an outdoor table, sending an empty cigarette packet skittering into a gutter. Had Patrick Brontë settled his numerous family in Orvieto or Montefalco, they might have dried out their sodden lungs in the Umbrian sun and lived to plant flowers on the paternal grave.

No description of the Yorkshire moors on which the Brontë children failed to flourish is without the attributive "windswept." Trees are stunted; the vegetation—scant heath and broom—clings to the earth. In the dales there is no shortage of stone and abundant water. Hiking trails wind along cheerful streams, but the moors are bleak; even the stone is a dingy gray.

Chloe turns from the photograph glowing on her computer screen. She has passed an hour virtually touring the town of Haworth, including the Brontës' cramped parsonage and the two houses that may have served Emily as models for Wuthering Heights and the Grange.

A tale of two houses, after all. As Lockwood describes it, the house at the Heights has little to recommend it. The walls are thick, the windows small and deep-set to keep out the incessant wind. The front yard is walled and there are a few fir trees at one end; it is there that young Catherine Linton and Hareton Earnshaw plant a garden of primroses as Heathcliff paces, indifferent to them, near death and mad with joy at the constant presence of his long-deceased, dark-angel Cathy. The interior of the house is gloomy, lit by the fireplace, candles, oil lamps, fire of some kind burning all day and into the night. Like hell. There are touches of refinement, an oak sideboard laden with plates and tankards, the painted canisters arranged along the fireplace ledge. The chairs are painted green, the floor is white stone, but the ceilings are low, the heavy beams exposed. A farmer's domicile, crude and serviceable; the barn is attached to the house.

Thrushcross Grange, by contrast, has French doors giving onto a curved drive, crimson-covered Empire furnishings, a white ceiling edged in gold, a chandelier, and red carpet. There is a piano. Ellen Dean refers to the house as "the Hall." When Catherine Earnshaw leaves her home to become Mrs. Edgar Linton, she is, socially speaking, moving up, but she has literally to go downhill to do it. Like her own house, Catherine is haughty, yet crude. Her ceilings, as it were, are low.

Chloe sketches two rectangles on a page. Suppose, though it is on a hilltop, all her renderings of the Heights feature a low horizon line, so that the house is dwarfed by the stormy sky it seems to generate, while the elevation of the Grange is always high, so that it's viewed from below, necessitating an ascent, offering, presumably, a wider view of both the heavens and the world of men.

The message is clear: social status trumps geography. The Heights must look up to the Grange, the Grange looks down upon the Heights. Heathcliff, the outsider, the foundling, brings a plague on both houses. This is the first visual serendipity Chloe has had, and it sends a familiar sensation of ease along her spine. There's a rightness to it that comes from the text, from the physical arrangement of the imagined world. She sets her pad aside and goes to the woodstove, where she throws another stick onto the fire. The leaves are all on the ground now, brown and sere; she's progressed from sweater to quilted jacket for her daily walk across the field. Through the bare trees she can see the roof of the house and part of the terrace. Brendan isn't there; he has gone to the library to take out more books.

And to get away from his wife. He will skip the lunch they usually share, and maybe the afternoon coffee as well. By dinner the argument will be no more than a tender area, a bruise better left untouched.

It started when Toby called to say he and his pregnant girl-friend had decided to spend Thanksgiving day with her father in Louisiana. The original plan had been for the couple to come up on Wednesday, spend Thanksgiving with the Dales, leave for Louisiana on Friday, and return to New York late on Sunday. It was too hectic, Toby explained; the break was too short and Salome wanted more time with her father, who was not yet apprised of her condition. It was Toby's good fortune that his father answered this call. "It's fine," Brendan said. "We'll go to the Burdocks'. They ask us every year and we never go."

"It was hard to get tickets," Toby said. "Most flights were already packed. We had to take what we could get and they were really expensive."

"Do you need money?" Brendan asked.

"No, Dad, thanks. Just tell Mom I'm sorry about it. She's not going to be pleased."

"She ordered a bird," Brendan agreed. "But she can cancel that. Or we can just bring it to the Burdocks'."

Chloe, sitting at the table, sent him an envenomed look over her coffee cup.

"No, it's perfectly understandable," Brendan concluded. "No need to apologize. Give a call when you get in, just to let us know you made it. Right. Right. Bye, son. Love to Salome."

"They're not coming," Chloe said as he hung up the phone.

"No. They're flying out of Newark Wednesday morning, straight to New Orleans. They had trouble getting tickets."

"Right," Chloe said.

"And Salome wants to spend more time with her father."

"Has she told him yet?"

"No."

"Why can't she go by herself and let Toby come home?"

"Well, I think the reasons are obvious."

"Do you?" Chloe said.

Brendan went to the window and stood looking out. "Mike's got something, it must be a vole."

"We're not going to the Burdocks'."

"We could. They always have a crowd. We'd be welcome."

"So your idea is that I call Millie and say, gee, our son has decided to skip Thanksgiving with us because he's knocked up his girlfriend and they have to go to Louisiana to give her father the news, so even though we don't have a lot to be thankful for, we thought we'd come to dinner at your house."

Brendan mumbled something, not looking away from the window.

"What did you say?"

He turned to her. "I said why would he want to come here?"

"Who?"

"Toby."

"Oh, I don't know. Because we're his parents. Is that a good reason?"

"Is it good enough for you?"

Chloe doesn't remember how she answered this question. It was a taunt, actually, an accusation. All her married life she had whined about the tyranny of holidays. After her parents retired to a condo in Florida and Brendan's moved to Arizona, the travel arrangements were complex and expensive, but there was no way around it; to say "We can't make it this year" was unthinkable, they must drag themselves across the country and sit down to tables overcharged with food and have conversations that steadfastly skimmed the surface of every subject. Then, over a period of five years, the first one suddenly, two lingering and suffering, one in dementia, their parents had all passed away. Now Brendan and Chloe were free of obligations. Brendan's question implied that Chloe was intent on imposing the same onerous regime she had so resented upon her son. This stung her and she had retorted coldly, but what did she say? Whatever it was, it shocked Brendan. "What's wrong with you?" he said, drawing away from her, his eyes icy with incomprehension and distaste.

That girl is what's wrong with me, Chloe thinks. That devious creature with her cold eyes and hot body. She's got a peasant's build, strong back, wide hips, designed to breed and pull roots out of the ground. In ten years she'll be fat. And she'll be here, dangling babies, my grandchildren, who will run around the house like vandals, pulling down the curtains, peeing on the carpets. Chloe snorts at her own grim prognostication. She does a quick sketch of a stolid Salome, her feet planted wide apart, her hands on her hips. The hair is a cloud of hornets swarming out to the edges of the page. It's a good likeness. She would show it to Brendan, but now is not the time. Maybe later, when it all comes true. Carefully she prints a line across the bottom of the page: *Run for your life; it's that hornet-headed girl.* It might make an amusing children's book. She slips it into a file of other such sketches and turns her attention to the problem of the two houses, Thrushcross Grange, where the pallid Lintons pass another decorous afternoon over cups of milky tea and cream cakes, and Wuthering Heights, where young Catherine Earnshaw is slamming out the door with a kestrel clinging to her arm, intent on a rendezvous with her boon companion, Heathcliff, the ruthless gypsy who waits for her and her alone out on the windswept moors.

❖❖

It's their first trip together. Toby is relieved to find that Salome's approach to getting somewhere is the opposite of his parents'. Their trips are micromanaged, with nothing left to chance, hotel rooms, transfers, train and plane tickets all purchased months in advance. Salome bought their tickets a week ahead, indifferent to all variables but price, so they are leaving at an early hour. She scoffed at the airline's requirement that they arrive two hours ahead of the departure time. They were on the street, bags in hand, looking for a cab at five-fifteen, plenty of time, she assured him, to catch a six-thirty flight, and she had proved correct. At the airport she appeared more interested in getting coffee than catching the plane. The loading procedure irked her—her method was to get on last. Toby distracted himself from his uneasiness about the meeting to come by observing his companion. He was, he knew, more widely traveled than she was, though he had not, as she had, escaped from a war zone, but now they were going to her home, a place as exotic to him as Lilliput was to Gulliver. He would have liked to spend a night in New Orleans, but Salome explained that it was impractical, as her father was driving from Empire to pick them up and he would want to go directly back.

And so his only experience of the Crescent City is the view from the window as the plane descends from the clouds, dropping low over a body of water so large he takes it to be the Gulf of Mexico.

"It's the lake," Salome corrects him. "The Gulf is hours from here."

"I thought New Orleans was on the Gulf," Toby says. "I thought there would be a beach."

"There's not much in the way of beaches," she says. "There's one at Grand Isle. Beaches are in Florida."

Toby peers out the undersized window; they are over land. Mile upon mile of tiny green squares framing black roofs roll out beneath them. "It's very flat," Toby observes.

Salome laughs. "It is flat," she agrees.

At the airport the smell of mildew and the whack of icy air from the air-conditioning assault the passengers as they file obediently into the carpeted terminal. Salome walks quickly, her backpack slung from one shoulder, her head lowered as if she expects to meet resistance. "Are you nervous?" Toby asks, keeping pace beside her.

She looks up, frowning; he expects a flat denial, but her expression softens and she slows down. "A little," she says. "I don't know why." They come to the maze of the security check, where bemused travelers pull off shoes, patting their hips and sides as they step up to the fake doorway, and past that to the huddle of those who are waiting to greet the soon to be liberated. Toby scans the group and, with perfect confidence, picks out Salome's father. He is standing a little apart, at the far end, his light eyes fastened on his daughter. He's a big, solid man, broad-shouldered, thick-necked; he appears rough hewn from something more durable than flesh. His frown is kept in place by deep, chiseled creases; his hair is white, coarse, wiry stuff, like a foamy scouring pad bursting over his forehead. He shifts his weight from foot to foot, controlling his impulse to rush into the crowd and pluck his daughter from it. "Tata," Salome says, stepping out ahead of Toby. She doesn't run, but there is a skip in the gait that propels her to her father's arms. He stoops to receive her and scoops her up against his chest. His eyes roll upward, the granitic frown lifts into a smile of surprising sweetness. Well, she's his only daughter, but Toby can't fail to note the contrast between this greeting and the reserved handshakes and cheek pecks that he exchanges with his own parents when they meet in such venues. Salome slides down her father's chest, landing with a flutter as Toby separates from his hustling fellow passengers and arrives at her side. She grasps his hand, presenting him eagerly. "Tata," she says. "This is my Toby."

My Toby, he is thinking as he holds out his hand to be swallowed in the hirsute paw of the Oyster King.

"Toby," he says, stress on To. "I am Branko."

✢✢

The house is a tract house of distilled ugliness, a white brick box with small, high windows, a carport tacked on at one side, a treeless, patchy lawn. A rectangle of fake stained glass set in a peeling blue steel door adds a touch of irremediable sadness. Inside it is dark and smells of boiled potatoes. Toby follows Salome past some heavy furniture crowded upon an expanse of brown carpet to the kitchen, where the linoleum and cheap plywood cabinets don't come as a surprise. There is a sliding glass door opening onto a square of concrete, which has the effect of a klieg light, blasting the fierce sun into the room. A table covered in a red cloth and surrounded by sturdy chairs sports a bowl of oranges. Branko extracts three beers from the refrigerator and passes them out to his guests. He raises his can to tap the other two in a mock toast. "Toby," he says. "Welcome to my house."

While the men sit at the table, Salome examines the pots on the stove. "Mrs. Yuratich is still coming?" she says.

"Sometimes it is her daughter," Branko says. "She is becoming too feeble."

"She must be ninety," Salome says. "Do you want a glass for your beer?" she asks Toby.

"No," he says. "The can is fine."

She takes a chair between them. "Here we are," she says. "At last."

"You are tired from your trip," Branko says.

"No. I'm not tired."

"I'm fine," Toby agrees. "This beer is good."

Branko beams at his daughter. "You are well," he says.

Salome shoots a meaningful glance at Toby. "I'm fine, Tata. I couldn't be better. I'm glad to see you." Her father lays his hand over hers and says something Toby doesn't understand. If I weren't here, he thinks, they wouldn't speak English. In ways that Branko Drago does not fathom, though he will, and soon, Toby knows himself to be an intruder, an interloper, yet, though everything is unfamiliar, he feels for the moment curiously at home. The long ride in Branko's truck, down the straight, flat highway between the sloping green levees, one holding back the Mississippi River, the other the Gulf of Mexico, had an eerie, somnolent beauty to it that thrilled him. They crossed the river on a ferry, a disembodying experience; the line of trucks waiting as the boat whirled toward them across the water, the clanking of chains and gates, the voices of the ferrymen as the vehicles crawled onto the deck, then the release, the floating away. "Can we get out?" Toby asked.

"Of course," Branko replied, throwing open his door. They went to the rail and Toby looked down at the churning brown water, the green expanse of the steadily approaching shore. The wind blew Salome's hair back from her face, the spray moistened her cheeks. She smiled at him, resting her hand over his on the rail, and he had the sensation that they were crossing some mythical river together, the Lethe or the Styx, on their way to another world altogether, from which they might never return.

In the kitchen the phone rings and Branko rises to answer it.

He switches to Croatian, gradually raising the volume and turning his back on the room. Salome leans over the table and brushes Toby's cheek, then his lips with hers. "Do you want to take a walk?" she says.

"Sure." Salome speaks to her father, who turns, nods, waves them away. As they go out through the sliding door, she says, "He gets so agitated. I worry about his blood pressure."

"What's he talking about?"

"The boat," she says. "It's always the boat." She leads him across the yard to a cracked and buckling sidewalk, past two more tract houses, one of which has parted company with its carport, and along a grassy path that leads to the levee. Clouds roll in from that direction; the air is cool and heavy with impending rain. They climb up the steep slope of the green hill to the top, which is as wide as a road. In fact, there are brown ribbons of tire tracks worn in the grass. Toby expects to see open water, but he is looking down into a forest of trees rising above the undulating shallows. In the rippling marsh grasses against the bank a shattered rowboat covered in vines shifts idly with the tide. "Is this the Gulf?" Toby asks.

"It's out there," Salome says. "You just can't see it from here." She leads him down to a tree that has extended its thick roots in a ledge, creating a shady seating area. She draws Toby down beside her and they sit, their arms entwined, looking out into the swamp. "This is my secret place," she says.

"I can see why. It's mysterious."

"It is, isn't it?" They are quiet, listening to the sound of water ruminating in the shallows; a bird cries and is answered by a comrade farther out from the shore. "When we first came here," Salome says, "I was miserable. I missed my mother so much, the kids at school were awful to us; my father was struggling just to keep us alive. He wasn't born to fishing; he had to learn a whole new trade. My brother and I didn't get along; we still don't. I used to come here after school and cry. I cried and called out to my mother to come back, to come get me. I cried so hard, I thought she must hear me.

"One day I cried myself to sleep, and when I woke up it was dark. I sat here, there was a light," she points to the wrecked boat, "down there. She was sitting in the boat, holding up a lantern and watching me. She was wearing a dress I recognized, a dark blue wool, and her light blue jacket, and she was waving to me and saying, 'Don't cry, *moja draga*, don't cry.'"

"How old were you?" Toby asks.

"I was ten."

"It was a dream."

"I guess so. But I felt better after that. I thought, she knows I'm here. And I love this place, because it's the last place I saw her."

Toby gazes down at the boat, imagining the lonely child waking in the humid darkness to a vision of her lost happiness. Salome leans against him, nuzzling his cheek. He pulls her in closer, kissing her eyes, her lips, moving his hands over her breasts, intent upon driving out sadness with desire. If it can be done, it will be here, in this place. She clutches his back, shifting under him, her eyes damp with tears. She whispers his name, fumbles with the button of his jeans. No one can see them here; they are hidden from everyone but her mother. Her eyes shift down to the boat, back to his face; she opens her lips beneath his. He has arrived at the source of her foreignness.

※※

Dinner is potatoes, cabbage, and boiled shrimp. They toss the shells onto a newspaper Salome has spread on the table. Branko is asking questions about Salome's classes. His interest in her teacher's credentials is interrupted by laughter from two men coming across the yard to the glass door. "My brother," Salome says to Toby. The men push inside, provoking a swell of greetings and introductions. Salome has to reach up to hug her brother, Andro, who frowns at Toby over her back. His friend, Mat, of more modest demeanor and size, waits his turn to take Salome in his arms. "Here's our scholar," he says, holding her at arm's length, pulling her in again. "What are you doing up there?" he chides her. "We need you here."

"No," Branko assures him. "She's too good for you now. Poor Mat."

Andro, helping himself to a beer from the refrigerator, says coolly, "Well, she thinks she is."

"Nice to meet you," Toby says blandly to Mat, who holds out his hand.

"Mat Barrois," says Mat.

Andro hands out beers and the two men pull up chairs to the table.

"Are you hungry?" Branko says. "Eat."

They decline. They have had dinner at a café. The talk turns to recondite matters of boats and leases.

Toby watches Salome, who enters this conversation with ease and a certain authority. Mat defers to her. He has pushed his chair in between Salome and her brother. The table is small, so he is close to her. His hand brushes her arm, his eyes linger over her face, at one point he puts his arms around her and says, "You see. We're lost without you, girl." Toby finds this offensive, but Salome evidently does not. She pats Mat's hand, takes another long pull of her beer. Should she be drinking so much? Toby tries to catch her eye, but it's hopeless; she has deserted him for these large, crude men who are laughing too loudly. Andro flashes him an occasional penetrating look, makes a point of offering him another beer. Branko extends his laughter to include Toby, and he smiles back, though he doesn't get the joke. He is trying hard not to hear a voice that isn't at this table, but is familiar and appalling, which says, "You know nothing about her. How can you even be sure . . ." He dismisses it, tunes it out like a radio, but it makes him sullen. He could bring all this excessive jollity to a screeching halt with a simple announcement. *She shouldn't be drinking so much because she's pregnant.* That would do it, and why not?

Their plan is to tell Branko after dinner; presumably Salome is waiting for these two to leave, but she doesn't appear to be impatient for that event. They all, including Mat, seem to know that Toby and Salome live together, that he is with her, to be included in all arrangements. Mat is talking about a dance in a hall down the road, a local band; Salome went to school with the accordionist, Rene. Why not take her friend out to hear them? "Mat's a Cajun," Salome announces to Toby, who has guessed this much. "All he thinks about is dancing."

Branko approves. He doesn't dance, but he likes the music.

"The women fuss over you," Salome teases him. "That's what you like."

"Yes," Branko agrees. "I am a good catch."

Andro laughs his bitter laugh. He will go because the beer is cheap. They are on their feet, clearing dishes, wrapping up the shrimp shells, stashing the leftovers in the refrigerator. Salome wants a shawl from her bag, and Toby follows her to change his shoes. They go through the dark living room to the hall. "I want to stop at the bathroom," Toby says. Salome takes his hand and whispers, "Tata likes you. I can tell."

"So far," Toby says. "But he may feel differently when we tell him."

"He'll be fine."

"I thought you wanted to tell him tonight," Toby says.

"No. Not tonight. There's no hurry. Let's wait until morning." She switches on the hall light, points to the door on the left. "That's the bathroom," she says.

❖❖

Toby wakes to the sound of Salome retching, which makes his own stomach uneasy. He's hollow-headed, his mouth is gluey and foul as a bog. The toilet flushing, the tap running, exacerbate the pressure on his full bladder. Salome comes in, decidedly green, and gives him a wan smile before falling into the bed. The mattress sags, rolling her into him. "Are you OK?"

"Oh God," she says. "I think so."

Toby staggers to his feet and crouches over the suitcase, bleary-eyed and dazed, though he knows where he is. "There's no one here," Salome says. "You don't need to put your pants on."

"Good news," he says, heading out the door. The floor in the hall is Formica, cool and damp under his feet. He passes the door to Branko's room, which is half open, revealing a dresser and the edge of a frameless bed with the sheets trailing off to the floor.

After relieving his bladder, he confronts his reflection indifferently. He ponders the stream of images that flow from the territory labeled "last night." One in particular recurs, troubling yet alluring; it is his lover in the arms of another man. All around her other couples are moving gracefully, as she is, animated by the insistent drive of the music wafting across the deck, into the clearing and beyond to the brooding darkness of the forest. The moon casts a thin light over the scene, made eerie by the torches which waft citrus-laden smoke into the atmosphere. The singer occasionally interrupts his patois with a bird call; the violinist imitates a sound that might be a wild cat, but the accordion and the drummer are relentlessly civilized, declaring an allegiance to the antique world of waltzes and country reels. With practiced ease and a confident eye, Mat Barrois works Salome from side to side, spins her out and back again. They never so much as brush against another couple, though the dance floor is crowded and everyone is moving fast. This floor is not really a floor; it is the earth itself, patchy with grass and hard from baking in the sun. The feet that pound it, to Toby's astonishment, are unshod. Barefoot girl dancing in the moonlight. It's a line from a song, a dreamy image from the past. This barefoot girl doesn't look pregnant, and as he watches her, Toby hears again the unwelcome voice suggesting that he knows nothing about her, that she has tricked him and trapped him. As he stands at the sink squeezing toothpaste onto his brush, he is reassured by the recollection of Salome's morning sickness. She's pregnant all right, and he really needs to talk with her about her drinking. It can't be good for the baby.

All evening he had sat with Branko, who was attended by women like a pasha in his harem; they rotated food and drink before him as he smiled, his big forearms resting on the wooden picnic table, his shoulders and head moving with the rhythm of the music, his eyes on his daughter. "You're not dancing," he announced to Toby.

"No," Toby said. "I'd just step on her feet."

Branko laughed, finished another beer. "Smart boy," he said. "She wouldn't like that."

In the breaks between dances Salome came to the table, hung her arms over her father's back, and helped herself to his beer. "Do you want to try?" she said to Toby. "I'll teach you."

"No," Toby said. "I'll just embarrass you."

"It's been so long since I danced like this. How I miss this place. Isn't this band great?"

"Yes," Toby said.

"What a night," Salome said. "It's good to be home." She came to Toby and kissed his cheek, filched a bit of cracker from the plate in front of him. "Are you having fun, darling?" she said, but before he could answer she had turned back to Mat, who stood waiting on the steps. The violinist ran up a scale that met the accordion coming down.

"Mat is a good boy," Branko said. "But he's not a college boy."

"He's a good dancer," Toby observed. A blowsy redhead appeared at Branko's shoulder, setting down two sweating glasses of beer. "Is this Salome's boyfriend from up there?" she asked. "Are you having a good time, honey?"

Toby took the beer and swallowed a quarter of it. "Yes," he said.

In truth, because she was always dancing, Toby had drunk a lot more than Salome; he owns to that. His memory of the ride back is hazy. He might have been stumbling, but Salome wasn't. She leaped up into the truck, laughing at Toby, who followed with less grace. When they got home she insisted on washing her feet, surely not the behavior of a drunken slattern. Toby brushes his teeth and slaps cold water on his face, then goes back down the hall to the bedroom. Salome is lying propped up on the pillows, grinning at him. "A little hungover?" she says. He stands looking down at her breasts, the curve from her waist to her hips. The sheet covers everything below that. Carefully he pushes the sheet down with his foot. One good thing about her pregnancy is that they no longer have to worry about her getting pregnant. "Not at all," he says, collapsing over her with mock solemnity. His brain sends out a shock wave to his eye sockets as he gathers her in beneath him. She is giggling, wrapping her legs around him. He's not the only one who needn't take precautions now, he thinks, but Salome's lips open beneath his and he uses his tongue to bury this perilous thought in her mouth.

❖❖

Chloe wakes to the sound of gunshots. Run, turkeys, run, she thinks. Brendan snores peacefully beside her. She leans across him to check the clock: 5:30. She is wide awake, fiercely so, her head pumping with rage and shame at that rage. She thinks of her son—down there it's an hour earlier—asleep in that house with those people: she pictures something on piers with screened porches, a boat tied up to a dock outside, and marsh all around. Maybe herons. "They're having duck," Brendan said when he hung up the phone. "Salome's brother shot it; they'll be going to the aunt's house."

"Sounds like fun," Chloe said acidly. She didn't speak to Toby. If he had asked for her, she would have, but he didn't. She has not, except politely, distantly, spoken to him since the conversation on the bench. The kiss he gave her when they left was cold, his lips barely brushed her cheek, his body drew away from her, and she had accepted it without comment. Of course he was angry; she had offended him, and now she is being punished. Because of what she said.

A volley of gunshots, very close to the house. Brendan opens his eyes. "Maybe we should invite him to dinner," he says.

"It would be like the first Thanksgiving," Chloe says. "The settlers invite the savages."

Brendan chuckles. "Aren't you ashamed of yourself?" he says.

She isn't, really, though she's conscious that she should be. She sits up and feels about for her slippers.

"Are you getting up?"

"I might as well," she says. "I can't sleep."

In the kitchen she sets the kettle to boil and stands looking out at the early morning mist. Something drops from one of the trees near the pond, something heavy, ponderous, a chattering sound, and down comes another and another. An amazing sight: the trees are raining turkeys. As they hit the ground they scramble up the hill, their heads bobbing, ruffling their big, largely useless wings, chortling to one another. A new day in the kingdom of the turkeys, and none got eaten by a coyote in the night. Soon they have formed a troop and set off on their progress into the forest.

The kettle whistles, Chloe turns away thinking about the poacher, the Lebanese. He can't be much of a shot, but he might get a turkey for his dinner; there are plenty enough of them. She pictures his triumph, arriving at the hovel with one of these enormous birds across his shoulder, the family rejoicing, the youngest—the beloved cripple Tiny Khalil—cries out "Allah bless us, every one." Later, gathered around the table, the children wide-eyed at the feast, the kindly mother explains that on this day Americans celebrate the bounty of their country, and look, here is this great American bird their father has brought to them, proof of the continuous blessing of their new land.

Chloe opens the refrigerator, pushing past the turkey roast to get the milk. Thanksgiving for two, is it too sad to contemplate? A remark of Brendan's from the very early days of their marriage floats back to her: *I didn't think you would be so bourgeois.* Why? Because she's an artist?

He was right, she is a bourgeois. She cares about rituals, furniture, flower arrangements, comfort; she dislikes risk. Risk averse, they call it in investing circles. She loves beauty; on this ground she defends herself. If more people did, why would that be such a bad thing?

The tea is brewed; she goes out to the terrace, sipping against the chill. It is neither dark nor light—impossible to tell whether the sky will be overcast or clear. The car crouches like a sleeping animal, its nose resting in the drift of leaves from the beech, now bare. There are sounds, birds, branches rustling in the breeze. From down the road a car comes closer, then goes farther. Her heart rate is elevated; this happens a lot lately, and it makes her feel frail, mortal, frightened. Another shot, far away this time; he's moving off. She looks toward the pond, toward the bench.

"You don't know her at all," she said to him. "How can you be sure it's yours?" Or did she say, "What makes you so sure it's yours?" Something like that; something she shouldn't have said. He was silent, sitting there, his shoulders slumped, listening to her moodily, his brow literally furrowed.

"I thought you were smarter than this." Yes, that too, and some warning about the future. About foreigners, people from an entirely different culture. About Catholics. "Is she even a citizen? Is she trapping you like this just to stay in the country?"

"Are you finished?" he said eventually.

By that time she was weeping. "Darling," she protested. "All I want is your happiness."

He looked at her, his eyes cold, distant, not hostile, almost curious. She knew that her face was splotchy, her hair mussed, that she was unappealing. "I don't believe that," he said.

But he didn't walk away; surely that was something. He stayed with her until she stopped crying, until she said, "Let's go back," and he walked beside her across the lawn to the porch, where the others scarcely looked up from the papers. He went to Salome and leaned over her shoulder to see what she was reading. "What's Friedman on about?" he said.

"Iraq. He's an idiot," she said. "He should read his own book."

✢✢

By that time tensions were high all over the region and our filthy little town was like a fish swimming in toxic water; all the hatred was concentrated in our systems and it was killing us. The men had their disgusting club where they lifted weights and pissed out the windows. One of them pissed on an Orthodox woman on her way home from church—my husband said it was an accident, but I doubt that—and her sons came down to the club to avenge her honor. There was a big fight; they hit one another with the weights and somebody had a knife, so there were injuries on both sides. One of the sons had broken ribs; a club member had a concussion. Hostilities were declared and it was neighbor against neighbor, though no one could do anything openly because the police were putting on a show of being neutral. It was just slander and talk about how they had no right to live in our town at all, how they should be forced to leave, all of them, all at once. We still had the "Unity and Brotherhood" posters up in the schools and in the town offices; it was ludicrous. At the market both sides cut one another. The young men stood in the streets in packs like wolves giving each other evil looks and making snide remarks.

One day when my mother-in-law was beating the linens, I went by myself to see if there was anything besides cabbage to buy and that's where I saw him again. He was standing over a barrow of carrots. I went up and pretended interest in the carrots; they were sad-looking things, but I picked up a bunch and asked the price. "Too high," I said and dropped them back into the barrow.

"You are right, madam," he said. "Those are far too dirty and limp to satisfy a woman like you." Well, it was a rude remark, but it made me

laugh and we exchanged a charged look. I thought: it's been too long since I laughed like that, or felt so drawn by a look. It made me bold. "I've seen you before," I said.

He nodded. "The first day I came to this town; I will never forget it. It gave me some hope that it might not be as horrible here as I feared."

"And is it?"

"Worse," he said. "Until I came upon these magnificent carrots. Now I am thinking it's not so bad."

We were having the same thought: where, where in this godforsaken town will we find a place for our first kiss? How, when every neighbor is spying on every other, will we be able to carry on a love affair in secret?

Did you think you'd be sleeping with the enemy?

No. That's absurd. I never had thoughts like that.

The opportunity to acquaint Branko Drago with his daughter's expectations has, in Toby's view, come and gone more than once. Perhaps Salome is not as sanguine about her father's re-action as she says she is. "Are you going to wait until we're on the way to the airport?" he asks her. It's Friday afternoon, they're leaving on Saturday. Salome is cooking a fish stew while Toby drinks a beer and peruses the world on his computer at the kitchen table.

"I want to tell him when it's just the three of us," she says. "I don't want Andro there."

"Because he won't approve?"

"You've seen him," she says. She has a point. Andro is what Toby's father would call a sociopath, his mother a "piece of work." His temper is an explosive device ever at the ready, and he keeps it fueled with alcohol. In his dealings with other men he vacillates between fawning servility and arrogance; for women he has only contempt. At the dance he got into an argument with a man twice his size who backed down when Andro bared his teeth and snarled at him like a dog. At the Thanksgiving feast, which lasted well into a black night illuminated by endless bottles of šljivovica and much singing of a tune called "Marijana," Andro was preoccupied with the seduction of a doe-eyed girl who could not have been fifteen.

"Do you think he'll try to hurt me?" Toby asks.

"Not if my father tells him not to."

"I don't get it," Toby says. "He knows we live together."

"I know. But it's different if I'm pregnant. Don't ask me why. Look at your mother. She knew we were living together and she had a fit."

"My mother didn't try to hurt you."

"She wants me to have an abortion. Don't you think that will hurt me?"

Toby doesn't want to talk about his mother. "Why is your brother so hostile to you? Has he always been like that?"

"No," Salome says. She is pulling the heads off a mountain of shrimp. "When we were little he was my protector. The war changed him. When mother and my brother died, well, we all changed. We had to leave with the clothes on our backs."

Toby turns off the computer. "That's why there are no pictures," he observes.

"Pictures of what?"

"Of anything. All the pictures in this house were taken after you came here."

"That's right," Salome says.

Toby swallows his beer. He's heard of the dead brother, but not wanting to revive painful feelings, he's never questioned Salome about him. "How did they die?" he asks now.

"Who?"

"Your mother and your brother."

Salome gives him a close look, then turns to the sink to rinse her hands. As she dries them, she frowns thoughtfully at him. "I mostly know what I was told. I remember little bits of it. I was only nine. My grandfather had died about a month earlier; he'd been sick a long time. There was always talk of war. There were Serbs in our town and everyone hated them. Andro was fourteen; he wanted to be a fighter. Then there really was a war. We saw it on television. My mother refused to watch it; she said it was idiotic. One day there were soldiers in the street. They rounded up some people and shot them in a field. No one could go out that night. Josip, my brother, was twelve. He played the violin, he was very talented, and he couldn't understand why he couldn't go to his teacher. He was very upset about that. In the night he snuck out of the house and he didn't come back.

"My parents were having a big fight; it went on for hours. Andro was in on it; he was yelling at my mother. I had to stay in the bedroom with my grandmother. I couldn't make out what they were saying, even though they were shouting. Maybe I did hear, but I don't remember. In the morning my mother was gone. Tata was weeping. He said we had to leave at once; a car was coming for us. When I asked where my mother was, he said we were going to a new house and she would meet us there. Grandma refused to come. Tata heard much later that she died and the house was burned.

"What an awful story," Toby says. He is thinking of his own childhood, catching frogs, climbing trees.

"My grandmother said something that night I never forgot."

"What was it?"

"She said to my father, 'That's what you get for marrying a tramp from the city.' "

Toby shakes his head, out of his depth.

"She and my mother never got along. Mother loved dancing and music and reading. My grandmother thought all that was a waste."

"Did you find out what happened to her?"

"After we got here, Tata told me. She went out to look for Josip and got caught in one of their roundups. They killed her. They'd killed Josip too, just because he was in the street after the curfew."

"What a nightmare."

Salome shrugs, resigned rather than indifferent. "It was a war," she says. "No one talks about it here, but many families have stories like ours. The ones who were here before, like my uncle, they helped us out. That's why we came here. We were refugees." She turns back to the counter, occupies herself peeling onions.

Toby looks on, working his brain over the disturbing images, soldiers in the streets, the boy climbing out the window in the night, his violin clutched beneath his arm, flashlights, shots fired, the child shivering in her bed, her grandmother glaring at the door, the raised, angry voices, the weeping father, the family huddled in the early morning mist outside the door waiting for a car driven by whom? A friend? A stranger? "Who drove you out?" he asks.

"I don't know who he was. I'd never seen him before. Tata seemed to know him, but they didn't talk much. We went through checkpoint after checkpoint—the man had some identification he showed that seemed to work—all the way to Slovenia."

"And then you came straight here?"

"We were in a camp for a few weeks. My father spent every day trying to reach my uncle, making deals with the authorities. His hair turned white. Then we got on a plane and came to New Orleans. My uncle was waiting for us at the airport. He had rented this house for us. We were the lucky ones." She takes up the dishcloth. "These onions are making me cry," she says.

"Not so lucky, if you ask me," Toby says.

"No," she agrees, dabbing her eyes with the cloth. "Americans are the lucky ones."

At dinner Branko is tired and Andro is sullen. There has been trouble with the boat. "What do you do all day here?" Andro says to Toby, who looks to Salome.

"We talk," Salome says. "And we read. You should try it."

"They are on vacation," Branko puts in, "from their studies."

"Your life is a vacation," Andro observes to Salome.

"Andro," Branko says, "be civil. You shame us in front of Toby."

Andro wipes his face with his napkin, pushing back his chair. "I'm off," he says.

"Your sister cooked this food for us. You can at least thank her for that."

Andro, shooting a cool look that glances off Toby on its way to Salome, mumbles a few words in Croatian. There is a brief three-way exchange that doesn't appear hostile. Salome nods at her father as she speaks. Andro, at the door, turns to Toby and says, "Good night."

"Good night," Toby pipes up, feeling childish. He has learned a few words of Croatian, but good night isn't among them. *Hvala lijepo*, which means "thank you," is and he doesn't think that's what Andro said to Salome. "Where's he going?" he asks her.

"Out with Mat," she says.

They eat quietly, washing the food down with beer. Toby thinks a glass of white wine would be welcome, and then, hearing his mother's voice in his own brain, disowns the thought; beer is better with seafood. "This is delicious," he says to Salome. "Very spicy. What makes it red?"

"Paprika," Salome says.

"Yes, very good, darling," Branko says. He is swabbing his bowl with a crust of bread. Toby and Salome exchange a significant look: the moment is at hand.

"Tata," Salome says. "Toby and I have something to tell you."

Branko looks up from his dish, his expression open and expectant. He's like a big dog, Toby thinks, affable, not too bright, but willing. There is something innocent about him, something easily wounded, which is odd, given what he's been through: the war, the death of his mother, wife, son, the narrow escape to a new world. As Salome said he would, he has accepted Toby without reservations. It's as if he has always been there, part of his daughter. Salome is clearly the only woman in his life; he defers to her, solicits her advice, trusts her to manage his finances, but he is not possessive of her, is willing to let her go off to college, live with a stranger, bring the stranger home. Toby admires him for this liberality, the opposite of his own parents' cautious solicitude. It accounts, he concludes, for that quality he most prizes in Salome, her confidence in her own ability, her indifference to criticism.

But it would not be a good thing to excite the wrath of Branko Drago, there is no doubt about that. As Salome begins to speak, Toby notices that his mouth is dry. He clutches his beer, brings it to his lips. "Well, it's this," Salome says. "I'm going to have a baby. Toby and I are very happy about it." Toby puts down his glass and looks at Branko. It's hard to tell how he's taking this news. He blinks, there's a slight twitch at the corner of his mouth; otherwise, he's the same. For a moment, Toby fears he hasn't understood and Salome will have to repeat the carefully chosen words. Branko takes up his napkin and wipes it roughly across his mouth, his eyes resting on Toby, but lightly, with nothing more probing than interest. Toby arranges his features in what he hopes is a "happy about it" expression. Branko turns a more penetrating look upon his daughter, who has primly folded her hands in her lap.

"Have you spoken to the priest?" Branko says.

"I will. I'll call him in the morning. I wanted to tell you first."

"So," Branko says.

"We'll have a wedding here over the Christmas break."

It's the first Toby has heard of this plan. He had assumed they would go to a justice of the peace somewhere, maybe in the city or near his parents' house, sign the forms, take the vows: that would be it. Dinner out, a weekend on the Cape at an inn with a big fireplace. The only change he envisioned was that he would henceforth refer to Salome as "my wife," which he is ready and eager to do. Suddenly he imagines his parents here, in this seedy kitchen, toasting the bride with a beer while Branko and Andro loom in the shadows and Mrs. Yuratich cooks up a pot of bean soup on the stove. He glances at Salome, who is silent now, gazing at her father, waiting, they are all three waiting, for Branko's reaction.

"So," he says again. He pushes his chair from the table, rises ponderously, and goes out into the living room. They hear him pulling out drawers, opening cabinets. He reappears with a bottle in one hand and three slender glasses that he holds by their stems in the other.

Salome smiles at her father. "Uncle Jure's orange wine," she says.

"This is the last of it," Branko says. "I saved it for a time when there is something to celebrate." He sets the bottle and glasses down with surprising delicacy.

"My Uncle Jure died three years ago," Salome explains to Toby. "He had an orange grove down in Venice and every year he made this wine. A month before he died, a hurricane came through and destroyed his grove."

"He made wine before he came here," Branko says. "The hurricane was the death of him. He didn't want to live without his oranges."

"My aunt divided up the bottles among us, and this is the last one."

Branko pulls the stopper from the bottle and pours the bright liquor into the glasses. "It is a traditional Croatian wine. I think you will like it, Toby."

"I know I will," Toby says, taking a glass. Salome and Branko raise their glasses for the toast. "To my grandchild," Branko says. "And to his father, Toby, and his mother, my Salome." They tap their glasses and sip the thick, sweet wine. "It's like sherry," says Toby.

"What will you name the baby?" Branko asks. "He will be an American. Will you give him an American name?"

"Maybe," Salome says. "If it's a boy. If it's a girl, I'll name her after Mother." Toby sips the wine attentively; more news. He has the sense of being carried along by a powerful tide, one that could drag him under or throw him up on the shore—he's dispensable. Salome and her father smile at each other over their glasses, like newlyweds at a banquet. When Toby's glass is empty, Branko is quick to refill it. "Toby," he says. "Look how happy we are. I will be *djed*."

"Grandfather," Salome translates.

"*Djed*," Toby repeats uneasily.

Exactly how dark is Heathcliff? Chloe closes the novel and lays it on the side table. Ellen Dean says he is a gypsy, which means he might be from Eastern Europe, perhaps a Romanian. But Mr. Linton says he is so dark he may be a "Lascar or an American." If he's a Lascar—Chloe has checked this—he could be from the subcontinent, which is vast and many-hued. Brits call Indians "blacks" and even "niggers," though Americans don't, reserving these epithets for people of African descent. Americans automatically qualify the word Indian, which could be East or American. With a dot or with a feather, someone said recently—who was it? It struck Chloe as amusing, also a useful distinction, and she tried it herself in a conversation with a Jewish friend who responded sharply, "I hate that. It's rude." After that, Chloe thought it rude too, though she isn't sure why. What might Indians use to distinguish between Americans and Brits? With a gun or with a brolly? This amuses Chloe. Is Heathcliff a "black," is he a "nigger"? Or an American with a feather?

When he first appears at Wuthering Heights, he is a bundle in Mr. Earnshaw's coat. The patriarch has returned from Liverpool, very late and exhausted from his journey. His children clamor for the gifts he has promised them: Hindley asked for a violin, Catherine, in keeping with her disposition, a whip. What they get is a boy, a filthy street urchin who barks a strange language no one understands. Earnshaw's wife calls the boy a "gypsy brat" and swears her husband has gone mad. Earnshaw explains that he found the creature—who may be three or four: "big enough to walk and talk," Ellen says—wandering in the black streets of Liverpool, and finding no one who would claim it, resolved to bring it home. He urges his wife, "e'en take it as a gift of God; though it's as dark almost as if it come from the devil."

Prophetic words.

Chloe's head aches from reading, from trying to see beneath the surface of the words to the place where everything can be rendered in lines. She takes up her camera and goes out to the deck. In her virtual touring of Haworth, she's noticed that junipers are common, often stunted and twisted by the wind. She wants to take photos of the juniper in the field behind her studio that was split by lightning a few years back. She sets out along the trail, her shoes crunching the dry leaves underfoot, fiddling with her lens as she goes. It's chilly, damp, the cold seeps through her sweater, and she considers going back for her jacket, but she is nearly there and it won't take long. The field opens before her, brown now, the long grasses flattened. The juniper dominates the scene. One third of it is broken, folded down like a peel, the grayish foliage smashed into the ground. In the slanting light it casts a shadow, an elongated, up-side-down V. For vanquished, she thinks, for victim. She wants it towering, so she drops down in the grass and angles the camera up at it, which is good, but loses the shadow. She takes the picture anyway. She stretches out flat on her stomach and gets a long view; interesting, but not ominous enough. She decides to do a few from the other side, so that the broken limb appears to pour out toward her from the upright trunk. This is good; it's like a tree waterfall, and the thornbush off to the right gives a sense of how tall it is. She gazes up into the scraggly branches; juniper is such a shabby tree, so unlovely and brittle. Quite the volunteer in this field. Knee-high junipers cluster in cozy groups here and there, giving out when they lose the competition for light at the edge of the hardwood stand.

Chloe is beginning to get a feel for the tree, for its age and deep indifference to the harsh elements in which it has stood, she guesses, for perhaps a hundred years. Height, about forty, maybe fifty feet, it's hard to gauge. Shape, generally conical, though triangular now with its broken shaft; bark, peeling, reddish; leaves, if you can call them leaves, more like flat blue-green fronds tracked with tiny brown dots. She goes up close, shoots up into the crown, squats to frame a bit of the forest inside the angle formed by the splintered limb. One close up, then she backs away, sits down with her legs out before her, feeling the moisture soaking through her pants, which is just too bad because this is an excellent shot. She snaps one, then another, leans down on one elbow and frames a section of the undergrowth edging the field. It's not a picture she'll use, but the contrast appeals to her, the various shades of gray, brown, and ocher. There's a lot of texture out there.

As she clicks the shutter, she sees, in the corner of the frame, a man. He is standing next to an old locust, his arm raised against the trunk, his rifle pointing down in his other hand. Without thinking, Chloe shifts the focus to put him dead center and presses the button with the satisfying sensation of having pulled a trigger, of having gotten off a good one. In the next second, the man steps back into the shadows of the forest. She can hear the rustle of the brush as he walks away.

She has taken a photograph of the poacher.

All the way back to the studio Chloe is triumphant. It was one thing to have seen him, to have carried the story back and described him to Brendan, who may have had some iota of doubt that the encounter really happened, but a photograph is real, undeniable evidence. No one can tell her he isn't there, and someone may be able to identify him and put a stop to his intrusion in their lives. They can scare him with a photograph. And she will get a good look at his face now, which remains steadfastly dim in her memory. She recalls the photographer— David Hemmings, wasn't it?—who accidentally snaps a picture of a murder in the old movie *Blow-Up*. He winds up with Vanessa Redgrave at his door looking for the negative. Times have changed. Chloe won't have to go through the tiresome darkroom process, the trays of poisonous developing fluid, the sheets hung out to dry with clothespins. All she'll have to do is press the zoom button and presto, there he will be for all the world to see, on her property with his rifle in his hand, spying on her.

I saw him in the viewfinder, she will tell Brendan. He was standing by the big locust, watching me.

And Brendan will ask, "How long?"

When she reaches the studio, she strides up and down the deck, looking back into the trees, nervous and defiant. I'm going to make you stop, she is thinking. I'm going to get rid of you.

In the department office, Brendan slides the jumbled contents of his mailbox into his briefcase. Most of it, the book catalogs, college announcements, advertisements for local book sign-ings, will wind up in his trash can, but there's no stopping the tide of it. David Bodley, coming in from the hall, greets him in his practiced, hearty manner. "Professor Dale is among us! Why aren't you out fishing somewhere?"

"How are you, David?" Brendan says.

"Buried in work, students lined up in the hall, and every one needs an A or they will not graduate. You remember all that, professor. Or is it too long ago?"

Amy Treadwell, passing by, calls out, "Hello, Brendan. Are you slumming?"

"Amy," Brendan says. "How are you?" and to David, "It hasn't been that long."

"Not to you. You're off fishing." David chuckles at his own lame humor. "So how's the book going? Nearly done, is it?"

"Slow," Brendan says. "It's slow, but it's going."

"Good for you," cries David. They go out together into the hall. David turns off at his office where a student is waiting, a shapely young woman with jeans slipping off her hips, spiky hair, and a silver stud beneath her lower lip, clearly passionate about history. "Right this way, Ms. Pettijohn," David commands, ushering her through the door. "Let's have a serious talk about the Battle of Gettysburg, shall we?"

Brendan lets himself into his own office, closing the door behind him. He doesn't miss teaching, but he does miss this room, the high ceiling, walls of books, gleaming hardwood floors, and long window giving out on the tree-shaded, manicured lushness of the quad. The college has a large endowment and everything—the floors, the windows, the furniture, the doorknob—is polished with money. He opens his briefcase and pulls the mail out in a wad. The radiator clangs and groans. Because the college can afford it, his office is overheated. Brendan opens the window a few inches and looks out at a clutch of students moving aimlessly along the sidewalk. The neo-Gothic tower of the library looms in the background, framed by ancient sycamores. Cool air swirls around his waist and up to his chin. For a moment he is conscious of nothing but the aesthetic charm of the view.

At the desk he sorts mail. The teacher's union is offering an alternative health insurance plan; two book catalogs, one devoted entirely to studies of the Civil War; and a brochure extolling the virtues of a taped lecture series by famous scholars in various subjects, including, he notes, the rise of Islam. They hate our freedoms. He deposits this lot in the trash can. Next a schedule of departmental meetings, another for a reading series, a brochure, three-color, expensive, professional, from something called the Rowalt Historical Society advertising a conference in Chicago, special rate for participants at the Allegro hotel. A newspaper clipping, folded, no note attached—why is this in his mail? Small headline, *Professor Wins Award*, and then the announcement that Professor Michael Newborn has won the Cardogan Prize, ten thousand dollars, for his "groundbreaking" biography of the thirteenth-century emperor Frederick II, titled *Unholy Emperor*. A few lines about Professor Newborn, where he went to university, current position, previous books, concluding with a brief quote from his remarks at the ceremony on the importance of history as a discipline. Brendan reads to the end, then goes back to the top. He is aware of the quiet in his office. The only sound is the clock ticking out the seconds it takes him to read the article a second time. A door closes down the hall; outside a girl calls out, "Becky! Wait for me." Brendan folds the article and places it on his desk. He doesn't feel sick, but something is going on in his stomach and in his chest, a sensation of tightening. His head too feels constricted, crammed with questions. Who put this in his mailbox? Was it a friend, and if so, why didn't he or she attach a note? Though what could one say, friend or foe? *Thought this might interest you. Tough luck. Michael Newborn is a charlatan.* If not a friend, then who, someone who disliked Brendan, someone who would be watching now to see if he'd been brought down a notch? And then there is the question of how he really feels about the information. How does it affect him? He is, he knows, years away from publication, so what difference does it make that Newborn's book has won a prize. Might it not increase the public's interest in the *Stupor Mundi*?

Michael Newborn has a bombastic, windbag style full of insinuation and pretension. He's eager to flaunt his knowledge, which, it can't be denied, is considerable, and disparage his critics. The thesis of his book is that Frederick was actually a heretic, that he disdained the church he represented, that he wished the pope and all his works ill. His fascination with Islam is offered as proof of this conjecture. He also pushes a theory about religious wars in particular and human history in general, which is that war is possible only when the enemy is perceived of as inhuman, when "he" becomes "it." Hence the eternal reliance upon animal metaphors; our enemies are dogs, pigs, snakes, swine. The warrior's refrain is "I will kill him as if he was an animal." This "it" theory offends Brendan; as an observation he finds it simplistic and obvious. Something happens before one's enemy becomes an "it" and that's what interests Brendan. Something happens to the "I." It's not how we see our enemies; it's how we see ourselves. Brendan has a dim memory of dismissing Newborn's book and espousing this counter-theory to someone at a faculty gathering. Was it David? Maybe Amy Treadwell.

Newborn was nearly sacked a few years ago for harassing a female student, an unusually courageous one, as his reputation for sexual predation upon the student body had been an open secret in the academic community for years. A bore and a brute, but a success.

The phone rings. He snatches it up, still frowning at the clipping, which reminds him of the diminishing value placed upon common decency in his profession. "Professor Dale," he says.

"I got a picture of him."

"Of who?" Brendan says, thinking *Of whom*.

"The poacher. I was taking pictures of the blasted juniper and he was standing behind it in the woods watching me. I blew it up on the computer. I'm looking at it right now. You can see his face clearly."

Brendan slides the clipping into his desk drawer. Chloe's obsession with the poacher is veering into a territory previously unexplored, and he has, so far, been unable to dissuade her from it. Living near the forest doesn't mean we must go exploring there, he thinks, but he knows her reply, which is not without historical, legal, and possibly moral force. *But it's our forest.*

"What does he look like?" Brendan says.

"I still think he could be Lebanese."

Salome and Toby are in the kitchen drinking coffee when Andro appears at the glass door, his face flushed with emotion. "Here it comes," Salome says, getting up to meet him. "Tata told him."

"What is it to him?" Toby asks, giving Andro scowl for scowl as the door rattles on its flimsy track and he bursts into the room. He grabs Salome by the arm so roughly her head snaps back and she cries out. He is shouting something Toby doesn't understand. Salome answers him, struggling to get away, but he tightens his grip, pulls her in close, and slaps her across the face. Toby turns over his coffee cup and his chair as he hurls himself at the enraged Andro, who knocks him to the ground with a well-aimed fist to his chest. Salome is shouting, "Toby, stay away from him," and Andro is bellowing in Croatian. Toby stumbles to his feet and runs headfirst into another blow, which knocks him into the table leg. He feels the skin tear on his cheek, close to his eye. "Stay away from him," Salome shouts again, and Andro aims a kick at him, punctuating harsh streams of Croatian with a phrase Toby understands: "I'll kill you."

"What's wrong with you?" Toby shouts, rolling away from the boot which, in some hyperconscious region of his brain, he registers as smelling of fish. "Leave her alone. She's pregnant, for God's sake." He scrambles out the other side of the table with the idea that he will jump on top of it and attack his opponent from above, but as he pulls himself up, Andro releases Salome and lunges out the door, upbraiding her still, but tearfully now. Salome follows, weeping, protesting. She pauses in the doorway to watch her brother loping across the yard and out of sight. Her shoulders tremble, a wheezing animal sound comes from deep in her throat. Toby goes to her side and wraps her in his arms. "Are you OK?" he says. "Did he hurt you?" She clings to him, burrowing into his sweater. "I don't understand," she says.

"He's crazy," Toby assures her.

"He's crazy," she agrees.

"What was he saying to you?"

She doesn't answer. He strokes her back, rests his bleeding cheek against her head. He doesn't understand either; in fact, he's so shocked and confused he has almost no sense of what really happened, but he's relieved to discover that he was not, for one moment, afraid. His brain had been so busy with the problem of saving Salome from her brother that he had felt only grim determination. Now anger rises up in him, and outrage. "He ought to be locked up," he says. "We should talk to your father about it. He's dangerous."

"No," Salome says. "It's over now. He didn't really hurt me."

"What the hell is his problem?"

Salome leans back in his arms and looks up at him. "You're bleeding," she says.

Toby touches his cheek, considers the red smear on his fingertips. "I hit the table leg," he says.

Salome leads him toward the bathroom. "Let me clean it," she says. "It's going to be an awful bruise. What will you tell your parents?"

"I'll tell them your brother is a lunatic. What was he saying?" He sits on the edge of the tub while she runs water over a cloth in the sink.

"I didn't understand it," she says.

"You mean he wasn't speaking Croatian?"

"No. I understood him. I just didn't understand what he meant." She applies the warm cloth to his cheek.

"Ouch. Well, what was he saying?"

"Sorry," Salome says.

"So what was he saying?"

"It was about my mother."

"Your mother? What about your mother?"

She takes the cloth away and pretends to examine the cut, but her eyes fill with tears and a sob escapes her. "It was too horrible," she says. "I can't repeat it."

We met in the woods, near my father-in-law's potato field. There was an old stone shed he used to store farm equipment and rusty dull tools he didn't use anymore. When my husband took over he traded two old tractors

for a new one with a tiller attachment, so now he could plow up the entire world without getting out of his tractor. I can't remember how I managed to tell Milan, that was his name, to meet me there, but I did. I told my mother-in-law I was going out to pick the last of the wild elderberries, an errand she approved of as the bushes bordered the neighbor's patch of woods and she wanted to get the berries before he did. So, on my way, I picked a bucket as fast as I could. When I got to the shed, he was there, leaning against the drainpipe with a blanket tucked under his arm. My heart lifted at the sight of that blanket: it spoke to me of his solicitude for my feelings. I was not to be bent over a filthy manure spreader and rammed from behind like a farm animal. I showed him where the key to the padlock was hidden behind a broken stone above the windowsill. He took it and opened the door. We hardly spoke, but he was smiling and so was I. When we got inside, I started trembling. "Are you cold?" he said, and I said, "No, I don't think so." "Then you are afraid," he said, and I said, "No, I'm not afraid." He put his arms around me and kissed me.

I wasn't afraid, but after that kiss, I should have been. Who knows why such things happen? When I try to remember it, I can only think I wasn't myself. It seemed that hurried lovemaking in the musty shed was the most important thing I'd ever done, and like so many foolish young women, I thought it would change my life. Well, ultimately it did, but not in the way I imagined. Milan was equally ardent and wanted to meet me as often as possible. It was all we thought about: how to get away from our families and meet in the shed. It wasn't easy; we never had much time. We didn't talk much, except to make plans for our next meeting. Of course I was flourishing from all the sex; everyone remarked on how well I was looking, and I was kinder to my poor stupid husband. His mother watched me with that cold eye of hers. She'd spent forty years bent on domestic tyranny and she wasn't giving up now. My laughter, my teasing the

*children and my husband, my good appetite and pleasure in drinking wine
and šljivovica, all this was an affront to her.*

*Outside our house things were getting worse and worse. People in the
market said there would be war, but not in our town; it would be nearer
the border. And they were right, that's where it started. I met Milan the
day after the shooting at Borovo Selo. The television was full of it. We never
talked about such things, but for some reason I asked him where his family was from and he said from Knin. I had a premonition when he said
that; I started coughing and couldn't stop. He had to pound me on the
back.*

Where is Knin?

*In the Krajina. Everyone knew the paramilitary thugs from Knin were
going to all the small towns and arming Serbs to be ready for war. They'd
been doing it for months. They were armed to the teeth at Borovo Selo.*

And was Milan one of those?

Yes. He was one of them. But I didn't know that then.

They are up early, talking softly in the kitchen so as not to disturb the young people, who may still be asleep upstairs. "So
what do you think really happened down there?" Chloe says.
She sets a plate of toast before her husband.

"Thanks," Brendan says. "What do you mean?"

"To his face? What do you think really happened?"

"I take it you don't believe the story about the deck."

"Do you?"

According to the story about the deck, which Toby told
twice, once at the train station when Brendan picked them up

and again in the kitchen, when he greeted his mother, Toby had stumbled on some steps at a dance—Cajun music, a great band, his parents would have loved it—and scraped his cheek on the edge of a wooden deck. It looked worse than it was, he concluded. As Chloe listened to this explanation, which was simple enough, Brendan watched the play of emotion across her features: dismay, incredulity, anxiety, and finally the retreat into her habitual long-suffering cynicism, the reliable what-did-you-expect of her strategically low expectations. She didn't believe her son.

"It looks like he got hit by a baseball bat," Chloe says.

"He never was much of a liar," Brendan agrees.

"She put him up to it."

Brendan doesn't doubt this, but he isn't going to pursue it.

"And what's come over her?"

No denying this either; Salome is edgy, not herself. She ate almost nothing at dinner, snapped at Toby when he asked her if she was feeling poorly, then went off to bed at nine, pleading exhaustion. "It was a long trip," Brendan says. "She's pregnant. She got worn out."

"No. It's not that. She's different. Something happened. Maybe the father lost it and hit Toby."

"He told me the father was fine about it. Can't wait to be a *djed.*"

"A *djed*?"

"Grandfather."

"When did he say this?"

"The father?"

"No, Toby."

"In the car."

"He's so distant with me," Chloe complains. "I feel cut off from him."

"He'll get over it."

"You think it's my fault."

Brendan chews his toast, contemplates his wife. The big blonde, his mother had called her, *Die Valkyrie*, which really was unfair, as there was nothing particularly Teutonic about Chloe, apart from her thick golden hair. When she was young she wove it into a single long plait at bedtime to keep it from tangling in her sleep. Now she keeps it short, in a neat, dopey pageboy with bangs to hide the fact that her hairline is receding. She sips her coffee, her eyes fixed on him over the rim of her cup, urging him to absolve her, to pity her, because she is now and always has been innocent. He swallows the chewed bread, feels it stick in his throat momentarily, and then plunge down his gullet into the dark interior, where digestive juices swirl it along, reducing it, transforming it by some mysterious process into energy and excrement. He knows what he's supposed to say to his wife, it's scripted. Chloe puts down her cup, expectant, confident. Something in the slight pursing of her lips as she swallows irks him out of compliance. "You tried to make him choose," he says. "He chose."

"I tried to make him think," she retorts.

"There's no reason to blow your top at me," he says.

The phone rings. Chloe snaps it up, barks a petulant "Hello." She sends Brendan a grimace, mouth pulled down, brows raised, mock surprise. "Oh yes, hello," she says. "This is Toby's mother." Her tone is moderate, friendly. "Of course. Yes, she's here. I think she's awake. She's upstairs. I'll call her."

"Branko calling," she says, laying the phone on the table. She goes out to the staircase, leaving Brendan alone with the phone that contains the Oyster King. Should he pick it up and say something cordial? They have common interests, after all. He can hear Chloe exchanging information with Toby. Salome is awake; she will take the call upstairs. Chloe treads heavily back through the dining room. As she appears in the doorway, they are assailed by a raised angry voice issuing stereophonically from the phone and the young woman upstairs. "Hang it up," Chloe whispers. Carefully Brendan replaces the receiver in its cradle. In a stream edged with hysteria, Salome's voice continues, pausing only briefly to gather breath and force. Brendan and Chloe sit quietly, their eyes raised to the ceiling, timid as rabbits in a subterranean warren. "What on earth is going on?" Chloe says.

"I wish I knew." Toby is slouched in the doorway, wrapped in his bathrobe, his feet bare, hair damp.

"Darling," Chloe pleads. "Tell us what really happened down there?"

He adjusts the cord of his robe while the shouting overhead turns to weeping. "I don't really know," he admits. "Her brother blew up when he found out she was pregnant. He attacked her. That's how I cut my face."

"He hit you?" Brendan says.

"He knocked me down and I hit a table leg."

"My God," Chloe says.

"He's a lunatic," Toby says, dismissively. "He was yelling at her in Croatian, so I had no idea what he was saying."

"And she didn't tell you?"

"She won't tell me," he says. "But she went off the deep end after that and there's some argument going on with her father now. They were shouting all the way to the airport."

"Is he against your marriage?" Chloe asks.

Toby flashes his mother a fierce look. The weeping from above has abated, the volume is normal, the tone is winding down.

"You'd like that, wouldn't you?" Toby says.

❖❖

The women have retreated to their rooms; the men are at the woodpile, gathering kindling, choosing logs to be split and stacking them near the chopping block. Everything around them is brown, dead, and the sky is white. "What's the father like?" Brendan asks, man to man.

"Big," Toby says. "Nice, actually. We didn't see that much of him because he's always out on the boat."

"Did you go on the boat?"

"No. I wanted to, but Salome said I would be in the way. Basically I wasn't invited."

"Well, it's his livelihood."

"It's hard work. Everyone is pretty poor down there."

Down there. "What's it like? Palm trees?"

"No. No palm trees, no beaches. It's marshy, very flat, green, water everywhere, a lot of egrets. It's eerie; it feels foreign. A lot of Croats; they've been there a long time. Some came because of the war, like Branko, because they had relatives already there to help them."

"I think this is enough," Brendan says, taking his place at the block. He examines the ax, his comrade of many winters. "Your mother wants to buy me a new ax, but I've never seen one I like better than this one."

"She's never satisfied."

"I'm worried about her," Brendan says. He raises his ax high and brings it down with controlled force, splitting the log neatly in two. Toby hands him the next candidate from the stack, which Brendan stands upright on the stump. "She's obsessed with the poacher."

"Is he still around?"

"She took a picture of him," Brendan says. "By accident. Then she printed it and took it to the police."

"Does he know she has a picture?"

"He may. He saw her. She was taking pictures of that old juniper and she caught him in the background. He was watching her from the woods."

"That's really pretty creepy, Dad."

"It is. I agree. But what's to be done about it? The police said they could arrest him and fine him for trespassing, but that might just enrage him. They told her about a guy over in Croton who went after a poacher. He got him arrested, but only for a few days. As soon as he was released this guy's barn burned down in the middle of the night."

"The poacher burned his barn?"

"They can't prove it, but that's what the police think."

"This is bad."

"It is. I say we just let our guy hunt. He's been out there three years now and hunting season isn't that long. He thins the wildlife a little; he doesn't leave carcasses lying around. Obviously he needs the meat and we don't. But your mother thinks I'm just nuts. She wants to blow the photo up, nail it all over the place on the trees with a sign that says, 'No hunting, this means you.'"

Toby laughs.

"She's confrontational. She wants to put his picture in the paper. I can't talk to her about it." Brendan adjusts the log so that it leans away from him. "Maybe you could talk to her," he says.

This suggestion meets with chilly silence. He raises the ax and brings it down powerfully, but his aim is off; the blade goes in at an angle and sticks halfway through. He has to wrestle it free. "I'm not really talking to Mom that much," Toby says. "Haven't you noticed?"

Brendan rests the ax against the stump. "Of course I've noticed," he says. "And so has she. It's making her sick. If you don't mind my saying, she's anxious enough about your situation without you making it worse."

"I just don't understand what her anxiety is about. It's not as if Salome is a drug addict or some self-destructive loser flunking out of school. We're not going to rob a bank, for God's sake; we're going to have a baby. She's an intelligent, mysterious woman and I'm in love with her."

"Women are seldom as mysterious as they seem," Brendan observes.

Toby flinches. "Well, so be it, Dad, that's fine with me. I want to know Salome, I want to know everything about her. That's my mission."

Brendan smiles. His son's ardor does him credit. He's seen

too many young men paralyzed by diffidence. "That's your mission," he repeats.

❖❖

This is the state of affairs. Brendan is in his study, his family is tucked away upstairs in their beds, every one of them disgruntled. His son, who by virtue of his parents' care and diligence has not, until a few months ago, had a care in the world, is now responsible for an unborn child and has been forced to defend his mate with his fists, an experience foreign to Brendan, and one that appalls him. Yet Toby is not alarmed, is, rather, dismissive. "He's a lunatic," and that's that. Brendan, who has always taken pride in his son's competence and equanimity, is forced to admit that there is more to Toby than he guessed; another side, passionate and heedless, bent on unsettling the status quo. It's not hard to understand the attraction of Salome to such a young man; she's so sexually confident she's frightening and so curvaceous, with her shapely buttocks, firm breasts, straight spine, and those dark, penetrating eyes, and that luxuriant hair; she's a dish.

And then there's Chloe, once his ironic helpmeet, now nervous and contrary, spoiling for a fight. Was there a time when she was to him, as Salome is to Toby, mysterious and alluring? She must have been. But now when he thinks of her, teary in her pajamas, protesting the injustice of her son's attraction to a woman she doesn't trust, who threatens her in the tender, vulnerable core of her motherhood, there's nothing mysterious about her and certainly nothing alluring. As plain as the nose on your face, actually; as clear as glass. She wants to take on everything, the poacher, a man she knows nothing about, and this girl, who is, Brendan suspects, more than her match. She feels her territory has been invaded and she is under attack. She wants to throw the intruders out, go back to the way things were, but this, she must realize, is not an option, and so she's panicked. They have a poacher and they have a pregnant soon-to-be-daughter-in-law; the outsiders are insiders now, staking their claims.

And nothing, not patience, kindness, an open mind, good-will, none of the resources Brendan usually brings to bear, nothing he can say or do, will disperse the atmosphere of dis-trust and hostility in which they must all greet one another at the breakfast table in the morning.

＊＊

Salome complains about the red tape, but Toby is surprised at how easy it all is, how few questions are asked. They have trouble finding the right building, then, after standing in a long line in the cold, they're confronted by a sign that says the bur-eau accepts only money orders. "Where are we going to get a money order?" Salome whines, but the guard says, "Across the street. At the Rite-Aid." So they leave the line, plunge into the wide, thronging boulevard, and after another line in the drug-store, come back to the first one. "It's nice down here," Toby observes, gazing past the imposing court buildings and the green stripes of grass flanking City Hall to the monumental base of the Brooklyn Bridge, gracefully lifting a multicolored stream of cars into the cloudless chilly blue of the sky. "It's very federal."

"It's very cold," Salome says. Slowly the line inches forward.

At the gate the guard only glances at their driver's licenses and motions them inside. "Marriage license," Salome says to the officer near the rank of bronze-enshrouded elevators. "Third floor," he says, and he smiles at them, as if he's pleased they've decided to come.

Upstairs it's a nondescript hall and various offices, one of which issues the licenses. Another line, a short one. The clerk is bored but not impatient, and the form asks for minimal information, their addresses, birth dates. Their driver's licenses are noted, the money order passes across the counter, the paper is stamped a few times and that's it. They have a license which, in twenty-four hours, will allow them to return and, for an additional twenty-five-dollar money order, have the ceremony in the "Wedding Chapel" across the hall. Salome folds the license and stashes it in her purse. She's tense, officialdom makes her nervous, but Toby finds the experience agreeable, somehow validating. He is an adult, the state confirms, accepts, yields to this fact. There's a festive air about the place. Many of the couples are young, of various ethnic origins and unsure of themselves, but ready and willing to hold hands and jump feet first into the melting pot. He takes Salome's arm as they get back into the elevator. "That was easy," he says, and she leans against him with a sigh.

Marriage, which is an honorable estate. Is it part of the ceremony language, the ritual language? Toby has been raised without religion, but he's heard this line somewhere, perhaps at a relative's wedding. They cross the imposing lobby, through a side door to the cold sidewalk. Salome pulls up the hood of her coat and draws on her foolish pink mittens. My wife, my child. An honorable estate. Toby puts his arm around her shoulder, surprising himself with the thought: *and only twenty-four hours to get out of it.*

The allotted time has elapsed and they are back in the line on the sidewalk, this time with Bruce Macalister, blowing his nose into a disgusting handkerchief, the collar of his inadequate gray wool coat pulled up against the icy wind. The Marxist is to be their witness, a role he's accepted without much grace, fretting that it might somehow compromise his conscience. An earnest consultation with that faculty has resulted in his unenthusiastic attendance. He doesn't possess a driver's license, so he's brought his passport, which has a stamp from Venezuela, where he spent a few weeks fomenting revolution. He imagines that this stamp will result in his being turned away, if not arrested. But the guard only looks at the photo and hands it back without comment. "You take yourself too seriously, Bruce," Salome chides him as they pass into the foyer. Toby, coming up behind, fingers the ring box in his pocket. Salome flashes him one of her arch conspirator smiles, as enveloping as her embraces, and he smiles back, his heart in it now.

Last night, after an unusually tender bout of lovemaking, Salome rested her head against his arm and spoke frankly for the first time since their visit to her father's house. She knew she had been cold and difficult since then and she was sorry for that, grateful to Toby for being patient with her.

"Is it because of what your brother said?" Toby asked.

"It is, in a way. And what my father said. I can't tell you yet; I want to, but I don't think it would be right."

"But it's about your mother."

"Yes."

"Is it about how she died?"

She made no answer. Toby stroked her hair. "I guess it's more about how she lived," she said.

"It was a long time ago," Toby said, thinking, how long? Twelve years? Not that long.

"Sometimes I can hardly remember her face."

A crash from the apartment above startled them. Then there was a rumble, something heavy—a couch? a body?—being dragged across the floor. "Who knows what they do up there," Toby said.

Salome chuckled; their neighbors, two men, one old, one young, one fat, one thin, were a running joke. Salome called them the "Contrasts." She pressed her lips against Toby's arm, put out her tongue, and licked him, catlike. "I love you, Toby," she said.

Toby petted her shoulder, allowing all manner of thoughts to run through his brain. It was one of his pleasures, entertaining conflicting notions in the privacy of his own head. He pursued the most outrageous thoughts; if he was angry, he amused himself plotting the perfect murder. He rehashed and weighed the opinions of his parents, which were evidently lodged in the pores of his brain like blackheads, ready to bloom into ugly pimples unless he squeezed them out regularly. His father's observation that women were seldom as mysterious as they seemed surfaced and he dismissed it. Women were exactly as mysterious as they seemed, no more, no less.

Certainly there was nothing mysterious about Salome's anxiety to be married. She was pregnant and no one, save her poor, dumb father, who couldn't really help her, was pleased. It was universally assumed, even by her father, that she had trapped Toby, and perhaps she had, but only because he didn't object to being trapped. He recalled a stuffed fox in a trap he'd seen at a museum diorama, the trap all steel joints and sharp teeth, the poor fox stretched out on his side, his leg twisted cruelly below the hip, his glass eyes starting from their sockets. Toby didn't feel like that at all. On the contrary, he felt free. The panic at the edge of everything they did together now was the requisite variety, but the real threats to their happiness came from outside. An erection pulsed at the thought of them all, his parents, her father and brute of a brother, Mat Barrois, Bruce Macalister, who had sucked in his breath and said "Damn" when Toby told him Salome was pregnant. Yes, damn, Toby thought, damn them all. He pressed himself against Salome's legs, which yielded at once, sliding apart, still slippery from the last time. He didn't speak, nor did she, and words faded away, replaced by something more urgent. As he plunged inside his bride-to-be, he heard a few phrases, drifting away—*no matter what* and *from now on* and *forever.*

Salome loosens her coat as the elevator doors slide open and they file inside. She extracts her mother's lace shawl from her purse and drapes it over her hair, pulling the edges over her cheeks. "Here we go," she says. Macalister astonishes them by pulling a disposable camera from his coat pocket. "I brought this," he says to Salome. "So you can have pictures."

Salome reaches up and touches his cheek in a gesture Toby finds far too intimate. "How thoughtful, Bruce," she says. "That is really kind." Toby chimes in, "That's great, Macalister."

❖❖

In the coffee shop, the day Toby told him, Macalister said, "Damn. What are you going to do? Is she going to have an abortion?"

"No," Toby said. "We're getting married."

"You're going to marry Salome?" The Marxist eyed Toby as if he'd announced his plans to blow up the Stock Exchange. "Are you sure that's a good idea?"

"Am I sure? Why shouldn't I be sure?"

"Well, how well do you really know Salome?"

"Jesus, Macalister," Toby said. "You sound like my parents."

"I'm just surprised. It feels sudden, that's all. Don't pay any attention to me."

"It's too late for that," Toby said. "Do you know something I should know?"

"No. Absolutely not. Nothing against Salome. She's beautiful, she's smart. I'm just envious, obviously. I wish you both the best. And the baby."

"Oh," Toby smirked. "The baby too."

"You'll be a good father."

"But will I be *the* father? Is that what you're thinking?"

"Not at all."

"Salome told me once that you were in love with her."

Macalister blushed. "I didn't think she knew."

"But you are."

"Toby, what chance could I have with her? Look at me. I'm a Marxist. I don't have any money and I never will—it's against my politics to prosper."

"So you think what she sees in me is money."

"Don't put words in my mouth. I only mean she doesn't see me as even a prospect."

"So she's right, then. You are in love with her."

"I'm your friend, Toby. I think you know I'm an extremely moral person. I don't go around following every impulse I have. I weigh my actions."

"So if I were to abandon her, it would be your moral obligation to step into the breech."

"Do you think I'm waiting for you to fail? You're not going to abandon Salome, Toby. What are you saying?"

"I just don't trust you, Macalister."

"That hurts me," the Marxist said.

The elevator doors slide open upon a cluster of well-dressed young Asians, laughing and talking as they toss a bouquet of sweetheart roses from one to the other. The bride pursues her bouquet; the groom adjusts his bow tie. Macalister plunges into the party, which yields before him. "Congratulations," he says, and a chorus of "Thank you" replies. As they pass into the hall, Salome takes Toby's arm and the bride, exchanging with her a candid glance, says, "Good luck."

"Look this way," Macalister commands. He has sprinted ahead and framed the converging wedding parties with his camera. They turn, good humor animates their faces as they are momentarily frozen and documented in time, the safely married and the soon to be, gathered at the gaping elevator door. The camera clicks. "No turning back now," says Toby.

❖❖

The party at the newlyweds' apartment went on late into the night, but because he had an early class, Toby was up at seven, dry-mouthed, head throbbing. He careened into the shower, which only made his head feel boiled. When he got out, to his surprise, Salome was up, tending the coffeepot and buttering toast in the kitchen. He wrapped his wet arms around her terrycloth shoulders and pulled her in close. "You don't have to get up," he said. "Go back to bed."

"I was awake," she said.

He sat at the table and rubbed his face with his hands. "My head is killing me."

"I'm not surprised," she said. A glass of water and two aspirin appeared before him, followed by a cup of black coffee. "So this is married life," he said.

That was, he calculates, thirteen hours ago. The headache had adhered to his sinus passages throughout the day. In class he took careful notes because he knew nothing would leave an impression. He didn't expect to see Salome until two, when she was due at the graduate office for her work-study job, which consisted of processing and filing applications. He had lunch, as he always did, at their regular table in the student café. Upon his arrival, the conversation shifted from politics to marriage. He understood that his peers viewed him as having done something daring, something they did not intend to consider for themselves anytime soon. "I admire you," Susan Davies said,

patting his coat sleeve, and he saw something that was not admiration in her eyes. Was it pity, was it envy? "It's not difficult,"
he said. "Anyone could do it."

"Anyone could," Brent observed. "But it's so . . ."

"Mature," Susan filled in. "Have you told your parents?"

"They knew we were getting married," Toby said. "They just
didn't know when."

The subject failed to produce further comment. Macalister
appeared, heavy-lidded and red-cheeked, to inform the gathering that it was snowing.

On his way to his last class, Toby stopped by the graduate office in the hopes of seeing his wife, but she wasn't there. He sat
through a long lecture about the collapse of Russian Commun-
ism, which included film of Reagan and Gorbachev in Reyk-
javik, the former bundled up and looking chilly, the latter with
his coat open, genial but vexed. Toby's professor disliked Reagan and didn't try to hide it. Gorbachev, in his view, had vision;
Reagan was myopic, dim, and heavily scripted. Gorbachev, like
many visionaries, was more popular outside his country than in
it, whereas Reagan was adored by Americans, who found him
warm and fuzzy. He was like slippers: he kept Americans from
thinking about how cold that cold war really was.

Communists, Toby thought, as he slogged across Washing-
ton Square in the steadily accumulating slush. He'd worn his
sneakers instead of boots, and he could feel the cold wet seep-
ing into his socks. Salome despised communists in general, but
she found Macalister's passion for Marxism somehow amusing,
even charming. Well, everyone did; it was hard to dislike his excitement about what was, after all, a kind of idealism. Macalister had stayed late at the wedding party, he and Brent, who

owed his indefatigable party spirit to his Southern upbringing. When the group wore down to four, Macalister produced from his book bag his wedding gift, a bottle of Russian pepper vodka. "The only good thing the Russians know how to make," Salome exclaimed, getting out the juice glasses and the ice. And so, after hours of cheap wine and beer, they did themselves in with the vodka.

That is, the men did themselves in. Salome drank only a thimbleful, because of the baby. Toby downed glass after glass, accompanied by increasingly raucous and ludicrous toasting. Once Macalister was out the door, Toby, reeling from the fumes of his own breath, collapsed across the bed and hurtled into sleep as off a cliff. In the night he woke to find Salome beside him, her arm wrapped around his waist, her breath soft against his shoulder. Later he woke again; she was up, he could see her through the doorway working at her computer. But when the alarm went off she was with him again. He recalled this, climbing the stairs to the apartment. Had she really gotten up, or had he dreamed it?

Inside the apartment all was orderly. The dishes were in the rack, the table had a fresh cloth on it. He had an hour before she would return from work and no inclination to do anything but sleep. She would find him in bed, she would join him there, they could have sex, then go out for Indian food. As he drifted away, he noticed that there was a chair drawn up beside the wardrobe, which struck him as odd.

In his dream he had an exam; he was late for it; he hadn't studied. The professor was wearing high-heeled boots. The dream was obvious and banal, and he woke from it feeling disgusted with himself. The room was dark. The clock said eight fifteen. The apartment was so silent it seemed to be listening. He sat up, called her name. Again his eyes were drawn to the chair against the wardrobe. He followed the ladder-back up to the top. They kept their suitcases there, and he saw at once that Salome's case was missing.

Still, still, he persuaded himself, there was an explanation for her absence. She had stopped in the library after work; she took the case down because she'd left something in it and failed to put it back up again. A cursory tour of the apartment revealed nothing amiss. He tried calling Kim Weh, who worked with Salome in the graduate office, and, on impulse, Macalister, but got no answers. He left the same message with both, "This is Toby, call back when you can." Perplexed, dissociated, apprehensive, he went into the bathroom to brush his teeth and was brought up short by the porcelain rack attached to the sink. Her toothbrush was gone.

"Damn," he exclaimed, abandoning hygiene. In the bedroom he rifled her dresser; half of her underwear was missing. He stalked into the kitchen. Her computer was on the sewing table shoved up against the window. At last he discovered a Post-it stuck to the lid. "Darling Toby," it read in her most careful hand. "Read your e-mail."

"What in hell," Toby said, reeling back to the bedroom. His computer was soaking up power after a day in his book bag. He flipped it open and went through the excruciating steps, to the Net, to his server, to his e-mail, it took a lifetime. And there it was—SDRAGO—in the in-box. *Darling, forgive me. I have to go on this trip. I can't tell you where or why, and it's better if you don't know.*

I will be back. I love you, my darling, don't worry about me and don't try to follow me. I'll be moving around for a time. As soon as I can, I'll call you. I love you, I love our baby. Your wife, Salome.

Toby read this message several times, but could make no sense of it. "What does it mean?" he said, clutching his brow.

She had gotten up in the night; that much was clear. She was at the computer, buying tickets, making plans. Then she had told him good-bye without a hint that she had any intention of going anywhere but to her job, and then she packed and left him this idiotic message.

If she bought airline tickets, he reasoned, the confirmation would be in her e-mail. He returned to her machine, cursed his way through the process, starting it up, yes, welcome, thanks, to the Internet, to her server, to her e-mail, typing in her ID and password, to her in-box, watching the mindless whirling yin-yang until three messages popped up on the screen: two clearly spam, and one an announcement from the poli-sci office about the exam period. He tried the out-box: wiped clean, saved messages ditto. Of course, she knew he would try this. She wasn't stupid.

But he is. And she knew that, she had counted on that, thirteen hours ago when he swallowed the aspirin she gave him and observed from the bottomless well of his ignorance, "So this is married life."

How long since they've done this? Too long, weeks, certainly. So long he's started dreaming of doing it, and not only with her. He wakes from such a dream, his erection pushing into the fold of sheet between them. He scoots close to her back, slip-ping a hand over her breast, expecting what he's been getting lately, which is no response, but to his surprise, she pulls his leg over her hip and turns her face to him, nuzzling his shoulders and his neck. They go from there, in the old way, in several of the old ways, yet it is exciting, interesting. He has to make an ef-fort to hold back as she urges him on. At last their bodies reach an agreement—this is it, go for it with all you've got. She is moaning and he rises up, driving into her with abandon, his heart pounding, blood pulsing to his fingertips, his throat tight. He hears a groan of pleasure escape his own lips, as if from a distance. Precisely at the moment of the benign explosion, as they cling to each other with cries of delight, gunshots ring out in the chilly morning air outside their window.

He laughs, collapsing over her, and she laughs too. "Oh, my God," she says, and "Can you believe it?" he says. Easing free of her, he rolls onto his back. She curls up to him, smiling, rests her cheek upon his chest. "Your heart is beating fast," she says.

"I wonder what it would be like to actually be shot at the moment of orgasm."

"Do you want to try it?" she says.

"No. Thanks. I think this was close enough."

"That was fun," she says.

"It was," he agrees. He strokes her back and they drift into sleep, pleased with each other, all grievances on hold. As he ad-justs the pillow one last time, Brendan thinks, *Thank God for sex.*

By the time the coffee is made, Chloe is no longer amused by the poacher's precision firing. "I talked to Joan yesterday. She thinks I shouldn't be in the studio alone."

"Do you agree?" Brendan is circumspect; the subject is potentially dangerous.

"I'm not afraid he's going to kill me, if that's what you mean."

"Is that what she means?"

"I think she's thinking rape."

"Good Lord."

"She offered to loan Fluffy to me."

Brendan snorts. A thin spray of coffee dots the tabletop.

"It's ridiculous, isn't it? But she managed to make me anxious."

"He's been out there three years now."

"I know. But I thought he was only there around dawn. I'd never seen him. Now I've got his face on my computer and the neighbors are worried about me, and the police say anything I do to antagonize him could make it worse. And then there's the rabbit head and Mike's getting wounded."

"The vet didn't think Mike was shot, darling."

"He's like Saddam Hussein. We know he's out there, and we know he's armed, and we don't know what he wants to do. He's a threat to the whole community."

The analogy is irresistible; Brendan joins in. "He hates our freedoms."

"He does. I know he does. And he kills our rabbits."

Brendan nods over his coffee. No denying this charge. "So," he says. "Do you think we should take him out?"

Chloe doesn't answer. She's looking out at the yard. "It's snowing," she says.

"Is it?" Brendan joins her, holding his cup. The snow drifts softly from the flat white sky, thick flakes already collecting along the wide shelves of the blue spruce on the drive. He puts his arm around his wife. In its purity and silence the snow is magical. As they watch, the enchantment is intensified; the brush at the edge of the wood parts and a stag steps cautiously into the open, his branched antlers as magisterial as a crown. A wondrous sight. "It's like a dream," Brendan says.

"If you painted it, it would be sentimental," Chloe agrees.

For the second time in only a few hours, Brendan and Chloe are entirely at peace with each other.

In the morning Toby leaves a second message on Macalister's answering machine, sends an e-mail—*Where are you?*—and calls at the bookstore where the Marxist works part-time. "He's not coming in today," the bored clerk informs him. "He went home for a family emergency."

"What kind of emergency?" Toby asks.

"I don't know. I didn't talk to him."

"Where is home?"

"How should I know?"

"Right," Toby says. "Thanks." He hangs up. Macalister is from some little burg on Long Island; he doesn't recall the name. He's with her. They planned this. But why? And where are they?

The phone rings; he pounces on it.

"Hello, Toby," Branko says. "This is Branko calling."

Toby injects courtesy into his voice. "Hello, Branko. How are you?"

"I'm not very good. I must speak to Salome very soon."

"She's not here."

"She will be back soon?"

Should he tell the truth, or play for time? "I don't think she'll be back until tonight," he offers. There is a pause in which they consider together, over the thousand miles of phone line that stretch between them, the unhelpfulness of this reply.

"You think she might not come back tonight?" Branko says.

"Well, not until late. If she goes to the library."

Another pause. "This is terrible," Branko says, softly.

"Are you all right?"

"Am I sick, no. But I am very upset."

"Is the boat OK?"

"The boat is never OK, but it is still floating. Toby, perhaps I shouldn't tell you this, but I think you are part of my family now, so I will tell you. I am ashamed to admit it. Salome has stolen money from me."

Toby sinks into the chair near the phone. "Oh, God," he says.

"Yes," Branko says. "Oh, God. This is what I said when I discovered two thousand dollars are missing from my bank account. Why would she do this! Have I denied her something?"

"She's gone, Branko," Toby blurts out. "We got married, and today when I was at school, she packed up and left."

"Where did she go?"

"I don't know. I think she may have gone off with my friend, or that he helped her somehow. He's gone too."

"This is not a friend."

"He's in love with Salome."

"Toby, my brain is spinning. But you say you are married? Is this what I am hearing?"

"Yes. Two days ago. At the courthouse downtown. My friend was our witness."

Branko changes his tone. "So you and Salome are married. I congratulate you."

"Thanks," Toby says.

"And surely she left you some message."

"She left me an e-mail. She says she has to go on a trip and I shouldn't follow her because she'll be moving around and I'll hear from her soon."

"I see."

"Do you know where she went?"

"I don't know for sure."

"But you have some idea."

"This is terrible."

"It is terrible."

"I think she has gone to Croatia."

"To Croatia!"

"She was very upset by what her brother said."

"She was. I know that. But what did he say?"

"It was cruel, Toby. Salome's mother was killed in the war."

"I know this. Looking for her brother with the violin."

"What?"

"Her brother, who went out to find his violin teacher."

Another pause. Was there a brother? Was there a violin? "Yes. She was killed. But Andro has told Salome maybe she is not dead. He has no reason to say this; but he wants to hurt her because he is jealous that Salome is a smart girl and goes to college. Andro never did well in school."

"I don't understand," Toby says truthfully.

"Of course you don't understand. You have never been in a war. But my children have."

"But is there some chance that her mother is still alive?"

"They told me she was killed. We had to leave quickly. There was no time to search for her and my son Josip. Many people were killed. I had to get my children to safety."

A surge of affection for this strangely articulate man who treats him as an equal takes Toby by surprise. Branko, he understands, needs comforting, but there is no one to comfort him. He has been the strong one, the one who pulled his family out of danger by sheer force of will. He recalls Salome's remark that her father's hair turned white while they were in the refugee camp. "Branko," he says. "Don't worry. Salome isn't stupid and the war is over."

"We must find her."

"Where do you think she'll go first?"

"Not the town. The town is gone," Branko says. "There is nothing there. They killed even the cows and the dogs. The fields are mined."

"Then she won't go there."

"Why didn't she tell me? Why did she steal from me?"

"Can you get by without that money?"

"Of course. It was a savings account. The money doesn't matter. I would have given it to her if she asked."

"How did she get it?"

"She takes care of all the money. She wrote a check to herself."

Just after they got back, Salome said she had to go to the bank on some business for her father. Toby had thought nothing of it: she went every few weeks to a branch of the Fleet Bank in Brooklyn. "There's nothing we can do," Toby concludes, "but wait to hear from her."

"I have such a bad feeling, Toby. It's not good to stir up all this about the past. I am so angry with Andro."

Toby sighs. He wants to say Andro should be behind bars, but his education forbids such honesty. Branko is suffering enough. "I'll call you," he says. "As soon as I hear from her."

"Leave a message on the phone," Branko says. "If I'm not here, I will call you back."

"I will. I promise I will."

"Toby, you have made me feel it will be all right with Salome. You are married. She will come back to you soon."

"I know it, Branko. I don't doubt it for a minute."

"Good-bye, Toby. We will talk soon."

"Good-bye, Branko," says Toby. The line goes dead. He hangs up the phone, then picks it up again to see if there are any messages, but the dial tone is unwavering.

Toby spends the next few days in an agony of waiting. He leaves the apartment only to go to class, deliberately avoiding his friends. He needs to study for exams, he tells himself, opening another can of tuna, and he tries, but his notes make no sense to him and he reads the same passage in the text over and over, his ears pricked for the computer chime. When an e-mail is announced he rushes to the screen, but it's mostly spam. Macalister checks in at last; he's on Long Island, where his father has had emergency surgery. Very frightening, but he is out of intensive care and on the mend. Love to you both.

Toby doesn't know whether to believe this story or not. He pictures Salome standing behind the Marxist. "Put 'Love to you both,' " she says, and Macalister laughs. "That's good," he says.

Each night, late, evidently after a few beers, it's Branko calling. "My son is getting in trouble with his friends here, and now Salome has run away and stolen money. Toby, I'm asking myself what I did wrong as a father." Toby accepts the role of counselor, but his heart isn't in it. "I'm sure I'll hear from her soon," he repeats. "I'm sure she's fine. I'll call you as soon as I hear anything."

His thoughts are clouded; moods assault him like guerrilla fighters. He is angry—her behavior is intolerable, unforgivable; afraid—what if something happens to her, what if he never sees her again; jealous—surely she has made a fool of him, is laughing at him in the arms of Macalister, or someone else, someone he doesn't even know; hopeful—there, an e-mail is coming in, it's a message from her. He buys a bottle of cheap scotch and applies himself to it. This consolidates the raging emotions into one: maudlin self-pity. He takes the wedding photo from the bookshelf and sits on the couch, resting it on his knees while he drinks. There they are, smiling serenely amid the raucous Asians. The elevator looms like a dark cavern behind them. Toby notices that Salome's eyes have engaged those of the Asian bride; they are exchanging an arch sororal look. It's a fine thing to have landed a mate, they agree, saluting each other in this moment of their triumph.

Nonsense. Look how lovely she is, how her hand is tucked

confidently in his elbow, how her body inclines to him, no matter what her eyes are up to.

Her lying eyes. Tears appear on the glass and Toby goes to get a dishcloth to wipe them away. And while he's at it, a little more scotch.

When the call finally comes, it's 3 A.M. The ringing rattles his sleep like a cage door and he hurtles past it into consciousness, pulling the phone into the bed and fumbling with the buttons. It's pitch dark in the room, but there is her voice.

"Toby, darling," she says. "It's me. I know it's the middle of the night, but I'm about to get on a train."

"Where are you?" he says. His voice is calm, neither anger, fear, nor jealousy colors it; it's as if she was twenty minutes late for a lunch date. *Stuck in traffic? Oh, poor you.*

"I'm in Zagreb," she says. "I'm on my way to Ljubljana."

"Are you OK?" He switches on the lamp, blinds himself, and switches it off again.

"Yes. Yes. I'm fine. I wanted to call you sooner, but it's not as easy as it should be. I'm using a phone card at the station now. We may get cut off and I won't be able to call you back. The train is leaving in a few minutes."

"I've been worried to death," he says.

"I'm sorry, darling. Forgive me."

"Couldn't you even send an e-mail?"

"I couldn't."

"What are you doing?"

"Toby, please trust me. I think my mother is alive and I'm trying to find her. I know she wasn't killed when they burned our town."

"How do you know?"

"The Red Cross traced her to Slovenia. Then they lost her."

"Wow."

"My feelings are so confused. I must try to find her. You understand, don't you, darling?"

"Your mother's alive," he says. He hadn't seriously considered this possibility, though he sees now that it was always there. "I'll tell your father. He's been calling every night. He's going nuts."

There is a pause; are they disconnected? "Don't tell him anything," she says coldly.

"He's worried about you."

"Let him worry," she says. "Let him ask himself why he didn't look for my mother for twelve years, why he pretended to us that she was dead. Do you know how many people are looking for family members they were told were dead? Well, I'll tell you. A lot."

"He said he had to get out in a hurry. You said that yourself. And they told him she was killed."

"They. Who are they? That's what I'd like to know."

"The police, I thought."

"No matter what I find, I'll never forgive him." The line clicks, stutters.

"Are you there?" Toby says.

"It's a signal. We're going to get cut off. Sweetheart, are you OK?"

"I'm not great," he says honestly.

"I miss you so."

"Why didn't you tell me where you were going?"

"I thought you might try to stop me. And I didn't want you to know I took the money from my father."

"He's not upset about the money. He's just worried about you."

"Toby. Don't take his side!"

"You should have told me."

"I love you, darling. You do believe me?"

"I want to be with you. Where should I go? Ljubljana? That's Slovenia, right?"

"No, not there. I may not be there very long. I'll call you to-morrow, I promise. Or I'll send you an e-mail and you can come meet me. You will come?"

"Yes, yes, of course I will. Just tell me where to go."

"What about your exams?"

The clicking starts again, very loud this time, then a hum and the line goes dead.

"Damn," Toby says. He listens, pushes a few buttons, but nothing happens, and then he gets a dial tone. "Damn," he says again into the blackness of their bedroom. "What am I going to tell Branko?"

Everything we learn about Catherine Earnshaw comes from Ellen Dean, the housekeeper at Wuthering Heights, and Ellen has it in for Catherine. Not without cause. Catherine runs hot and cold to everyone, even those who love her, even Heathcliff, and she is merciless to her inferiors. Her methods are a child's: first wheedling and petting, then tantrums, including kicking, biting, and beating her own head against the floor. Her doctor is convinced it's best not to cross her.

After she marries Edgar Linton and moves from the gloom

of the Heights to the sunny comfort of the Grange, Ellen expects the worst, but to her "agreeable disappointment" for a time all goes well. Catherine is "over fond" of her husband and affectionate to his sister, Isabella. She has the upper hand, as Ellen observes, "there were no mutual concessions; one stood erect, the others yielded; and who can be ill-natured, and bad tempered, when they encounter neither opposition nor indifference." This honeymoon felicity ends with the return of Heathcliff, which results in the protracted business of Catherine's illness, madness, and death, all brought on, according to Ellen, by sheer willfulness and bad temper. Catherine closes herself up in her room, refusing food, making herself sick, and when she is feverish, she opens the window so she can catch her death in the frigid air. Ellen Dean struggles with her, but finds her "delirious strength much surpassed mine." And, of course, worse luck for Ellen, during this struggle Edgar Linton at last decides to pay a visit to his wife.

Chloe recalls a similar dramatic standoff engineered by her own mother, Deidre, though to far less tumultuous effect, when after living twenty years in one house she was required to move to another. The old house, the one Chloe grew up in, was a fifties faux-colonial, poorly constructed, the Sheetrock so thin a whisper in the kitchen could be heard in the back bedroom. The shingles buckled, the deck leaned, the roof leaked. After years of hating the place, Chloe's father had found another house, larger, brighter, more solidly built, with a garden instead of a yard, a commodious, modern kitchen, twice the storage space, all on a tree-lined street not ten miles from the old house, which was now referred to by her mother as "our home," dearer than life, never to be abandoned.

In a weak moment Deidre had agreed that the new house was a good deal—perhaps she thought it was so good it would fall through. When it didn't and she was faced with moving, she plunged off the deep end. Did it dawn on her that she had freighted her wretched suburban bungalow with a barge load of junk and now it would all have to be packed up and moved? She refused to get out of bed. She couldn't breathe. She wouldn't bathe. Chloe's father called one summer afternoon and said, "You have to come and talk to your mother. This is women's business. I can't say a thing to her."

Chloe drove out to the house in her own fit of pique, to find her mother wrapped in blankets in a darkened room, face to the wall. "Mother," she said, sharp as a pick to ice, "what are you doing? Have you no shame. Dad has gone out and bought you a bigger, better house and you can't rouse yourself to be grateful? There's nothing wrong with you. Get up and go take a shower."

And that's exactly what Deidre did, but she remained erratic and fragile, and the heavy lifting, cleaning, and clearing out was done by Chloe and Brendan. In a month Deidre was inviting their friends from the old neighborhood to see how she had come up in the world. "Twice the storage," she said, throwing open meticulously arranged linen and china closets. "The garden was landscaped by a professional." And because she had been so ostentatiously demented, her pleasure in her new house was taken as a sign of her return to health, and no one ever said a word to her about it.

There was a lesson in this, Chloe thinks, placing a sticky tab in the margin of the novel. Catherine Earnshaw battling her maid at the open window—it might be an interesting moment to illustrate. It reminds her of a painting she saw some years ago, in Madrid, the Countess of Something, a slender figure seen from the back with a full skirt swirling around her calves and a volcano of black hair curling down her back, evidently attacking a little old lady who holds out a wooden cross in self-defense. The countess was known to be mischievous, the card on the wall explained, and the artist had caught her in the act of "teasing" her maid.

The artist was Goya, who spent the first part of his career concealing his disaffection for light, his horror of human flesh, and his distrust of human nature. Or divine nature, for that matter. Chloe had steeled herself to look closely at his painting of Saturn eating his son, so disturbing was the image: the bleeding torso and lifeless legs of the child, the god's lips strained apart, his eyes bulging with determination and horror. Goya had sat down and thought about it; how does one actually eat a child? And the answer was: head first.

And why does one eat a child?

To keep him from replacing you.

Chloe looks out through the snow-laden trees to the path. Mike, lounging on the deck, lifts his head but doesn't get up, and in the next moment Brendan appears, his head down, hands stuffed in the pockets of his fleece jacket, tramping through the snow in his duck boots. He arrives at the steps, bats at his jacket and his pants, shedding snow. It's unusual for him to appear in this way; he must have some message of import. She gets up to invite him into her domain, conscious of the warmth from the woodstove, the homeliness of the teapot and shards of cinnamon toast on the table next to her chair. "Is something wrong?" she asks as he steps inside and bends over his knees to unzip his boots.

"No, I don't think so," he says. "I hope not. But I thought I should tell you. Toby called to say he's coming up this evening."

Chloe pulls up her guest chair, a spavined wicker porch reject lined with pillows. "Tonight?" she says. "But it's Wednesday. Would you like some tea?"

"Sure," he says, and sinks into the chair, looking about himself contentedly. "It's nice and warm in here."

"Did he say why?"

"He said he wants to talk to us about something."

Chloe lifts the cozy and pours out the tea from the pot. "I'm afraid this isn't too hot."

"It's fine," he says, sipping.

"Is he coming alone?"

"I think so. He said 'I.' He'll be here on the eight-thirty train."

Chloe takes up her poker and slaps open the doors of the stove. "They've broken up," she says.

"That seems unlikely."

"Does it? Why else would he come home alone in the middle of the week?" She jabs at the embers, which produce a flurry of sparks.

"I don't know."

"They've broken up and he's feeling dramatic. He'll be hungry."

"He did sound serious."

"We'll have to pretend we're not relieved," she says.

"*You'll* have to pretend. If that's what it is, which I doubt."

"You won't be relieved?"

"No. Not at all. I think I'd be disappointed."

She narrows her eyes. "Are you out of your mind?" she says.

"Well, how could it make things better? Salome's still pregnant. He's still the father of that child. You said yourself that means she's in our lives for good."

"Maybe he's not the father. Maybe he found that out."

"How could he find out?"

"How long did he know her before she got pregnant? Two months? She could have been pregnant when they met and spotted him for a fool."

"You really should do something about that imagination of yours."

"You're an innocent, I know. I shouldn't soil your purity."

"It's just so crude. And I don't think Toby is as stupid as you think."

"Thank God they didn't get married," Chloe concludes, closing the stove with a whack of her poker.

Toby is unshaven; his eyes are sunk in bluish circles, and there is a Jesuitical intensity in his gaze that unnerves his mother, who is disguising her feelings, as always, poorly. She was right, however; Toby is hungry. He demolishes the roast chicken efficiently and steadily, angling his knife in the flesh to get the last bits away from the bones, washing down big mouthfuls with deep draughts of beer; he's on his third. Chloe watches him, her fingers circling the stem of her wineglass. Brendan allows his attention to drift from one to the other. It's pitiful, but fascinating, and he is aware of a prurient interest in what happens next.

"Have you been eating?" Chloe says. "You look thin."

"I'm starving," Toby says, reaching for the plate of potatoes.

"Have some spinach," Chloe says. She picks at her own food, anxious and miserable. Toby hasn't told them the reason for his visit. So far it's as if he simply wanted to come home for a meal, as he did sometimes in his first year at college, when he lived in a dorm, long ago, before he changed, before Salome.

"When's your last exam?" Brendan inquires. They are near the end of the term.

"I've got one tomorrow," he says. "One paper due Friday and I'm done." Pendulous over the table is the question of where and with whom Toby plans to spend the month-long recess. Brendan isn't touching it, and Chloe, to his surprise, forestalls it. "That's good," she says. "Do you want some pie?"

Toby wipes his mouth with his napkin, surveying the bare bones on his plate. "Pie would be great," he says. "And coffee, if you have any made." When his mother has gone to the kitchen, he finishes his beer. "So, Dad," he says. "How's the book going?"

"Fine," Brendan says. "Slow."

Toby smiles. "You just keep at it," he says. "I admire that."

This praise touches Brendan with unexpected force. So his son has noticed that he is dogged and admires him for it. When he sits at his desk, rummaging about for the right pen, making pointless notes on file cards, arranging facts, rewriting obstinate sentences to present those facts attractively, getting steadily nowhere, he is, in his son's view, up to something worthwhile. I do it, he wants to say, because I don't know what else to do. But he won't say that. He is not in the practice of discouraging the young. Chloe appears with a tray, and Toby jumps up to help her. They bustle about the table, laying out the plates of apple pie, filling the coffee cups, passing the milk pitcher and the plate of cheese. "It's the last of the local apples," Chloe says. "They're so cheap I bought a bushel." They settle at their places, delve into the thickly crusted pie, still warm and fragrant, and it feels, momentarily, as if nothing is altered, as if Toby has returned from a brief adventure to resume his life as a promising and dutiful son.

"A lot has happened in the last few weeks," he says.

His parents, chewing quietly, give him their attention.

"First, Salome and I are married. We decided not to wait."

Chloe's fork clangs sharply against her plate. Toby produces a ring from his pocket which he slides onto his finger. She covers her face with her hands and props her elbows on the table. "Oh no," she moans. "Oh no."

Brendan swallows, staying focused on his son. "And there's something else?"

"Yes," says Toby. "It looks like I have to go to Trieste as soon as I can."

Milan was humorous, very ironic, which was surprising; they don't generally appreciate irony. Like so many men, he wanted to have a secret life. It made him feel like someone else, someone he'd rather be, that was obvious. For that reason, I think, I was important to him.

You mean he wasn't in love with you?

Well, we weren't Romeo and Juliet; we weren't children. But the worse things got in our town, the more our families cursed each other's families in our kitchens, the more exciting it was in the toolshed. We began taking risks. Everyone was taking risks. Some stole from their neighbors, a few tried to murder them. Milan and I had sex; we were harmless. It was our way of telling ourselves we weren't like the others.

The others were gorging themselves on hatred. Every night they sat in front of their televisions and worked themselves into a frenzy. After Borovo Selo the rhetoric was poisonous. It was impossible to know what really happened there. The Serbs said the Croat police attacked them; the Croats said they had gone in to rescue their men and been trapped in an ambush. It was far away from us, up near the border with Serbia, but it was close too, and it was the incident everyone had been waiting for, to see what the government would do, if the Croats would fight, if Belgrade would send the federal forces to defend the rebels in the Krajina, if the Serb paramilitaries would listen to anyone. Our town was spoiling for a fight. The health club nuts dragged a teenager who said Croats were all Ustashe into the gym and beat him half to death. In the night somebody lit his family's gas tank and their house went up in flames. The next day they packed up what was left and drove out of town. Some of the children coming out from school followed the truck and threw stones at it.

Milan was furious. He was waiting for me with the blanket and he didn't say anything until after we had sex, but he was rough with me and I knew what it was about. He pulled away at once, stood up, lit a cigarette while I gathered my clothes together. "Your son was one of them," he said.

"One of what?"

"At the gym."

I didn't know it, but I believed it. My oldest boy was fourteen and he was in a testosterone-fueled rage most of the time. He kept a photo of a dead Croat family in Slavonia on the wall by his bed; he'd gotten it from *some magazine, the same picture that was on the television every night. His latest theory was that Serbs were not really Slavs. "Why don't you go all the way," I said, "and say they're not human."*

"What can I do about it?" I asked Milan. "He doesn't listen to me."

"What about your husband?"

"You live here," I said. "You know what it's like for the farmers. His father is paralyzed, his mother is a witch, and he's got three children to support. He's up at dawn, he works until dark."

"And his wife is fucking a Serb."

"Well," I said. "He doesn't know that."

He smiled, but not in a friendly way. I got up and brushed myself off. "What do you tell yourself?" he said.

"Don't worry," I said. "I don't tell myself lies, unlike everyone else in this town."

He bent down to pull up the blanket. "The tables could turn, you know," he said. "Your husband is not a bad man, but his father is Ustasha. You should tell your son to be careful."

"Is that a threat?"

He didn't answer and we stood looking at each other coldly. Outside our little hideaway it was summer; the grass was spongy underfoot, the trees were dazzling, fresh green, their blossoms scattered on the ground, and as we stood there silently appraising each other, a bird gave a long, throbbing trill. "What do they say in your house?" he said softly. "Do they say there will be war?"

"My mother-in-law says yes, my husband says no."

Milan nodded. He put his arms around me and pressed his lips against my hair. All at once I was sad; tears stung my eyes and I clung to him. "Let's hope your husband is right," he said.

What Milan said stayed with me all the way home. I was chastised. That night at the dinner table, a meal I prepared carefully, as if I might not get to do it again, I looked at my family and I saw how miserable they were. Much of the suffering was caused by the cruelty of my mother-in-law. She sat at the head of the table—she had replaced her husband, who was slobbering in his wheelchair in the corner—wiping a piece of bread around her bowl to soak up the last of her soup. Her face was like an ax; she had hard, glassy eyes, crooked, yellow teeth, her lower lip sagged, showing the purplish line of her gums. She made grunting sounds as she ate. My younger son was terrified of her. He sat across from her, occasionally sending her anxious glances. He was a tenderhearted boy. He liked reading, which she detested, and she was capable of throwing his book in the stove if she found him with one, so he had to be careful every minute. My husband sat next to her, eating doggedly, the solid agrarian. Now and then he paused to speak to one of the children, or to pet our little girl, who always sat next to him. Those two were in love; they were an island of peace in this hellish kitchen. He'd brought her a little half-dead orange kitten he found in the barn and showed her how to nurse it back to life. She'd been up every hour in the night for a week to feed it with bread soaked in goat's milk, and later thin gruel. Now it was tearing around the house like a tiny lightning bolt. She was pleased with herself. She and her father talked about the kitten constantly; he was never impatient with her. I knew he was worried about everything. Money was tight, the fighting in Slavonia, which was all we heard about on the television, horrified him, the crop was critical; he'd had a very bad year, all the farmers had. His father was a burden, his mother a cross, and then there was me. He knew the life we had was not what I wanted, that he had failed me, and it made him sad and shy. He was polite to me, as if I was a visitor.

My older boy, who was eating hurriedly, was a walking time bomb. He worked alongside his father when he wasn't in school, but he still found time to run with the worthless pack of curs at the health club, plotting mayhem. I'd seen him standing with some of them at the market, smoking cigarettes, *laughing too loud, ogling the women who passed. He was the youngest of them, and he affected a servile, ingratiating manner it made me sick to see. At home he was all braggadocio and bombast. He'd taken to standing up to his grandmother, which I didn't discourage. He looked on me as a possible hindrance to his schemes, not much more. Sometimes if I drank too much, he gave me cold looks and said I was disgusting. Once he took my glass, poured it into the sink, and stormed out of the kitchen. His teeth were always clenched and his eyes were shifty. At best his thoughts were unclean. I didn't want to think about the worst.*

This was my family. I felt sorry for them, one by one, except the old woman, and I wished them a better mother, a better wife than they had in me. But I knew this wish wouldn't make me any better than I was.

That night my father-in-law died in his sleep. The old woman came into our bedroom before dawn and announced, "Get up, your father is dead." Later that same day the bodies of four Serbs washed down the river and jammed in the curve at the top of the town. Each one had been shot once in the head and their hands were tied behind their backs with clothesline.

What happened to them?

No one knew; no one wanted to know. The police fished them out and buried them in a big trench behind the station. My husband told me about it in bed that night. He whispered it to me. By that time every house in our wretched town was full of whispering.

❖ PART TWO ❖

It takes a few minutes for the photos to come in. While she waits, Chloe turns to the table and examines the Resingrave block nestled on the leather sandbag. The engraving is nearly done. The window frame and the swirling, spiraling sky, which occupy two thirds of the block, are finished. The twisted fir, the graveyard, and the figures of two men, one digging and one wrapped in a cloak looking on, can be seen dimly through the toner. Chloe is pleased with the texture of the sky, which contains, for those discerning enough to notice, the wind-driven silhouette of Emily Brontë's hawk.

For weeks now, Chloe has been working long hours into the night, inspired by the not particularly earthshaking observation that windows constitute a recurring motif in *Wuthering Heights*. She's finished three engravings: the famous scene in which Heathcliff's luckless tenant Lockwood dreams the waif Cathy is scratching at his window, begging to be let in from the cold; Cathy's struggle with her maid to close the bedroom window;

and Ellen's discovery of Heathcliff flat on his back in his bed, soaked by the rain driving through the open window, wide-eyed, grinning, dead. Though Heathcliff's moonlight disinterment of his beloved Cathy in the graveyard has nothing to do with a window—he confesses it to Ellen after the fact and she is appropriately horrified—Chloe has a reason for framing the scene in this way. The other windows are all interior to the engravings; the characters appear before them. This scene, near the end of the book, is the only one in which the window frame is moved to the outer edge of the print. Two questions are thereby raised: Who's the viewer? Who's dead?

The computer bell summons her to the screen.

Dearest. All is well. We'll call you Sunday afternoon. Truly wish you were here. Love. Brendan.

That's the message, which he may have composed with Toby looking over his shoulder. Chloe clicks the attachment square at the bottom of the screen and there they are, admiring the Hapsburg facade of the Palazzo del Governo on the impressive Piazza Unitá in Trieste. The sea is black behind them, the sky a mass of threatening dark clouds, the wide stones beneath their boots slick with rain. It looks cold. Brendan has on the down-stuffed coat he calls the "bear," the hood lined with fake fur. Toby is huddled in his old L.L. Bean parka, sporting a new Russian-style fur hat with flaps over the ears. Salome is wrapped in a headscarf, babushka style, and her thick woolen coat. They are all smiling big "cheese" smiles. Toby's arms are draped across Salome's shoulders; Brendan has rested his hand on his son's arm.

Who's the viewer? Who's dead?

Not the mother, as it turns out, and that's the fantastic part.

This woman who has been presumed dead by her family for twelve years has actually been very much alive and living in Trieste. She has made, in all this time, no effort to locate her family, and the Oyster King, evidently, has been too busy harvesting the seas to ascertain that his beloved wife was not, as he believed, killed in the war. It took her daughter two weeks to find her.

Not only is she alive, but she must have a computer, or access to one. The camera is Brendan's. It was his Christmas present. He had been reluctant to take it with him—thieves were always a problem in Italy and expensive cameras were irresistible to them—but Chloe had insisted; it would mean he could send her photos right away.

And here they are. She clicks to the next one—a café, architecturally Viennese, but the long marble-topped bar with the row of espresso machines behind it proclaims that this is Italy. The happy threesome leans against the bar, their tiny cups behind them. Toby is nuzzling Salome's ear, she and Brendan are laughing.

Why all this glee? Brendan should be weeping. The tickets cost a fortune, and he is on half-pay for another semester. His mission is not tourism, it is talking sense into his son, who has the lunatic idea of leaving school and staying in Italy to "help" the formerly dead woman. Another photo, same café. They are sitting at a table before plates of enormous cream cakes. The cheerful trio lift their glasses of prosecco in a lighthearted toast. The camera is excellent; Chloe can actually see the bubbles in the wine.

One by one they'd gone. First Salome, who disappeared in broad daylight, leaving Toby in the dark for a week, and for no

reason. Why couldn't she have just told him where she was going, why the secrecy, why the drama? First she was in Zagreb
consulting with the International Red Cross, and then she was
in Ljubljana in Slovenia, and then Trieste, where in short order
she was reunited with the lost mother. *I've found her, come at once,*
she wrote to her pining husband, who stopped off at home to
eat an enormous meal and borrow his father's credit card before doing exactly what he was told.

Chloe was incredulous. "You gave him your credit card?"
she said, but Brendan shrugged. "It's got a limit on it. And
what else could I do? She's his wife."

Phone calls followed, very expensive, charged from phone
booths. Why? Didn't the mother have a phone? "Yes," Toby
explained. "But it's so expensive and she doesn't have much
money." That she was poor is not surprising, but Toby informs
his mother that she is also "remarkable." "An amazing woman.
Never met anyone like her."

To the repeated question "When are you coming home?"
Toby offered only, "Soon." Soon became later, Christmas was
a phone call, and then there was the "important news" that the
newlyweds were planning a leave of absence from the university and a longer residence with the "remarkable" woman.
"What's her name, for God's sake?" Chloe complained.

"Jelena," Toby said. "It means Helen."

"Really," she replied acidly. "You don't say."

"Calm down, Mom," Toby said.

But she wasn't the one who was nervous, it was him; otherwise, why would he talk to her as if she was suddenly an idiot?
"You'd better talk to your father," she said coldly, handing off

the phone to Brendan, who did his interested and understanding routine, which was not useful at all.

Chloe closes the photos, transfers them to another file where she keeps pictures. She's required to give the new folder a name. She could just call it *family* and dump them in with all the others, but something feels wrong about that. It's her family without her in it, photographed not by her but by someone else. The viewer. And who is that? Is it the mother? A stranger passing by? She types *Trieste* into the allotted space and sends them away. But because she doesn't ever entirely trust the computer, having come to it late and fighting all the way, now she has to go to the file and make sure the pictures are there. This brings her to a screen covered with icons, too many—she should get rid of some of this stuff. Her hand lingers on the mouse, moving the cursor aimlessly, reminding her of the Ouija board of her childhood and the long, hot summer afternoons passed with her cousin Marianne, who was an adept at extracting horrifying messages from the dead. The cursor stops over the file labeled *The Poacher* and she clicks it. There's a hesitation; he is being retrieved. Abruptly his face fills the screen.

Zigor. That's his name. Basque, not Lebanese.

Brendan hadn't approved of her taking the photograph to pass around at the cocktail party, but Chloe insisted. "Joan thinks it's a good idea," she protested. "Someone may even know his name." And someone had, though not his whole name.

"It's Zigor," the contractor said, bending over the photo. "His last name is something you can't pronounce, no vowels and a lot of X's. It's Basque. He's a Basque. He's working for

Jake Hardy over in Croton. Zigor was a plumber in Bilbao—is that where the Guggenheim is?—I think he worked on the Guggenheim, for God's sake, and he wound up here. His English is pretty poor, but he speaks Spanish. That's how Jake talks to him. There's not much Zigor doesn't know about pipe. Pipe is a universal language."

"A Basque," someone said. "As in ETA."

"Zigor is harmless," the contractor insisted. "He wouldn't hurt a fly."

"Well, he's killing our rabbits," Chloe said. "And he almost killed our cat."

"The vet doesn't think Mike was shot," Brendan observed once again.

"I don't care what the vet thinks," Chloe retorted. "This guy is wandering around on our land at all hours with a rifle. I told him he can't hunt there and he ignored me."

"He probably didn't understand you," the contractor said. "His English is pretty poor."

"He understood me," Chloe said.

"A Basque," Brendan said.

"If you see him," Chloe said, "tell him we know who he is and if he comes on our land again, I'll have him arrested."

"I couldn't make him understand all that," the contractor said, handing the picture back. Chloe sent a pleading look to Joan Chase, but her hostess only frowned and changed the subject, clearly displeased to have the festive atmosphere spoiled by her neighbor's grievance.

Chloe wanted to call the employer and confront Zigor at the work site, but Brendan was adamant. "Hunting season is almost over," he said. "What's the point of making a scene now?

He's a plumber, he doesn't speak English, he's just trying to make a living. I haven't heard him at all in the last week. Have you?"

"No," Chloe admitted.

"And now that we know he isn't dangerous . . ."

"People with rifles are dangerous by definition."

"Promise me you won't do anything until I get back from this trip," Brendan said. "Then we'll talk about it."

But Chloe didn't promise. She changed the subject. Now she studies the poacher, this ambitious immigrant, expert in matters of pipe, gainfully employed by the Spanish-speaking contractor whose name escapes her at the moment. He looks different, she has to admit, less threatening. Clearly not Lebanese or even Middle Eastern.

In Madrid they insist Basques are the best cooks, which is odd as the Basques hate the Madrileños and occasionally set off bombs, blowing up potential restaurant patrons. Doubtless it's a kind of patronizing of an inferior, unworthy enemy, like Southern whites who are mad for "soul food," or Brits who go out to an Irish pub for the singing. They want to kill us, but they have their charms. See, we're not intolerant, so long as they stick to what they're good at.

As they drove to the airport, Brendan said, "They say you hear more Slovenian and Croatian than Italian in Trieste these days."

"Who says that?" Chloe said.

"The guidebooks."

"I'll bet the Italians love that."

"They might put up with the language, but they're not going to like the food."

They laughed. Those amusing Italians and their antipathy for any cuisine not their own.

"I've always wanted to see Trieste," Brendan said. "Though not in winter."

"You're not going to see Trieste. You're going to bring him back."

"Them back," he corrected her.

"Right," she said.

Chloe clicks the red X. Zigor turns blue, disappears. It's all such a waste of time and money; this awful girl and her baby and her dead mother who will have to be helped now because she's so poor and remarkable and because she's a refugee. Chloe decides to vent her frustration on sharpening her gravures. She has to use a jig now, as her hands have developed a slight tremor that ruins the edge. She takes down the tin of cutting oil and the hard Arkansas stone. The plumbing contractor's name comes to mind and she stops to write it down on a notepad: Jake Hardy. It shouldn't be difficult to find his phone number. Surely he can explain to the worthy Zigor the meaning of the words *posted*, *penalty*, and *arrest*. It will be doing the Basque a favor.

"It's not very nice, is it?" Toby says.

"It's fine."

"Mom wouldn't stay here five minutes."

"It's fine," Brendan says. The room is relentlessly dreary, threadbare carpet, sagging bed with soiled red coverlet, rickety table, twenty-watt lamp, an ancient TV attached to the wall by a rusty metal arm, a curtain for the bathroom door. They haven't looked in there yet, but the likelihood of a shower that sprays the entire room and runs down a central drain in the floor upon which a dying beetle feebly wags its legs is high. Toby is right; Chloe would say, "Absolutely not," and walk out.

The trip was long and Brendan is already feeling jet-lagged, but he doesn't much want to lie down on the bed. "Are you hungry?" Toby asks.

"Not much. I could use some coffee."

"There's a good café near here."

"Trieste is famous for its cafés," Brendan says. "I'll just wash up and put on a clean sweater." He lifts his suitcase onto the table—no place else to put it—zips it open, and extracts his venerable Dopp kit. Toby has witnessed the unpacking of this kit dozens of times in as many hotel rooms all over Europe, but never in a room as shabby as this one and never without his mother taking up her share of the physical and psychic space. Or more than her share.

"I'm glad you came, Dad," he says. "There's a lot I want to talk to you about."

"That's why I'm here," Brendan says, pulling the bathroom curtain aside. On the drain in the center of the floor a dying beetle wags its flimsy legs. "To talk."

Toby goes to the window, wrestles the heavy curtain aside, and looks out into the street. It's gray, wet, cold, and largely empty. He's thinking about sex, which has become a problem. Jelena's apartment is small, the girl, Vilka, is always there, they have no privacy. "Ask your father to let us use his room when he comes," Salome said. She's right, it's the obvious solution, but Toby feels awkward about it. He's been hitting Brendan's credit card hard in the last weeks; mostly on food, as Jelena certainly can't afford two more mouths to feed. This is why he skimped on the room. He looks back toward the bathroom, where his father is brushing his teeth, and his eyes settle on the bed. Grim, but Salome won't care. The thought of her naked on that disgusting bedspread provokes a pleasant stirring in his groin; he has to put the image firmly away. His father turns off the tap and comes out from behind the curtain. He's wearing a close-fitting winter undershirt that reveals his still-muscular shoulders—all that wood chopping—though his chest looks hollow. His expression, as always, is mild and inquisitive, slightly unfocused, as if he expects to be distracted at any moment by some urgent business proceeding inside his own head.

Toby has no wish to be like his father; he has known this for some time now, but this doesn't mean he wants his father to change. He appreciates the ironic distance that characterizes the paternal aura, disinterested yet benign, fresh as opposed to chilly. "He's coming to bring you back," Salome said as she read the e-mail announcing this visit. "Your mother is afraid to do it, so she's sending him."

"He's coming to talk to me about money," Toby said. "My parents aren't as rich as you think."

In fact, Toby has a fair idea of exactly what his parents are worth and how much has already been invested in his expensive education. He isn't ungrateful, but given who they are and what they value, it would have been out of character for them to do otherwise. He understands that his self-sufficiency, both moral and financial, is the hoped-for return on this investment, and he's not unwilling to gratify that expectation. But as an ideal, self-sufficiency isn't irresistibly compelling; it makes no

allowance for passion. Toby watches his father rummage about
in his canvas book bag, searching for his wallet. "So, how is
Salome?"

"She's fine. She's at her mother's. There's a sick girl there she
looks after while Jelena is at work. It's been a big help to her."

"Is the girl her daughter?"

Toby shrugs. In the three weeks he has been living in Jelena's
apartment, he has not penetrated the mystery of Vilka's identity. Jelena refers to her as the "child," and Salome maintains
that she is not related or even adopted. "My mother found her
somewhere," she said, "in the war."

"How old is she?"

"She must be ten or eleven. Something's wrong with her.
She can't talk. She just makes sounds, and sometimes she has
fits and we have to wrap her in a blanket."

"Good Lord," Brendan says. His father's amazement is a relief to Toby, who has been stoically keeping his own counsel in
an alien environment. Good Lord is right, he thinks, though he
has not been able to say this even to himself. He sinks down on
the bed—there's no other place to sit—and unburdens himself.
"It's pretty crowded in the apartment; it's only two rooms. Jelena works a lot; she translates at the consulate part-time and
she works for an English family, kind of a nanny-housekeeper-
assistant. She speaks Italian and English; she's really smart.
That's where Salome's brains come from. She's been through
hell, I think, but she doesn't talk about it. She smokes a lot. It
makes me anxious because of the baby. Smoking's not good,
is it?"

"Probably not," Brendan says.

"Salome is all mixed up. She hardly knows what she thinks

from minute to minute. She's angry with her father because he didn't even try to find Jelena after the war, and she's trying to make up for lost time with her mother, but Jelena is not the same person she remembers."

"Does she say that?"

"Yes. She says it to me. She spent twelve years keeping her mother alive in her memory. And now here's this new mother, with this strange child. She didn't recognize Salome when she opened the door; that hurt her. And then there's the question of why she didn't try to find her family."

"And why didn't she?"

"I don't think Salome has had the nerve to ask her."

"How do you feel about all this?"

"I'm in way over my head, Dad," Toby admits. "I'm just treading water."

"And you're seriously considering leaving school?"

"What choice do I have? Salome won't leave her mother now; she just found her. And I can't leave Salome, she's my wife, she's pregnant. This is my family now."

Brendan regards his son solemnly. "Any chance the mother would come to the States?"

Toby shakes his head; a rueful smile plays around his mouth. "That's really hard to picture."

A silence falls between them. Outside someone shouts. A car passes, making a whoofing sound on the wet pavement. Toby reaches into his coat pocket and pulls out an impressive fur hat. "We'll get you some coffee," he says.

"That's quite a hat."

"Thanks. Salome bought it for me. After we go to the café

we'll walk over to the apartment, if that's OK. She's waiting for us."

"I'm ready," Brendan says. "Lead the way."

The apartment is four flights up, tucked under the eaves of a building that, like much of Trieste, has seen better days. They pass a few tenants on the stairs, an old woman wrapped in what looks like upholstery and two young men, smoking and speaking rapidly a language Brendan recognizes only as not Italian. The staircase is dim, the plaster, once pink, has faded and crumbled, leaving large maplike areas of gray in a field of muddy beige. There is a strong smell of fried fish. Toby pauses at each landing while Brendan catches up, not panting, but with a steady plodding that bespeaks his general fatigue. At the top a narrow hall leads to a final door. Toby extracts a key from his pocket and turns it in the lock. A wail issues from within. He steps inside, looking back at his father nervously. "It's Vilka," he says. "She's having one of her fits."

Salome is kneeling on the bare floor, her back to the door, struggling to hold down a screaming, gyrating wraith of a girl whose face is hidden by a mass of black hair. "Help me," she calls to Toby, who rushes in, snatching up a blanket from the couch and dropping to his knees at her side. Together they restrain the child's flailing limbs and with practiced care roll her up in a tight cocoon. She doesn't stop screaming, but the pitch changes from bloodcurdling terror to pitiful suffering. "It's OK," Toby repeats. "You're safe. We're here, you're safe."

Salome pulls the weeping bundle into her arms and croons along with Toby, but in another language. Gradually the sobbing subsides.

Brendan hasn't moved from the door. As calm returns, he takes in more of the room, the bare table and wooden folding chairs, the grimy cooktop and steel sink crammed into a corner, pipes exposed beneath, and next to it a doorless cupboard in which a few dishes and pots mingle with canned goods and a waist-high refrigerator below. Against the far wall is a lumpy sofa covered in a brown throw, another military-quality blanket folded over the arm for an extra cushion. Next to it is a battered table with a shelf beneath that serves as a bookcase. Paperbacks are piled upon it in stacks. They're in English; a few words are legible on the spines: *Silas Marner*, Doris Lessing, *Disgrace*. A brightly patterned cloth, strung on a cord across an open archway, is the only touch of color in the heavy gloom. The light, what there is of it, drizzles in through the single dormer window. Toby and Salome are absorbed in soothing the child; for the moment they have forgotten Brendan, and he is left to decide for himself when and how he will enter the room, which is, in some consequential way, his destination. This room where his son is in "over his head." Yesterday he left Chloe at the airport and now he has come to the end of his journey.

What did he expect? He isn't sure, but it wasn't this. He glances back at the narrow, dusty hall with its line of flimsy doors. Behind each one, bleak lives wind down their days; no one with any hope left lives in this place. Brendan crosses the portal and closes the door behind him.

At the sound Salome looks up and meets his gaze with her

candid surmise. She eases the child, who is quiet now, into Toby's arms and comes to meet him, her hand extended as if she is welcoming him to a tea party. "Brendan," she says. "I'm glad you came. You must be tired from your trip."

This unsettles him further; her studied casualness, the tacit understanding that she is related to him, his daughter-in-law, carrying his grandchild. Is this ratty apartment her dowry? He has offered no resistance to her claim, but now, as she takes his hand and raises her cheek to be kissed, he understands the full extent of it. She's wearing a bulky sweater, but it's clear that she is, as Chloe would say, starting to "show."

"How are you, my dear?" he says.

Toby, watching this meeting from the floor, settles the mysterious bundle of the child in his arms. "This is Vilka," he says, smoothing the black hair away from her face. "She'll be afraid of you, so you shouldn't come too close yet. But she'll get over it." The child appears not to have noticed Brendan. Her dark eyes are fixed on Toby's lips. "I couldn't get near you when I first came, could I?" Toby says to her. "And now look at us."

"And she doesn't understand a word you're saying," Salome observes, a little coldly in Brendan's view. "Let's sit on the couch," she suggests.

Brendan follows and sinks into the thin cushions. He can feel the hard frame beneath. Toby lifts the child, loosening the blanket around her neck, and she turns her head, taking Brendan in with startled, inhuman eyes. Her complexion is milky white, her lips thin and bluish, turned up at the corners, but not in a smile. There's something elfin about her, something otherworldly. On her right cheek is a dark half-moon scar, as clear and neat as a brand. She makes a sound. Brendan doesn't think it's a word in any language. "Hello, Vilka," he says, smiling. Salome adds something in Croatian, which Vilka takes in by screwing down her eyes, as if she can't listen and see at the same time. "I told her you are our father," Salome says.

Toby pushes the blanket down farther and her thin arms emerge. She wraps one around his neck and lays her cheek against his chest. "Where is she from?" Brendan asks.

"No one knows," Salome says. "My mother found her in the war. In a camp somewhere. She doesn't like to talk about it. Would you like some coffee?"

"No, thanks. We've just been to the café."

"My mother will be here soon," Salome says. "Then we'll have lunch."

My mother. How precisely she pronounces the magic syllables that for so many years denoted only a childhood memory, a phantom mother, now returned from the dead. One mother, under God, incarnate, in Trieste. And Brendan is to be "our father," as she has dismissed her own to outer darkness. How clear moral choices are to the young. "It's a miracle you were able to find your mother," Brendan says. "So many were lost in the war."

Toby shoots him a warning look, but Salome's answer, though sour, isn't hostile. "It wasn't particularly difficult, actually, which is pretty annoying."

Brendan can think of no response that will lighten the mood, so he says nothing. Vilka, watching him closely, releases Toby and stands biting her fist. She's tragically thin, her sweater swallows her up, her cheeks are drawn, she looks shriveled, as if there was once more to her. "She wants her bear," Toby says. Salome gets up, disappears behind the curtain, and returns with a small stuffed animal, much chewed upon and shapeless, missing, Brendan notes, an eye. Vilka runs to her, snatches the toy, and, holding it close to her chest, barricades herself under the chairs at the table. "She'll come to you when she's ready," Toby informs his father. "Just don't reach for her. That really frightens her."

"I see," Brendan says. "I won't." In fact, he decides, he isn't going to reach for anything in this place. He is going to let it all come to him.

And shortly it does. They hear the sharp rap of footsteps approaching, accompanied by creaking protests from the floorboards; no one will be sneaking up on this apartment. "It's my mother," Salome announces, going to the door. She turns the bolt and pulls it open, blocking Brendan's view of the hall. "Let me take that," she says, and "Toby's father is here."

Brendan feels Toby's eyes upon him, but he's too preoccupied with concealing his surprise to exchange even a glance with his son. Jelena has come inside, closed the door, and stands unfastening the black fur hat that covers her forehead and ears. She shakes her head, loosening the wavy blonde hair around her face, then, using her fingers as a comb, rakes it back. Her eyes, dark and hooded, rest upon Brendan with distant interest; she looks him over. She hangs the hat on a peg next to the door and shrugs her coat from her shoulders.

Did he think she would be some wizened Balkan peasant, some overweight refugee dressed all in black with a woolen shawl, beaten down by war, penury, and suffering? The coat is cheap, fake leather with a fake fur collar, a knockoff of something better, and her boots are worn, but they have stacked heels and silver buckles. She is no longer a beauty, but she once was, and she can't afford to be fashionable, but she hasn't lost the habit of caring for her looks. Her pouting lips are painted a shade of red that matches the fluffy cardigan under her coat. She hangs the coat on the peg and turns to Brendan, who is on his feet, putting out his hand, American style, feeling unaccountably foolish now, like a boy. "I'm Brendan," he says.

She regards the hand pointedly, her mouth flickering with amusement. Then, decisively, she puts her hand in his and leaves it there without pressure while he pumps it briefly up and down. "So you are the American father," she says. "I am Jelena, but I'm sure you know that." When he frees her hand, she rests it upon his shoulder and touches her lips to one cheek and then the other. "Shall we greet each other in this way?" she suggests.

Vilka, who has crawled out from her table fortress, hurtles between them, grasping Jelena about the hips. Without comment, she gathers the child up into her arms and carries her to the table, where Salome is laying out plates, glasses, bread, sausage, cheese, and a jar of pickled vegetables. Brendan follows, admiring the straightness of Jelena's spine, the width of her shoulders. She's thin, but she looks strong. Her hands are large, with long tapering fingers.

"Do you want coffee, Mother?" Salome asks, and Jelena replies, "Yes."

Toby joins them. "Can I help?" he asks.

"You can get the cups," Salome says.

Brendan stands aside so as not to be in the way. There's a lot of tension in this domestic scene, and he determines that most of it is coming from Salome. Toby does the cheek-kissing routine with Jelena and takes down cups from the cupboard.

"What do you want to drink, Dad?" he says. "We could run downstairs and get some beer."

"Just water is fine," Brendan says.

Jelena slides Vilka to the floor and takes a chair. The child recovers her stuffed bear and curls up with her head on Jelena's boot.

"How are we all going to sit if she's under the table like that?" Salome asks. It's a testy question, but not without merit.

"Very carefully," Toby offers, which makes Jelena smile. "Toby is right," she says.

Salome drapes her arms around her husband's shoulders and kisses his neck. "Toby is always right," she murmurs. Toby grins at his father. He's got the hotel room key in his pocket. They worked it all out over Brendan's first cup of Italian coffee. After lunch the newlyweds will make an excuse. Salome wants to go to the *pesceria* to get fresh fish; she's making fish stew for dinner. Brendan will plead fatigue and stay in with Jelena. "An hour," Toby said. "If we could just get an hour alone together." Later they'll meet at the famous café near Piazza Unitá.

Brendan pulls a chair out from the table, careful not to disturb the child, who appears to be asleep. Jelena draws a pack of cigarettes and a plastic lighter from her sweater pocket. She taps the pack against the table, extracting a cigarette. "I don't suppose you smoke," she says. "Americans are very pure."

He takes the lighter and flicks up a tenuous flame. As she leans toward him, the cigarette between her lips, her eyes engage his with the same effrontery that characterizes her daughter's address. Yet it's warmer, he finds, not unkind, and devoid of cunning.

"Are we your first Americans?" he asks.

She sucks at the flame through the slender tube of tobacco, inhales the smoke, and lets it seep back out through pursed lips. "More or less," she says.

❧❧

The tombstones jut up ominously in the foreground, pointing to the two figures bent over an open grave. The perspective is low; the stones are much larger than the figures, and so are the shadows.

It's Heathcliff's second attempt to dig up his dead love. The first was the night after her burial, when he went to her grave alone, mad with grief. He gave up when he felt Cathy's ghost sigh in his ear; she seemed to entreat him to let her rest in peace. This time, eighteen years have passed, and Cathy's husband, Edgar, has just died. It is in the light of day and Heathcliff is in a colder frame of mind. He has achieved his goal; his vengeance on the two houses is complete; he is, in fact, the owner of both. His position is such that he can require the sexton to do the digging for him. He pries open the coffin and finds, to his surprise, Cathy's beloved face intact.

Necrophilia, on top of wife-beating and some active assistance in the deaths of his foster brother and his own son. It can't be denied that Heathcliff is driven by the ungovernable passion recommended by William Blake in the maxim Chloe once taped to her bedroom door. Some of his critics have described him as the epitome of the Byronic hero: melancholy, defiant, Satanic. Chloe doesn't agree. Byron's Childe Harold and Don Juan are paragons of reason compared to Heathcliff.

Don Juan's passion is seducing women, any woman will do—
they are as interchangeable to him as an artist's brushes—and
Harold is an injured idealist, disillusioned, defiant, and coolly
realistic by turns. Both are aristocrats. Heathcliff was never an
idealist and his origins are unknown. His history, Ellen tells
Lockwood, is a cuckoo's. His passion is vengeance, a steely pu-
rifying furnace that consumes him and reduces him ultimately
to ash. He wants to get even with those who took him in and
failed to love him. No, he's not the Romantic vision of an overheated female imagination. He's something new: the vengeful
orphan, the ungrateful outsider, the coming retribution of the
great underclass.

Chloe bends over the block, guiding the round graver along
the grooves, widening the line as it descends, lifting the tool
carefully at the end to keep the burr from falling back into the
cut. She's working her way around the gravestones, which are
light against a dark swelling roll of earth, like a billowing curtain ending in the line of the horizon. The stones in the foreground are large enough to write on, and she's considering
etching Emily Brontë's name and dates on one of them, to remind the reader here at the end of the novel that, like all the
characters who populate this mad universe of her creation,
Emily died young.

Chloe is moody and depressed. Why not? The newspaper is
packed with lies, idiotic speculation about whether a bunch of
empty warheads in Iraq that have a range of twelve miles constitute a threat to national security. And Friedman, that idiot, is
trotting out his sage advice to the Democrats; he thinks they
should run Tony Blair.

And then there's Brendan, who sounds like someone she

hardly knows. He's been gone two weeks now and they've had four conversations, one less satisfactory than the last. He's obviously distracted and Toby has somehow thrown him off his mission. Yesterday he explained that Toby would lose only time if he stayed out of school a term, there was no doubt that the university would take him back, he was an A student, after all, and couldn't they all use a break from tuition payments?

"What is he going to do there?" Chloe complained.

"It looks like Jelena can help him get some English tutoring."

Jelena. A name she's sick of, a name that makes her shift the subject pronto. "So what do you think of Trieste?" she said.

"It's pretty cold, pretty windy. The big piazza is stunning. I haven't seen much of the town."

And why is that? Because he's been busy trying to help Toby and Salome and Jelena. "I miss you, darling," he said, but she doesn't believe him. "I'll be home on Sunday."

Which is tomorrow. He's come to some kind of agreement with Toby, something that will be expensive, though evidently cheaper than tuition. "He can't leave Salome now," Brendan explained. "And she won't leave her mother."

It could be worse, Chloe reminds herself. They could wind up with the mother in the sewing room crocheting curtains, doing the whole house over in Bohunk chic. Chloe lifts the burin and backs away from the block. The bitterness of her thoughts is spilling over into everything. Even this work, which she undertook with such enthusiasm, seems pointless and stale to her now. Her head aches and her arm is numb from being too long in one position. She turns to the hot plate, slides the kettle onto the burner. It snowed hard in the night and she was trapped in the house all morning until the plow man came.

Then she had to shovel the steps to get out to the drive and again to get into the studio, which wore her out. She hasn't been eating much, or talking to anyone. She's annoyed with Brendan, but she'll be relieved to see him. The phone is too frustrating. Toby got on only once and said about ten words, formulas—*how are you, we're fine, did you get our pictures?*

"Yes," she said. "I like your new hat."

"Salome gave it to me," he said.

She gave you a hat. I gave you your life. This is what she thinks as she fills her teacup, dimly conscious of a sloughing sound in the snow-muffled silence of her studio. She looks out at the path, which is scarcely a furrow in the white expanse. At the moment when she's certain she's hearing approaching footsteps, the poacher comes into view.

He's walking determinedly, lifting his feet high with each step, his arms raised at the elbow to keep his balance. He's wearing a hooded jacket, sweatpants, and short rubber boots, into which, with each step, the snow is piling. No rifle, no dog. Chloe stands arrested, teacup in hand. Bits of the exchange she had with his employer rustle in her memory, chilling her. As he gains the deck, his head comes up and he sees her. He pauses, holds up one hand in a gesture that might be defensive or cordial, or both. His frown is deep, his eyes troubled. He pushes back the hood with his other hand and allows her the opportunity simply to take him in.

Carefully Chloe sets down the cup, noting the location of the cell phone on the table by her reading chair. "He's harmless," she hears the contractor say. She repeats this to herself, a new mantra, as she unlatches the glass door between them, pulling it open with a tug.

"Missus," he says at once. "Forgive me. I'm very sorry."

"You scared me to death," she says.

"I must speak." She steps back, motioning him inside. "Come inside, it's freezing out there." But he ignores her invitation. "You call Mr. Hardy," he says. Is it a question or a command?

"Did I? Yes, I did."

"You must call him."

"What is it you want?"

"I am not hunting." He says this carefully; he's rehearsed it. "I am not any more hunting. I'm sorry."

"I'm glad to hear it."

"You must call Mr. Hardy." He is trembling, whether from cold or an excess of emotion, Chloe can't tell. The icy air pushes in around him, gripping her neck and her ankles, as insistent as a dog's cold nose.

"Come inside," she says. "It's too cold. I can't stand out here and talk to you. It's ten degrees."

"What I do?" he says, addressing who knows who. But he steps inside and Chloe pushes the door closed behind him.

"I'm sorry you're upset," she says. "But you know I told you last year to stop hunting on this land."

He stands pressed against the door, literally wringing his hands. "I don't understand you," he says.

"I told you. Last year. This land is posted. Didn't Mr. Hardy tell you what posted means?"

"You call Mr. Hardy," he says.

"Why?" Chloe backs away. The headache she's had all morning is suddenly much worse; it's moved in behind her eyes and sends out hot wires down the back of her neck and into her sinuses. Even her jaw is throbbing. "Why must I call him?"

"I am losing my job," he says. "I am not hunting. You must call him."

"Stop saying that," Chloe snaps. She told Mr. Hardy she wasn't trying to get the guy fired; she just wanted someone to explain to him that he couldn't go around shooting on private property. It turned out Hardy hated hunters. One of them had accidentally shot his cow. "How do you accidentally shoot a cow?" he complained. "This guy didn't even have a license." Chloe wound up defending the poacher. "He's only shooting rabbits. And he doesn't have very good English. I just want you to speak to him."

"Fucking Zigor," Hardy said. "Wait 'til I get my hands on him."

So he'd fired him. Chloe frowns at the distraught Basque; there's nothing she can do for him and she knows it. Why doesn't he just leave her alone? "I wasn't trying to get you fired," she says.

Zigor looks at her wonderingly. He's about to say he doesn't understand, but that doesn't matter, because Chloe doesn't understand either. What she said. She understands that it wasn't what she meant to say, whatever that was. She tries to say something else, something simple, his name. "Zigor," she says. Yes, it comes out right.

He hasn't moved, but he's changed. He doesn't look so frightened, which is good, because Chloe has a few urgent things to tell him. The headache slices through the back of her right eye and splits her vision; there are two Zigors now, one the bright shadow of the other. She raises her hand, which is numb, and points at the table. "The phone," she says. He doesn't move; she will have to get it herself. That's when her legs give out and she sprawls across the floor.

"Missus!" he says, stumbling to her. "Missus! What is problem?"

"The phone," she says, or tries to say. By some miracle he understands her, spots the phone, and snatches it from the table. "What I do?" he says. "Who I call?"

"Nine-one-one," she says, but she only hears the nine.

"Yes," he says. "Nine-one-one. I am calling." He taps in the number. The reception isn't good in the studio; Chloe often has to go outside to use the phone, but she has no way of telling him this. She doesn't understand why she is on the floor, jammed between the counter and the bookshelf. Where is her tea?

"The lady is falling down," he says into the phone. Evidently someone hears him. "Yes, come at once. Is emergency."

The numbness in her hand has spread to her shoulder, an invasion of insects, not stinging, more like the palpitation of a million tiny feet.

"Address!" Zigor exclaims. "What is address?"

Here she can help him. "Forty-seven," she says, but only the four comes out. She tries again, "Four, seven."

"Four," Zigor shouts into the phone. "Is four."

No, you idiot, she is thinking. It's forty-seven. He bends over her. "Street," he says encouragingly.

This will be her doom and she knows it. The street is Elmwood. She tries it, without much hope. One side of her mouth isn't working at all. She has no idea what sound is coming out, but she concentrates all the force she has left into the two difficult syllables.

"Yes," he says, leaping up. "It is Elm. Number four Elm."

There's an Elm Street in the next town, but none in this one.

Maybe they'll figure that out. They must be good at that sort of thing. Zigor is shaking the phone. "No, no," he cries. "I cannot hear you." His English is improving by the second. Next he'll announce that the reception is poor. "Wait," he says, getting to his feet, casting her a look of such desperation that her heart fills with pity for him. He pulls the door open and rushes out on the deck, holding the phone tight to his ear. "Yes, now I hear you." The cold rolls in behind him, slapping into her like a tide rolling in. She remembers, not that long ago, lying on the beach at the Cape with her feet in the water. A wave rolled in to her waist, soaking her towel. Toby was nearby; he was just a boy, building a castle in the sand. He laughed as she leaped up from the towel, his voice full of delight. Look how the sea has surprised my mother. She laughed too. And the light was so bright, so bright.

But here the light is rapidly dimming. Is there a dimmer switch in the studio? She can't remember. There is a man out there; who is he? Is it Brendan? No, she doesn't recognize him. He's a stranger. He stands on the deck looking out into the forest and he is calling out: "Help us. You must help us."

And the forest answers ceaselessly: *I don't understand you.*

"Help us," the man cries again. He has some kind of accent. She can't identify it. "Please, help us." These are the last words she hears.

❖❖

Of course, not long after that, we were caught, and in the worst possible way. The hostility in the town made it unwise even to talk on the street. Everyone knew the war was coming. The Yugoslav army had Vukovar surrounded and people there were hoarding food. The Krajina Serbs had blocked the road between Split and Zagreb with tree trunks. Still we carried on as if it was something happening elsewhere, a squabble that would be settled by our leaders. Surely they wouldn't turn us loose on one another, knowing what they knew about us. We eyed our neighbors warily, but we weren't sure how to tell what we were looking for, how to know when the rumors were true and there was no turning back. How does it happen? How does a war get started? Not out there, but here.

One day you get up and look out the window and there's some small change, something so minor you might not notice it if you weren't already tense from waiting, a gate ajar in the neighbor's yard, the smell of rubber burning, a dog whimpering at his own front door. It's here. The war is here. It has begun.

In my case it was two trucks pulled up at the edge of the woods, and three men with rifles over their shoulders, standing in the dust smoking cigarettes.

I hadn't seen Milan in ten days. Every day I made some excuse to go out and I tore through the woods to the toolshed, but he wasn't there. We had no way to get a message to each other; we were forced to leave it to chance. That day I'd been in the kitchen all morning, putting up plum jam and pickles while my mother-in-law complained about how I wasn't sterilizing the jars properly and we'd all die of botulism. Then we sat down to lunch, all of us, and my husband talked about the weather, which was good for a change, but his mother assured him it wouldn't last and a drought or a hailstorm would wipe him out. The children were quiet; even Andro, the oldest, had nothing evil to report. He'd been working with his father all morning cutting hay and he wanted only to be released so he could go find his gang and plot crimes. After they'd all gone out again, I cleared up and drank a cup of coffee. The old woman fell asleep in her chair in the middle of a tirade about the Serbs, about what butchers they were and how *lazy they were. As soon as her chin touched her chest, I was out the door, still in my apron, and I ran to the toolshed full out. Somehow I knew he would be there and he was, as desperate as I was. We crashed into each other like trains and without speaking began tearing off our clothes. It was a hot day, we were both sweating, which bothered us not at all since all we wanted was to slide into each other and out of the world we were in. Our kisses were so avid, he held me so tightly; I thought I would faint. I slid down to my knees before him and took him in my mouth. Distantly I heard him speak. He said, "My God," and I thought it was from pleasure, but then his hands were in my hair and he pulled me up and I heard a crash, which was my son Andro swinging a scythe into the window. The glass shattered and rained down over me. Andro was screaming curses. Milan leaped out the door and knocked him to the ground, then jumped on top of him and held him down. It was an appalling sight, my naked lover straddling my crazed son, both of them cursing and threatening each other. I was trying to cover myself and pick glass off at the same time. "Don't hurt him," I shouted through the window, but neither of them was listening to me. Milan was grinding my son's face into the dirt, and Andro was weeping and sobbing over and over, "You bitch, you cunt, I'll kill you."*

While I was putting on my clothes, Milan told my son that if he spoke to anyone of what he'd seen his family would be dead the next day, did he understand, and he would be dead and so would his cunt of a girlfriend, Anelka; he'd cut her throat himself.

This was the first time I'd heard that my son had a girlfriend. "Go home, Jelena," Milan said. "I have a few more things to say to this nasty little spy."

"Don't hurt him," I said again, and I went down the path without looking back. When I came out of the wood, I saw them, the three men and the trucks. I didn't stop and they didn't speak to me, they just watched me. They had on military-style jackets, but I didn't recognize the color and

I couldn't see the insignias. They weren't from Belgrade, that much was certain. One of them said something to the other and they all laughed. I didn't hear what he said, but I thought it was about me. I kept my head down and hurried along the path to our house. And I knew then, even before I saw my husband's truck pulled up at an odd angle by the house, that this was it; the war had come to our town.

On this day of all days, I thought, letting myself in at the kitchen door. My husband rushed out from the bedroom and took me in his arms. "Where have you been?" he said.

"I went for a walk," I said. "What's wrong? Why are you home?"

"They've taken over the police station. They rounded up everybody there and took them to the river and shot them. They say there's a curfew tonight and anyone who comes out of their house after dark will be shot."

"Who are they?"

"They call themselves 'the wolves.' They're from Knin."

"I saw them," I said. "Just now. They were parked by Ante's field. Where are the children?"

"They're here. But Andro is still out. He went off after we finished haying. Did you see him?"

"No," I lied.

"I think they'll send him home. Right now they're just telling everyone to return to their houses."

"Did they tell you that?"

"Yes. I was on my tractor. One of them came over the field and told me it wasn't safe to be out and I should go find my family and bring them home. I said, 'Who are you?' and he said, 'We are the wolves of wolf town.' I thought he was joking and I laughed. And he said, 'Well, it's no joke. If you don't care about your family, we will kill them for you.' "

My little boy came out from the bedroom and ran to me. He had been listening at the door and he said, "Mama, what will happen?"

"Nothing," I said. "Nothing will happen."

"Why can't we go out?"

"Because we're busy," I said. "We're busy in our house. We have all these plums left and we're going to make plum cake. Will you help me?"

So I began to make plum cake with my son. My little girl came in; she knew something was wrong, but she didn't ask questions. She climbed onto her father's lap and showed him a bit of lace she was making; his mother had taught her how to crochet and she was crazy for it.

"What is Grandma doing?" he asked her.

"She's sleeping," she said. "She sleeps a lot."

We stayed in the kitchen, waiting for Andro. I didn't know whether to wish him dead or alive. We were so much better off without him, but it's not really possible for a mother to wish her son dead, so I was hoping he would come and that he would say nothing about what had happened. It seemed unimportant, though of course it was the most important thing in the world for him. I knew that. I knew he hated me and he would hate me until he died. I thought there was a slim chance that he would be quiet to protect the others, or at least his girlfriend. Perhaps he had gone to her and would stay with her until whatever was going to happen, happened.

But he came home and all hell broke loose. It was dark; the plum cake was cooling on the rack. We'd had a light supper, just potatoes and sausages, and the children were in the bedroom with their grandmother playing a game. My husband and I were sitting at the table, talking anxiously. We might have to leave, he told me. They might make us all walk out of the town and then they would pillage and burn our house. He'd heard that was what they did in Slavonia. First they went house to house and picked up all the rifles, then they gathered up all the townspeople and marched them out.

We heard footsteps in the yard, approaching the house. My husband got up and looked out the window. "It's Andro," he said. "He's OK." He opened the door and called out softly, "Andro," as if he expected the "wolves" to leap out of the bushes and take him away before he got to the door. In a minute he was in the kitchen. I saw his face as he crossed the threshold and I knew my fate was sealed. "Look," my husband said, "they've beaten him," but he pushed his father aside and pulled me out of my chair. He held me by one arm and gave me a backhanded blow across the face that made a sound like a plate cracking, then he dropped me on the floor. "You fucking bitch," he swore. "You cunt." He tried to kick me, but I scrambled away and his father caught him and held him by the throat. He started yelling too. "What are you doing, how dare you strike your mother?"

"She's not my mother; she's a whore," Andro said. "She gets on her knees in the shed and sucks Chetnik cocks! She's a traitor. I'll kill her."

I sat up and watched them struggling, holding my face in my hand. Andro had a swollen eye and a bloody lip; his clothes looked like they'd been washed in mud. His father held him, trying to take in what he'd just said. "Have you gone crazy?" he said.

My little boy appeared at the kitchen door. I didn't know how much he heard or what he understood. "Josip, go in with Grandma," my husband said sharply. "Close the door and don't come out until I call you."

"We wanted some cake," he said, poor darling. I got to my feet and went to the stove. Andro kept still and didn't say anything. "I'll bring the cake to you," I said. "I'll put it on a tray and you can pretend you're at a picnic." He went back in and I took down the tray, loaded it with cake, plates, forks, a pitcher of milk, cups, and followed him. In the room Josip said, "What happened to Andro?" and I said, "He got into a fight." My mother-in-law gave me a look of daggers, but I ignored her. I put a slice of cake by her chair and said, "Don't upset these children with your awful stories." She just grunted and grabbed the cake with her fingers. When I got back to the kitchen, Andro was sitting at the table with his arms out *in front of him and my husband was standing behind him, tears running down his cheeks. "Is it true what he says?" he asked me.*

How my heart went out to him! I wanted to comfort him, but I was the source of his pain. For a moment I thought I might just deny it, tell him Andro was lying. But why would a son make up such a story about his mother? Who would believe me? I closed the door and stood with my back pressed against it. "Branko," I said. "You deserve a better wife than I've been."

"God fuck me," Andro cried, pushing his chair back from the table. "Let me kill her." My husband shoved him back into his chair. "Shut your mouth," he said.

"Don't you know what's going on out there, you stupid farmer?" Andro replied. "They've got the town cut off; they're going to kill us, one house at a time, and she's been fucking them."

"Not them," I said. "One of them. Only one of them."

My husband took this like a blow. He clutched his head and reeled back into the stove. "Jelena," he said. "What have you done?"

"I'm sorry," I said.

Andro leaned forward and spat at me; I felt his saliva hit my shin. "When they come for us, I will put you in front of me and tell them, here she is, let her suck your cock, and please, when you come in her mouth, blow her brains out. Then I can die happy."

"Andro, be silent." My husband still had his hands over his eyes to keep from seeing me, to keep me from seeing his big heart breaking in pieces. I felt more pity than guilt, though I knew his suffering was my fault.

"Branko," I said. "Can you forgive me?"

"This fucking family," Andro raved. "May the earth push up our bones."

I felt the doorknob turning in my back and my mother-in-law croaked, "Open this door." I obeyed. She looked in at us, oozing contempt through her pores. "The boy has jumped out the window," she said.

"Josip," I cried, and I ran into the bedroom. My little girl was sitting

on the bed, wide-eyed. "Where did Josip go?" she asked. I went to the window and looked out. It was dark, but I could make out something moving near the road. "Josip!" I called. Branko came in. "Do you see him?" he said, and my daughter repeated her question.

"He went to his music lesson," I said. "You stay here in bed and I'll go tell him there is no lesson tonight." I pushed past Branko, who followed me back into the kitchen. Andro had taken down the rifle from the rack. "Where are the bullets?" he barked at his father. "Or do you plan to sit here and let them kill us?"

"I'll bring Josip back," I said, going to the door.

"Yes, go out there," Andro said. "They are waiting for you. And when you're finished fucking them, come back so I can shoot you from the window."

"Jelena, I will go," Branko said.

"No," I said. "They'll kill you. You know they will. I might have a better chance," and before he could stop me I was out the door.

I ran along the road toward the town. Why had Josip run away? Was it because of what he heard his brother saying in the kitchen? He was old enough to understand, in some measure, what I'd done. Perhaps he only understood that we were fighting. I came to the bend where the road entered the town between two rows of tall lindens, a sight that usually gave me pleasure as it was one of the few attractive features of our village. The moon was full, the air warm and fragrant, the field beyond the trees studded with great rolls of cut hay. But I felt only fear, and the dark trees seemed to brood over the road like watchtowers. I wanted to call my son's name, but I was afraid to bring attention to myself. It was oddly silent, not even a night bird rustled among the leaves over my head. Across the field I saw a building burning; the flames leaped up over the rooftop, but no sound reached me. Was it a barn or a house? The man who owned that place was on the police force. Was he one of the ones they had killed?

I heard three sharp cracks of gunfire and threw myself against the nearest tree. "Don't move," a man's voice called out, but I didn't think he was talking to me. I pressed myself against the trunk and peeped around it. Two men stood at the edge of the field, one with a rifle raised to his shoulder aiming at something flailing in the grass a few yards away. He fired two more shots.

It's some animal, I told myself. They've shot a wild pig. The one who fired the shots lowered the rifle and the other one strode into the grass to check on his work. He poked at the body with his boot. "He's dead," he said. Then he bent down and pulled up a thin little arm. I could see the red-checkered pajama sleeve clinging loosely to his elbow.

I fell to my hands and knees and vomited onto the ground. They heard me. "Don't move," the one with the rifle said, raising his weapon to his shoulder again. His comrade came galloping out of the field to have a look at me.

I sat up and wiped my mouth with my arm. "Shoot me," I said.

"Who is this?" he said. "The little mother?"

"Yes," I said. "You've just killed my son."

"That's your fault. No one is allowed out tonight. You should have kept him at home."

"He jumped out the window," I said.

The one with the rifle came up and they stood over me. "She's pretty," one said. "Should we shoot her?"

"Let's take her in."

"It would be better if you shoot me," I said.

One of them laughed. "You're right. It would be better for you. That's why we're taking you in." He poked the rifle into my back. "Get up, Ustasha cunt," he said. I didn't move. "We'll tie you up and drag you if you don't get up," he said.

"I don't care what you do, murderers," I said.

He began unfastening his belt, cursing me. When the other one yanked me to my feet, I managed to slip out of his grip. I ran for the field where Josip's body lay, but they caught me before I got beyond the road. Then I cried out and begged them to let me see my son, while they slapped me and cursed me and tied my hands behind my back. They put a rope around my neck and pulled me along like a goat, down the empty road to the police station.

It was all lit up, the only building that was, and there were a dozen or so of them lounging around on the steps or standing in the yard, smoking and strutting up and down. They cheered when they saw me stumbling along behind their comrades, and a few of them gathered round to welcome me with insults as I went up the steps. I didn't recognize any of them, though there was one, a boy of perhaps eighteen, who looked familiar. Inside more of them stood about in groups, drinking šljivovica from bottles and showing one another their weapons. I'd never seen so many guns in one place. It was hot in the room; they'd tossed their jackets on the desks and chairs; their faces were sweaty and red. When they saw me being led in, they made snide remarks. One picked up a gun and pretended to shoot me. "POW," he said in a loud voice. Another one, absorbed in conversation near the window, turned toward me.

It was Milan.

I thought, Well, I should have known, but I hadn't known until that moment that he was one of them. I stared at him, feeling sick again, confused by all that had happened. Was it possible that this man and I had greeted each other with ecstatic cries of passion only a few hours ago?

"Jelena," he said. "What are you doing here?"

The answer to this question was so obvious as to be ludicrous: my hands were bound, I had a rope around my neck, and two puffed-up roosters dragging me about; clearly I hadn't just stopped by for a chat. "We found her on the road," one of my captors said.

"They murdered my son," I said.

"Andro?" Milan said.

I couldn't answer. "Is this true?" he asked the roosters.

"He ran into the field," one answered defensively. "We told him to stop but he kept running." Milan was vexed and the roosters had turned to sheep, so I concluded he was their superior. "Untie her," he said. I hadn't stopped staring at him; it was as if my eyes couldn't entirely take him in. My wrists were freed; the rope was lifted over my head. Milan took my elbow and steered me into an inner office. He closed the door and sat down on a desk, pouring out a glass of *šljivovica* from the bottle there. "Drink this," he said.

"I don't want it," I said.

"You'd better drink it," he said. "You're in shock." I took the glass and swallowed it in a gulp. He was right; it braced me a little.

"What were you doing outside? Didn't you know there was a curfew?"

"Andro came home and told Branko about us," I said. "We were fighting. Josip heard us and he jumped out the window. I went after him."

"I see," he said.

"But I was too late."

"So Andro told him," he said.

"Yes." He took the glass and poured himself a shot. "I can't go back home," I said.

"No," he agreed.

"You seem to be in charge here," I said. He shrugged. "Can you get my family out?"

"We will be taking some people out in the morning."

"Not just out of town," I said. "Out of the country. Can you get them to Slovenia?"

"I don't know, Jelena."

"You killed my son. You owe me this."

He swallowed his brandy. "What about you?"

"I don't care what happens to me. How could I?"

"You can't stay here."

"Why not?" He gave me a long look, loaded with what we both knew was going to happen. They were going to burn the town to the ground. *"I'll walk out with the others,"* I said. *"Just tell my family I'm dead. Branko won't leave if he thinks I'm alive."*

There were shouts in the office and in the street; several shots were fired. Milan threw the door open and went out to his comrades. Through the open window I could see an old man with a hunting rifle staggering, one hand clutching his eye. Blood spilled out between his fingers. He was cursing the men who jeered at his fury. The rifle clattered to the road. Someone fired another shot that hit him in the chest, knocking him backward. His arms and legs flew up briefly over his body, then dropped back splayed at odd angles in the dirt. Milan appeared on the steps and made some remark to two of the men. They laughed. My mother-in-law was right about them, I thought. Butchers. A few gathered at the open door looking at me coldly, but I wasn't afraid. *"A fine day's work for you,"* I said. *"You've murdered a child and an old man."* They wanted to insult me, but they refrained because Milan was back inside giving instructions to a skinny pockmarked boy who nodded his head repeatedly, casting guilty sidelong glances at me. He reminded me of Andro. The gawkers scattered when the boy went out and Milan came to the office. He's enjoying this, I thought; ordering idiots around, making sick jokes about a dead man. I sat on the desk glaring at him while he closed the door. He shook his head, rolling his eyes. The burden of command; what was to be done about it? *"I'll do what I can for your family,"* he said. *"Someone will drive them out early tomorrow."*

"Thank you," I said.

"If Andro hadn't seen us, you could go with them," he observed.

"It's better that they go without me," I said. He took a pack of cigar-

ettes *from his pocket and held it out to me. "It was bad luck this morning," he said wistfully.*

"No thanks," *I said. He tapped a cigarette from the pack and held it
between his lips while he lit it. "Was that all it was?" I said.*

"What?"

"Bad luck." *At last he met my eyes and saw that I hated him.*

"It's a war, Jelena," *he said. "I didn't know it would come, neither
did you."*

"But you don't mind that it has."

"It was inevitable."

"Then you knew it would come." *He frowned, blowing out smoke, annoyed by my logic. Outside a truck pulled onto the lawn, right up to the door.*

"I'm sending you out now," *he said.*

"Where am I going?"

"Where do you want to go?"

"Not Slovenia."

"Then you'd better go East."

"I don't care," *I said.*

"I'd take you myself, but I can't leave here now."

"No," *I said. "You have an important position. I see that now."*

*I was ridiculing him and he knew it, but he didn't bother defending
himself; why should he? "Well," he said, opening the door. "You'd better
go as soon as possible." I followed him into the office where the men were
milling about; one of them was singing a song that sounded like a dog
howling. They were aware of me, but they made no remarks as we passed
out to the steps where the truck waited. The driver threw the door open and
Milan leaned in to speak to him. He was young, bullet-headed, surly by
nature, though he was respectful to Milan. I couldn't hear what they said.
They gave each other ridiculous salutes and Milan stepped back. "Good*

luck, Jelena," he said. I climbed inside, closed the door, and the boy started the engine. The old man's body blocked the drive and the boy maneuvered to avoid it, but I felt the wheels bumping over his legs. I didn't look back.

So Milan got you out?

I suppose you could say that.

Where did you go?

The boy drove for several kilometers without speaking to me. I was too stunned and filled with rage and sadness to think clearly. My body was numb and cold, though it was hot inside. The truck rattled over the road, which was riddled with holes. There wasn't another vehicle in sight. In the distance I saw another farmhouse in flames. It must have been burning for some time because there wasn't much left of it. I could feel the boy watching me and he kept his eyes on me until the farmhouse was behind us.

"Anyone you know?" he asked.

"No," I said.

"Too bad," he said. His eyes rested on my breasts and then momentarily on my knees. He was downshifting; the truck slowed and drifted into the shade of a tree at the side of the road. "So tell me, Ustasha cunt," he said. "Did you think that if you fucked one Serb you wouldn't have to fuck them all?" His hand came down hard on my leg and I saw that the nails were chewed and ragged as a child's.

"No," I said. "That's not what I thought."

"That's good," he said. "Because I have news for you, stupid cow." He brought his lips close to my ear and whispered like a lover. "You're going to fuck them all."

❧❧

What astonishes Brendan is that at no point on the long journey home, approaching hour by hour and minute by minute the af-

termath of the cataclysmic event, did he have the slightest suspicion that anything was amiss. Rationally, of course, he understands there was no way he could have known, but that seems a
poor excuse for the enormity of his unpreparedness. Even at
the airport when he spotted Joan Chase loitering near the entry
gate, her hands shoved down in her coat pockets, her eyebrows
drawn together as she scanned the arriving passengers, his first
thought was that there was no avoiding an accidental encounter,
and he steeled himself, because Joan bored him. Her eyes col-
lided with his, urgent and damp, but still he was clueless. "Joan,"
he said. "What are you doing here? Are you taking a trip?" Only
then did it occur to him that Joan was there to meet him; that
she was waiting for him, and that Chloe was not. She stepped
forward and rested her hand on his arm, the tears in her eyes
silently overflowing, and she said with commendable calm,
"Brendan, dear. Something terrible has happened."

Now, two weeks later, that moment has an icy clarity to it.
The preceding hours, leaving Trieste, changing planes in Milan,
stuffing down disgusting airplane food on the long transat-
lantic flight, are hazy; they yield little in the way of detail to the
inspection of memory. But that moment in the airport, the
light pressure of Joan's hand on his forearm, the sensation of
nausea and consternation as she spoke, the outrageous inter-
ruption of the warning about unattended luggage on the PA
system, the red suitcase of the man pushing past him, is fixed,
as vivid and lavishly ornamented as a scene in grand opera.

It can't be denied that Joan has handled everything with sen-
sitivity and efficiency. Brendan is indebted to her, possibly forever. It was she who directed the ambulance to the house when
the Basque, sweating and breathing hard, appeared on her

doorstep panting his refrain, "You must help us, lady has falling." Joan was at the hospital when Chloe was pronounced dead and she made the necessary arrangements to keep her there until the next of kin could be notified. Then she went to the house and searched until she found Chloe's calendar with the arrival time of Brendan's plane. Through all this she was calm and competent and after all this she was a daily visitor, dropping by with a casserole or a pie as if Brendan was an invalid in danger of starvation. When Toby arrived she courteously backed off, settling for a daily phone call to see if there was anything she could do for the bereaved father and son, though there was clearly nothing she could do.

When Brendan called Toby in Trieste, his first reaction was disbelief. He said, "Oh God, oh no," several times and then, "How is this possible?" By the time he arrived he was determined to focus his attention on the enormity of his father's loss; to play the role of the sympathetic son. He entered into the necessary decisions: should Chloe be buried or cremated, what sort of service would be appropriate, should the Basque be prosecuted or held in any way accountable? Joan Chase was hot on this topic, though there was no evidence that the man had ever touched Chloe, and it was clear that he had tried to save her life. "But he was there," Joan insisted. "He frightened her to death. Who knows what he said to her? She was feeling very threatened, we all knew that."

"Mom wasn't afraid of him," Toby insisted. "She'd seen him before, face to face." Brendan agreed. The doctors had concluded that the stroke was sudden and massive and could have been triggered by any number of coronary "events." Her blood pressure had been high for some time, her physician reminded

Brendan. The last time she'd had a physical exam she'd complained of palpitations, which was not uncommon in women her age. In fact, sudden-onset ischemic stroke, which was the name they gave for what happened to Chloe, was not all that uncommon in women her age. If they'd gotten her to the hospital sooner, she might have survived, she might have been paralyzed, partly or entirely, for life. No one could say.

Brendan had seen her, laid out on a chilly slab in the hospital morgue, her body covered by a green plastic sheet, her hair brushed back from her face, which was pale, waxy, oddly comforting, so definitely Chloe and yet absent of her. This was the familiar abode she had recently occupied, but she wasn't home. Brendan felt he could speak to her and he did. "My darling," he said. "Oh, my dearest." Then he wept, his shoulders shuddering with racking sobs, while the attendant stood by waiting to pull the sheet back over her face. Brendan was unapologetic; it was good and right that he should weep; his tears gave expression to his grief, which was at that moment nearly unendurable. At length he turned away, drying his eyes on the handkerchief he'd remembered to bring, and went out to sign the necessary papers.

Toby hadn't seen his mother. It could have been arranged, but he'd refused. Chloe had disliked the practice of displaying a corpse; she thought it barbaric, and so did her son. As far as he was concerned, she was simply gone. She'd wanted to be cremated, which was done forthwith. It was Toby's idea that the urn containing her ashes should be interred in the pretty cemetery on the hill near their house, which she had often admired for the serenity of its situation. "I don't like the idea of scattering Mom," Toby said frankly to his father.

Now it was all done, the service, the burial, the brief deluge of flowers, the sympathy cards and the thank-you notes. Life must go on. For Brendan this is not a complicated process, though a disheartening one, but Toby has a lot on his mind. He wants to get back to his wife, who calls him daily, but there are other matters he must clear up before he leaves. One of these, a sore subject between the young couple, is Branko Drago.

"Salome wants to cut him out of her life," Toby explains to his father. "But I think she should forgive him. He believed Jelena was dead and he had a family to raise. He had to start all over in a new world." They are in Chloe's studio; their mission is clearing things out, or, more accurately, getting some idea of what's actually in there. Toby takes a moldy loaf of raisin bread and drops it into a trash bag.

"Does he know Jelena is alive now?" Brendan asks. He's holding Chloe's teacup, still half full of milky tea. She must have been drinking it when the Basque appeared. *You didn't finish your tea, dear*, he thinks, dumping it into the sink.

"Yes, he knows. I called him before I left New York. Or he called me. He was calling me three times a day. I had to tell him."

"Did he sound surprised?"

"He sounded anxious."

"Do you think he knew already?"

"I don't know. I think he might have suspected, I mean, he must have, right? But so many years had passed. And if Jelena had wanted to, she could have found him, probably more easily than he could find her. That's what I think, but I can't say that to Salome."

"But surely that's occurred to her."

"All she sees is that her mother was taken away from her and now she's found her and it's her father's fault."

"What does Jelena say?"

"She won't talk about it. You know what she's like. She lives day to day. She just says, 'The past is over.' "

"Right," Brendan says. He can see Jelena, stubbing out her cigarette while her long-lost daughter serves her another cup of coffee and the damaged child she wrested from the jaws of war curls up like a dog for a nap at her feet. "What are you going to do?"

"I think I should call Branko. And then I guess I'll have to tell Salome what he says."

"Yes," Brendan agrees. "You'll have to tell her."

"Who knows," Toby says in his innocence. "Maybe Branko and Jelena could get back together. They're both single." He examines a stack of books next to Chloe's reading chair. "I didn't know Mom was interested in gypsies," he says. Brendan joins him. It's an oversized book of photographs titled *Romany*, with a picture of a beaten-down family gathered near their cooking pot in a makeshift camp. A boy of perhaps ten is in the foreground, his hand pressed against his forehead, his eyes, which are black, glaring fiercely at the camera. Behind him an old woman, swathed in layers of patterned fabric, brandishes a wooden spoon. Brendan takes the volume and opens the back cover. It's a library book now overdue. "She was looking for Heathcliff," he says.

"What?" Toby has moved on to a bundle of file folders tucked under the drawing table.

"For her book. She thought Heathcliff was probably a gypsy, so she was looking for a type."

Toby extracts a file and sifts idly through it. It contains sketches, mostly pen and ink: a fox walking on his hind legs, a whirling dervish of a dog he recognizes as belonging to their neighbor. "This is Joan's dog, isn't it?" he says to his father, holding out the sketch. Brendan takes it and laughs. "Fluffy," he says. "It's perfect. I'll have it framed and give it to Joan." Toby admires a page covered with sketches of hawks: in flight, perched on a limb, a detail of a head and another of an outspread wing. "Mom was good at birds," he observes. He lifts this sheet and looks at the next one.

"Damn," he says, but softly. Carefully he lays the open folder on the table and turns away from it, rubbing the bridge of his nose between his thumb and index finger. Brendan steps in behind him to see what he has seen. It's Salome, hands on hips, stolid and defiant, her wild hair a nest of insects. He reads the caption printed neatly across the bottom: *Run for your life; it's that hornet-headed girl.*

It really is too bad that Toby has come across this drawing. And it's a good likeness, there's no mistaking it.

"That's what we were to her," Toby says. "A joke."

"She meant nothing by it," Brendan assures his son.

"No," Toby agrees. "It's just one of her sketches." His voice breaks on the last word. His tears gather and overflow, a sob escapes him, he allows it, and another follows. Brendan wants to comfort him, but the circumstances—the cruel sketch, the sarcasm that provoked it—have diluted sadness with bitterness, and he senses that Toby will not find solace in anything he can say. Indeed, the phrases that come to mind—*she loved you very much, she was always thinking of you*—sound hollow, defensive, and false. Toby sits down in his mother's reading chair and covers his face with his hands, weeping for what can't be said, and his father waits, without speaking. On the walls the images Chloe fashioned so patiently, day after day over so many years, seem to brood over the sound of her son's suffering. "She never gave Salome a chance," Toby complains through his tears.

"She would have come round," Brendan says. "She just thought you were both too young . . ."

"She thought we were idiots," Toby retorts, and Brendan hears Chloe's voice clearly, close to his ear, *"He's an idiot."*

Perhaps Toby hears it too, for he leaps to his feet, snatches the sketch, rips it in half, wads it into a ball, and hurls it at the woodstove. Brendan is shocked; it is as if Toby has struck his mother. "Stop it," he says sharply. "Calm down. Show some respect for your mother."

Toby turns to him. "How can I?" he exclaims, but his anger is fading as quickly as it erupted and he's shamed by it.

"Forgive her, then," his father says. "It's the least you can do."

"I know," he admits. "I will. But I haven't yet." He surveys the room, his mother's lair, where he was always welcome. When he was a boy, he came here after school and she stopped whatever she was doing to make him toast and hot chocolate, to inquire about his day, to tell him what she thought about what he thought. "I can't stay in here, Dad," he says, calmly enough. "I'll see you at the house." At the door he glances back.

"It's OK," Brendan says. "I'll be up in a little while." He watches Toby's bowed shoulders as he trudges along the snowy path to the house.

It's a bright day, bitterly cold and still; the temperature was five degrees when Brendan arose. He'd put on several layers of clothes and slogged out here to get the stove up, conscious of doing the job Chloe had done every morning, though she never let the studio get this cold. The windows were glazed with ice. Brendan crouched before the stove, feeding the kindling to the flickering flames. The dry wood caught easily. Soon this room would be a warm refuge in a universe of ice. But a refuge for whom? Brendan tried hard not to picture Chloe collapsed on the floor near the open door, the cold air washing over and under her, hauling her away to the underworld. But he could feel her there, losing consciousness, battling the encroaching darkness, determined to fight her way back to the realms of light. The fire crackled merrily, sending fingers of warmth to caress his chilly hands and face. I'm alive, he thought wistfully. But my wife is dead.

Toby is mentally rehearsing the message he will leave on the tape when the ringing is interrupted by Branko's gruff "Hello." Why isn't he on the boat? "Hello, Branko," Toby says. "This is Toby." In the pause that follows he asks himself if he should add his surname, but that seems ridiculous; he is, after all, this man's son-in-law.

"Oh, Toby," Branko says. "Do not hang up. I must speak to you." Toby holds the line listening to a stream of Croatian passing back and forth between Branko and someone else; he doesn't think it's Andro. The voices are animated, but not urgent. Branko's responses are brief, as if he is receiving information. What a language! Toby thinks. Will I ever be able to understand it? Will our child speak it? Will I be an outsider in my own family? At length the conversation is concluded and Branko says, "Yes, Toby, here I am. Many terrible things are happening here and I am desperate to hear that Salome is coming home with you."

"What terrible things? Is it the boat?"

"It's my son. He's been arrested. A very serious charge."

Great, Toby thinks. The brother has killed someone. "I'm sorry to hear it," Toby says.

"We will get through it. I have engaged a lawyer, a good man but very expensive."

"What's the charge?"

"It was an accident. He got into a fight with a man here and the man was sent to the hospital. Then he died."

"Manslaughter," Toby says.

"Yes. This is a strange word. Slaughter is for animals, I think."

"It is strange, I agree."

"Tell me, Toby. Where are you calling from?"

"New York."

"I'm relieved to hear this. And Salome is with you?"

"No. She's still in Trieste."

"When is she coming back? How is she? Is she well?"

"She's fine."

"I am not sleeping worrying about her."

"There's nothing to worry about. She's helping her mother; she wants to be with her now."

"Of course, I understand this."

"Jelena has had a difficult time, but she's doing well now. She has a few jobs and she's taken in a little girl who lost her family in the war."

"I see," Branko says. A silence falls between them. Toby plunges into it. "Salome is still angry at you because she thinks you should have tried harder to find Jelena, but I think she'll get over it. Jelena has a phone. I could give you the number and you could call her there."

"How long do you think Salome will stay there?"

"We've both taken a leave from school. So conceivably we could stay until September, but I'm not sure we will. It's hard to say. The baby is due in July, so we have to decide where we want to be when it's born."

"My grandchild must be born in America," Branko asserts.

"I'm an American," Toby says. "My child will be an American, no matter where he's born."

"So you are hoping for a son. So am I."

Toby rubs his jaw in frustration. It's hard keeping Branko focused on anything for long. "It doesn't matter to me, really," he says. "Will you call Salome? What should I tell her?"

"Tell her to call me. She can call collect."

"She won't, Branko. She's too angry."

"I will wait until she isn't angry. Tell her that. She knows I love her. Tell her I wait for her call."

"Should I tell her about Andro?"

"I am a failure as a father. My children abandon me."

"I won't tell her."

"Toby, you must come back and finish your studies."

"I know that. I will. But Salome needs to be with her mother now, and I need to be with her."

"When are you going back?"

"Next week. I have to move all the stuff out of our apartment up to my parents' house. Then I'll go back."

"Tell Salome I'm longing to hear her voice."

"Yes. I'll tell her that."

Branko says, "Wait," and bursts into Croatian. Another voice answers him, a woman this time. "Toby," he says. "I must go. I have to meet with the lawyer very soon."

"All right," Toby says. "I'll tell Salome what you said."

"I love her. I miss her. Tell her that, Toby."

"I will. I'll try to persuade her to call you."

"Good-bye, Toby. You are a good son, the only one I have."

"Good-bye, Branko." The line clicks. Toby listens to the buzz for a moment before hanging up. He realizes he has failed to tell his father-in-law that his own mother is dead. He never got the chance.

The warehouse district is a recurring locale of his dreams; it is where he meets the dead. His parents, a cousin killed in Vietnam, Moira, an Irish girl he dated briefly in college, who committed suicide, Dr. Brasher, his college adviser, who expired while reading a student's dissertation—fortunately not Brendan's—and now Chloe. She walks toward him on the dock, past the gaping doorways of the warehouses. The air is resiny; it smells of tar and baled cotton. He can hear water churning under the pier, slapping against the rope-ringed moorings. Chloe's hair is long again and her skin glistens in the moist sea air. She's wearing a summer dress he's always liked: a black fitted top over a full polka-dot skirt and—this is odd, this signals *dream*—she's smoking a cigarette. As she approaches, he observes that she's anxious. Her eyes search his; she puffs at the cigarette, stamps it out with the toe of her sandal. A wind comes up, lifting her long hair like a golden cloud, swirling the skirt this way and that. She's speaking, but he can't hear her; the wind carries her voice away. "What?" he shouts. "What did you say?" He reaches out to take her hands.

"Where is Toby?" she says over the gale.

"He's in Trieste." Brendan opens his eyes in the chill morning light of their bedroom. "He's in Trieste," he says again.

In the shower he probes the still-tender bruises on the back of his right hand, the fading mementos of his latest, possibly his last, foray into the theater of civil disobedience. At first he'd thought he wouldn't go, no one expected him to. Chloe had been gone barely a month. David Bodley's invitation to join his colleagues, who were going down in a group, was extended, he assured Brendan, mostly by way of courtesy. "We don't want you to feel left out," David said. "But of course we understand if you're not exactly feeling up to standing in the street in fifteen degrees for no reason."

It was to be an international protest; marches were planned in over three hundred cities around the world. Colin Powell had held up his vial of sand at the UN and warned that if it was dry anthrax, which it certainly was not, it could do a lot of damage. The New York City police had refused a march permit, citing public safety, and the Homeland Security clowns had upped that ante by changing the color code of the eternal terror alert to orange. They advised people to stock up on plastic sheeting and be ready to seal themselves in their homes. The Pentagon was rolling out the great machinery of war; there was no stopping it. Even Tony Blair had finally figured that out. David was right; there was no point in going. It would be cold and miserable, but there was no point in not going either. "Thanks," Brendan told David Bodley. "I want to go. Chloe wouldn't have missed it, so how can I?"

The train was packed with cheerful, laughing throngs, all ages, all races, jostling signs and flags, trying to make room for the lines waiting on the platforms all the way down to Grand Central Station. It was going to be big, all agreed. At the station the mob flowed into the street outside, where sullen policemen directed everyone uptown. The mood was upbeat; their goal was First Avenue, as close to 51st Street as they could get, but it soon became clear that they were being herded away from this destination. It was bitterly cold, the police increasingly hostile. The crowd trudged north on Third Avenue, turned away at the cross streets by metal barricades, uniforms, and sticks: 57th, 61st, 68th. At last, at 73rd, they were directed across Third Avenue to Second, but here they weren't allowed to turn south. Brendan and his friends complained through their scarves. David Bodley stopped to give one of the cops a lecture about the right of law-abiding citizens to courtesy from the officers sworn to uphold that law. A shout went up from a group just ahead as a policeman on a horse drove them against a glass-fronted restaurant. One of them had fallen. The horse plunged back into the street, forcing the crowd to disperse. Brendan backed away as the powerful creature veered in his direction, and it was then that he realized he was inside a barricade. Across the street another shout went up, "Let them out, let them out," and a squad of uniforms surged into the crowd to secure the perimeter of the pen. The pressure from behind was making it difficult to stand. "What is the point of this?" David said to Brendan.

"It's ridiculous," Brendan agreed. The observation that the mayor was in Florida was passed around one more time. Brendan had his back against the barrier, and he could see a skirmish breaking out as people refused to enter the overflowing pen. He thought, as he sometimes did now, that he was glad Chloe wasn't here to see this. The barricade gave behind him and a group near the corner cried out, stumbling over the edge into the fury of the police, who greeted them with blasts of pepper spray. Brendan lost his balance and fell to his knees. It was all so unnecessary, he thought.

The horse was near, making everyone scramble again. A knee hit Brendan in the side and a man fell on top of him. "Sorry," the man said as Brendan sprawled beneath him. He could smell the horse, its dancing hooves were very close, but he couldn't see it. There was a searing pain in his hand. "Watch out," someone cried, and the man on his back rolled off. Brendan sat up, clutching his hand, to see the backside of the horse moving north, creating a wake behind. Careful to keep enough distance to avoid a hoof to his chest, he stumbled to his feet and followed the churning haunches halfway up the block and out the open end of the pen.

His hand throbbed and burned inside his glove; he was afraid to look at it. "That's it for me," he said to no one, as the potential auditors who pressed against him all had on earmuffs or fur-lined hoods. He turned west, head down, his wounded hand pressed against his chest. By slinking close to the buildings he was able to work his way back against the tide of the crowd. His colleagues had planned, in the event that they were separated, to reconvene at a bar downtown, far from the demonstration. It was a charming, cozy place with stuffed leather chairs and a fireplace. It was where he wanted to be. Politics would have to wait. *A horse stepped on me, for God's sake*, he would tell them. He was ready for a drink.

The glove saved his hand, Brendan's doctor assured him. No bones were broken. In the days that followed it swelled alarmingly, turned black, blue, green, and yellow. Though satellites can photograph bugs on a leaf from outer space, the press fell back on the universally accepted truth that it is impossible to accurately estimate the numbers of people standing in streets. It was agreed that the protests had been impressive, well in the millions. When asked for her reaction to the worldwide expressions of outrage, Condoleezza Rice observed that it really didn't matter what people thought.

In the kitchen Brendan cinches his robe and puts the espresso pot on the burner. Now that he's making coffee for one, he's switched to the stronger brew and the smaller pot. He puts a spoon of sugar in the cup and when the coffee gurgles, pours it in, stirring absently. An icicle is dripping steadily from the eaves; it's above freezing for the first time in weeks. The sky is white, feathery, like the underside of an enormous goose. He recalls his dream as he ambles into his study and switches on the computer. Why was Chloe smoking? She hated cigarettes.

In his e-mail he finds a message from Toby. It's easier now that he has his computer; no more missed calls and hurried conversations from phone booths to avoid running up Jelena's bill. Toby reports that he has taken on two English students. Salome has a part-time job in a bakery and they have found, at last, a small apartment nearby. Naturally they need money, but not too much. He's only asking if he can put three hundred dollars on the card. They are all well. Jelena sends regards to "my dear historian."

This last makes him smile. *My dear historian.* He can hear just the light mocking tone of it, not unfriendly, almost indulgent. *Send him my regards.*

When he told her his profession, she laughed. "A historian!" she said. "Fantastic. Tudjman was a historian, you know. Our noble president, *Doctor* Tudjman. Everyone knew he had a third-rate degree from a fifth-rate university. He wrote a book, he called it a history book, to prove the Serbs exaggerated the number who died in Jasenovac. Typical Chetnik strategy, he said. We Croats had to get over our Jasenovac complex; we had nothing to be ashamed of."

"What was Jasenovac?" Brendan asked.

"A death camp. South of Zagreb. This was during World War Two, when the Ustashe were running things. A lot of people died there. A lot of Serbs, a lot of gypsies."

"Was Tudjman right? Did the Serbs exaggerate?"

"Who knows? Who cares? That book was the beginning of the end of Yugoslavia. Suppose the German prime minister wrote a book saying the Jews exaggerated the number who died at Auschwitz. They were just trying to make the Germans feel guilty. Do you think anyone would be fooled, do you think the Jews would stand for it?"

"There are Holocaust deniers," he observed.

"Yes. How many? Can they get elected? They go to jail for saying it. But Tudjman was greeted as a man of learning setting the record straight. People admired him; they took him seriously and so he was elected president. Right away he threw out the Yugo flag and brought back the *sahovnica*, which to the Serbs means one thing—Ustashe. It was everywhere; the whole world was wrapped in that checkerboard. Then the government started firing Serbs who had jobs in the police force, also teachers, doctors, even tourist agents. They were overrepresented in these fields; that was the official story. Next you couldn't get a passport or take money from the bank without a card that proved you were of Croatian descent. People said Tudjman and Milošević made a deal: you inflame your murderers, I'll inflame mine, and we'll divide the spoils." She blew smoke out in an impatient huff. "It's not hard to start a war if you know how to rewrite history. You just dig up the old grievances, pour gasoline on them, and hand out the matches."

"I'm not that kind of historian," he protested.

"Of course not," she said. After that she called him *my dear historian*.

Brendan takes up a note card from the stack. Of course not. He's not writing the kind of history that could start a war. For one thing his audience will be limited to those who take an interest in events that happened seven hundred years ago, not a multitudinous group. He reads the card. *Processions of flagellants were a common sight on the roads all across Europe. Public penance = 13th-century psychotherapy?*

Why had he written this down? Because it had occurred to him that Frederick would have seen them, in groups or as solitary wanderers, condemned by the Church to be forever on the move, flogging themselves on the roads the Romans had built a thousand years before. Did they know the stones they stained with their blood had been laid in place by slaves captured in the far-flung provinces of the empire, the gloomy forests of

Germany, the verdant green of the British Isles; wild men, fair-haired and rosy-cheeked, who believed in tree spirits and fairies? The soldiers who chained them up and drove them back to Italy consulted virgins and holes in the ground, read omens, and built altars to a pantheon of capricious gods. Though master might beat slave into submission, neither master nor slave held his own body in contempt. Indeed, the gods of the Romans occasionally found humans so attractive they had sex with them, producing mayhem. They would have thought mortification of the flesh a form of madness.

But Frederick of Hohenstaufen was the *Holy* Roman Emperor, and in that word *holy* the body had become a problem. As he traversed the roads, supervising his vassals, overseeing the construction of his castles and hunting lodges, Frederick must have passed processions of flagellants, relentlessly beating the devil out of themselves, their bodies repudiated by their Church and the God who made them. It is ever Brendan's object to give his readers a sense of Frederick's world, of what it looked like, smelled like, what the food tasted like, and most of all what ordinary people were up to. So he had made this note to remind himself.

He turns the card over and reads the reference notation. A motion at the window catches his eye. It's Mike coming home from a night of carnage to top up at his food bowl. Though his reflections have distracted him, Melancholy, his new companion, follows Brendan to the door to let the cat in. Mike rubs his side against his master's leg. As he measures out a cup of meal from the jar, Brendan reminds himself that Chloe has been gone two months and three days. It's cold in the kitchen. The first flakes of snow are drifting down, the icicle is still dripping.

"It seems longer," he says to the cat, emptying the cup into the bowl. "Don't you think?"

I wasn't afraid; I was beyond that. We went through a few checkpoints where the boy got out of the truck and walked up and down, trading what was essentially gossip with other boys, all of them displaying their rifles or guns to show how important they were. They looked in the truck at me and laughed when the boy told them I was his captive. They pointed their guns at me and called me names. One of them spat at me and announced that I should have my throat cut there and then, why wait? and he would be happy to do it, but my driver complained that he had orders and they let us pass. We were going southeast. I thought we must be close to the Bosnian border. I had not much interest in what happened to me; I assumed it would be bad. What I thought about was whether Milan had told me the truth when he said he would get my family to Slovenia. I didn't even know if he had the authority to do it, much less the will. I thought he had some kind of perverse male-code respect for my husband, possibly because Branko was the only honest man in a hundred kilometers and because Milan was cuckolding him regularly. That might make him want to do one decent thing, since he was about to destroy a village. But there were a lot of people who wanted to murder Andro, and Branko wouldn't leave without him. I thought of my poor little girl and all the horrible stories we'd been hearing on the radio and the television about the things the Serbs were doing to children and old people. I tried not to think about Josip, about that bit of his pajama sleeve I'd seen, his thin little arm, the boot pushing into his side in the stiff mown hay. I didn't want to weep in front of the brute who was driving. I tried to figure out where we were, but it was dark. The road seemed to go on forever between fields of grain. The hills flattened out

completely. In the distance I saw the dome of a church dimly lit by what must have been streetlights below; a town, but I didn't recognize it. A rumbling grew louder ahead of us, and when the road curved we were driving into a blaze of headlights, a military convoy that stretched out as far as I could see. Trucks, armored cars, they even had a tank with soldiers in camouflage uniforms brandishing machine guns over the turret. The boy pulled the truck over, flattening a patch of sunflowers that slid down reluctantly, like interested bystanders. The lead vehicle slowed but didn't stop, evidently recognizing our right to be there. The boy waved out the window, exchanging a salute and encouraging shouts with the driver. He continued waving and offering his mindless enthusiasm as they rolled by, one by one, for a long time. When at last they had passed us, he turned on me, his eyes bright with excitement. Where did they get a tank? I was thinking, but I wasn't going to let on that anything surprised me. "They're going to Zagreb," the boy said. He swerved the truck back onto the road and drove on through the darkness that was now as blinding as the lights had been. "You're from there, aren't you?"

"How do you know that?" I said.

For answer he repeated my question, imitating my inflections exactly, his way of informing me that I had the citified accent he particularly despised.

"Have you ever been there?" I asked.

For answer he sneered. Zagreb, I thought. Would there actually be shooting in the old city where my embittered father was winding down his days? My mother had died of cancer the year Josip was born; Father hadn't forgiven her for that. My brother was a disappointment as well: he married a Dutch girl and moved to Holland, where he worked in her father's restaurant supply business. The last time I'd seen my father he'd had one subject: his determination to disinherit my brother. He refused even to see my children. He referred to them as the "farmer's children." I left him to

his enmity, which was clearly keeping him alive. Now he would have some-
thing new to rage against: soldiers on the streets of Zagreb.

The road narrowed and there were a few streetlights. We had come to
a little village, all white walls and red tile roofs, roses and honeysuckle
clambering everywhere, the doors painted a fresh blue, not a soul in sight;
a postcard town that ran one street deep for perhaps ten blocks, then yielded
to more fields of grain. We turned onto a dirt road that intersected two
fields, passed a barn, a chicken coop, and came to a concrete storage build-
ing. The boy parked near some cars pulled up in front. Light poured from
the open door. Two men in camouflage suits came out and watched him as
he climbed down from the truck. "What have you got for us?" one of them
said, and the boy laughed. "A piece of shit," he said. They had a brief con-
versation, the men looking over the boy's shoulder to appraise me. I couldn't
hear what they were saying. At length he came back and opened the door.
"Get out," he said. "You're staying here." I followed him to the men who
grinned at me, positively filled with mirth. "Don't worry, little housewife,"
one of them said. "We'll take good care of you." I realized I still had on
my apron. There were four other men inside, gathered around a table, play-
ing cards and drinking. "Are you staying?" someone asked the boy. "Do
you want a drink?"

"I'm going back," he said. "I have to drive the bus in the morning. I'll
take a beer with me." Someone handed him a bottle and he went back to
his truck, but before he got in he undid his pants and pissed into the dirt.
"Bravo," one of the men said, and another chuckled about the convenience
of country life. After he was gone, one of them turned to the men at the
table and said, "Well now, we have a guest for the night."

"Can she talk?" one asked.

"Can you talk?" the other repeated. "What's your name?"

I stood there feeling sick with fatigue and hatred and utterly without
hope. At the table their heads came up one by one, curious to see if I would

speak. The one closest to me, who was so amused he could barely contain himself, leaned toward me, his nostrils quivering, and I thought, He's sniffing me. He brought his hand to my cheek and patted it, as if trying to return me to consciousness. I raised my eyes to his and saw his rapacious curiosity and no mercy. I pushed his hand away and stepped back, showing him my contempt. "Jelena," I said.

"Jelena," he said, smirking, and a shout went up at the table: "Jelena!"

"Well, Jelena," he said. "What shall we do with you?"

I don't have to tell you what they did with me, but I will say that they didn't try to kill me. They didn't beat me, or piss on me, or sodomize me, or strangle me, all that came later. More or less, they took turns. I lost consciousness more than once and woke each time to find myself in another part of the room: facedown over the table, on my back on the bare floor, my wrists tied before me to a pipe on the wall. It's difficult to remember these scenes; in this way the memory is kind. Someone gave me some water at one point, holding the glass to my mouth. In the morning when I woke I was lying on a blanket in the corner of the room, my clothes were piled at my feet. All the men were gone and there was an old woman instead, stirring a pot at a camp stove near the door. She showed me a bucket of water and handed me a rag and a bar of soap. "Who are you?" I said, but she wouldn't speak. "I have to pee," I said. "Is there a toilet?" For answer she gestured to the field. I went out, naked as I was, and squatted there. The pain was intense. I was bleeding, I saw, but only a little, from being rubbed raw inside. I went back to the bucket and washed myself as best I could. Every muscle in my body ached and I could see bruises coming on my breasts, my ribs, and my thighs. I had a lot of itchy mosquito bites. I put my clothes back on and went to the door. The woman pointed to a chair and brought me a slice of bread, a piece of cheese, and a tin cup filled with bitter coffee. It was early, not hot yet, the fields were buzzing with insects. I ate the food, looking out at the rustling grain. It was a bu-

colic vista, peaceful and serene. Eventually we heard the sound of a motor. A bus rattled up the road and parked in front of us. When the doors opened, the driver from the night before jumped down, followed by nine of the prettiest girls from our town.

They were all frightened and weeping. Some of them had blood on their clothes. Another soldier came out behind them, herding them into the building, threatening to shoot anyone who didn't do as she was told. I knew a few of them by sight. One was the daughter of Ante Govic, whose farm adjoined ours. Though I couldn't give them any hopeful news about what would happen next, I went in with them to try to calm them down. They were all younger than me by at least ten years. Ante's girl, Maja was her name, came to me, put her arms around my neck, and sobbed. "They kicked in the door and shot my parents and my brother, and even the dog." Another girl said, "They put all the men from our street in a truck and drove them away. Then we heard shooting in the woods for a long time."

"Did anyone escape?" I asked.

"They rounded up some women and children and told them to walk out," one girl said. "They set our barn on fire and made us listen to the poor cows that couldn't get out," another cried. She was a child really, perhaps fifteen. "Why didn't they kill me too?" How could I tell her what was going to happen to her?

Later that day four of the men from the night before came back, all in one truck, and the boys on the bus drove away. "Jelena," one of the men called out as he strode in among us. "We're home." My heart sank as they went among the young women, asking their names and ogling them, but that night they did nothing to us. The old woman pronounced her cooking pot ready and we lined up to receive bowls of bean soup and bread. The men played cards, shouted, and sang, ignoring us. We huddled near the door. One of them went out and came back with blankets and a bucket, which he put in one corner. "This is your toilet," he said. That night only two of them stayed, smoking and talking with their rifles on their laps on either side of the door. We spread out our blankets and lay down in the heat, the mosquitoes buzzing in the air, the foul smell from the bucket wafting over us, the sound of weeping without end. I was dry-eyed. I thought, Now my family is dead and I should have died with them. I knew that I was alive for the very reason I should have been killed, which was ironic and cruel, as it seemed being alive with these men who might kill me or might not, who would certainly abuse me in every way they could think up—and in this area I suspected they could be imaginative—was what I deserved. Nothing in me then wanted to live.

The next morning the bus came again. A few girls got out and stood in the dust at gunpoint and then we were all herded into the bus and taken away. They had spray-painted the windows black, so we couldn't see out. Two of them sat in the front, turned to face us with their guns on their knees. The trip lasted, I don't know how long, a few hours, and then we pulled into a parking lot. One by one we filed out and stood looking at what was to be our prison for a long time to come. It was a country restaurant with a red tile roof and an awning across the front where once tables and chairs had been, where once people sat and drank and talked and ate and laughed. The sign was shot full of holes but legible, and when I read it I pinched myself to make sure it wasn't a dream. A soldier jabbed his rifle at my back, chuckling to himself. The sign said "Konoba Jelena." I looked over my shoulder at the smirking brute behind me. "Where are we?" I said, and he replied, "You're where you've always been, Ustasha bitch. You're in Serbia."

That's where we stayed, I don't know how long. There were fifteen of us at the start; our numbers went up and down as new girls were brought in, others taken away; we didn't know where. One died. She was a Bosnian girl, only sixteen. She bled to death after a particularly brutal session in what we called the "other room." We lived, as best we could, in the former dining room. We pushed the tables against the walls and slept on blankets on the floor. They gave us nothing but beans and a little oil and salt, sometimes a bone for seasoning, now and then a loaf of bread. There were always a few of them guarding us with the rifles and their curses. At night they came in groups and pretended that they were visiting some kind of brothel, and they did to us what they did to women in brothels, which made me feel sorry for those women as I never had before. They trooped into the "other room," laughing and tipping back their bottles of šljivovica or beer; they had an endless supply of alcohol. They would send one of the guards out for one or two of us. They knew our names. Because I was the oldest, I got called upon less often. Sometimes as they tossed out one exhausted girl and called upon another, they gave us lectures about how grateful we should be. If we knew what was happening in the villages, they said, we would know how lucky we were. We were fed and housed and we would be the mothers of Serb babies. They were making the next generation of Serbs with us; it was an honor. Then they'd drag one of us in and shout curses at her, slamming the door in our fortunate faces.

This harangue about the Serb babies puzzled me; it was repeated often enough to have the flavor of a party line. Did they seriously imagine that we would be able to love or even to want a child forced upon us in this place? It was the purest lunacy.

During the day when they were out murdering and pillaging and burning up the world, we talked about them, about how we might survive them, about escape. Our situation was bleak. Even if we were to get away somehow, we didn't know where we were and they did. We would certainly be picked up again or just shot. The only way, we agreed, would be to get one of them to break with the pack and help us. This seemed impossible, but there were moments after most of them had passed out from drink, when a word or a look might actually penetrate the miasma of fear and hatred in the "other room." For the most part they were young; they were boys,

*out amusing themselves with their engorged cocks and the joy of carnage.
In my opinion young men should never be allowed to have guns. When they
pick up a gun, it gives them an erection and then until both gun and cock
are discharged, there can be no peace.*

*They knew what they were doing, but they didn't want to know it. We
talked about how to get to them, which ones were weak, which hardened
thugs. Sometimes you were gagged, so there was nothing you could say and
it was best to close your eyes and shut down. Or you could look at them, try
to make them meet your eyes; occasionally a guilty boy would do it. If you
weren't gagged, there were things you could say. Once I said, "What would
your mother say if she could see you?" Which was a big mistake; I nearly
got my head slapped off. One girl said, "God forgive you," and another, "I
forgive you," wasted words in my view and obvious lies. We agreed that
there was one useful phrase you could say. It resulted in amazing largesse. I
got a handful of cigarettes once and Maja got a loaf of bread and a tin of
sardines. If the timing was right, and you managed to cross eyes with the
beast who was fucking you, you could say, "You're different."*

*I'm not suggesting that we ever felt for one moment that we had any
power over them. We lived in constant fear and our diet was so poor we
were always hungry. If one of us missed her period, the others all assured
her it was because we were starving, and in some cases I'm sure that was
true. When they were gone we never went into the "other room," though
nothing was stopping us. We didn't go near the door. We had one toilet
among fifteen, but we had a kitchen sink, so we spent a lot of time just
trying to keep ourselves clean. A day dragged by, but we couldn't wish for
it to end in yet another night. I think we each nourished some spark of
hope that the madness outside would end and the soldiers would disappear
and we would walk out into the sun.*

*A few girls were driven mad by the abuse. They tried to hurt themselves.
One day Anka, a lovely girl of twenty, sat down next to the wall and*

started banging her head against it. We pulled her away and she collapsed in my arms. I said, "Aren't they cruel enough to you? How can you want to make it worse?" Another girl, she was also a Bosnian, a Muslim I think, cried out, "Why do they hate us? Why do they humiliate us?" I tried to think of an answer that would help her in some way. "If a dog pisses on you, if a horse kicks you," I said, "do you think he wants to humiliate you? No, you think: He's just a stupid animal and a dangerous one. He doesn't know who I am or a thing about me. It's like that with them. Don't blame yourself because they are animals. They no longer wish to be human; it's a choice they've made. Look what they call themselves: 'the wolves,' 'the tigers.' They're absurd."

The girl nodded her head, considering my reasoning. One of the others, a farm girl from the village near mine, said with a wry smile, "The eagles."

"The eagles," another repeated. "They should call themselves 'the worms.'" We laughed. "The mollusks," said one, to more laughter. "The maggots," said another. We laughed until we wept.

When the Bosnian girl died, all laughter stopped. It takes a long time to bleed to death and a lot of blood. We begged them to send us a doctor, but they ignored us. She lay on her blanket on the floor, dazed, feverish, her eyes wide with fear, but she never spoke. It took all night and all day. The next night when they came and we told them she was dead, they were annoyed. "Couldn't you take care of her?" one of them said, as if it was our fault.

The days got shorter; there was a chill in the air. We could get no news from outside. It was as if we were somewhere out of time. Trying to stay alive, helping these young women want to stay alive, wore me down more than my evenings with our captors. The boredom was crippling. Quarrels sprang up among us, tears, accusations, and then numb despair.

One night we heard explosions in the distance and we saw red streamers bursting across the sky, obscured by clouds of smoke. The guards tried *to keep us away from the windows. They were nervous, distracted, muttering to themselves and holding their rifles at the alert. A small truck drove up and two soldiers jumped down. There was a consultation, with frequent glances back at us. Then they threw open the door and told us to come out single file and get in the truck. "It's not big enough," one girl said. For answer she received a rifle barrel against her chest and the command, "You first." One by one we filed out under the awning. It was a chilly night. I hung back, pulling up a few blankets. "Let us take these," I said to the one who motioned me into the line.*

"Leave them," he said. The women watched me hopefully. "Let her bring them, it's cold, let us have our blankets," they cried. The soldiers cursed them and threatened them with the rifles. "Get in the truck or we will shoot you here," one said. "It makes no difference to us."

One by one the women climbed into the back of the truck. It had high sides made of wooden planks with a space left between each one; it might have been used to haul a hog or a load of hay once. Now it was transport for women. I took my place at the end of the line, still holding the blankets. A soldier jabbed me hard in the back with the butt of his rifle. "Drop the fucking blankets," he shouted. I fell to my knees. Just then we heard two big explosions and the sky to the west turned red. The soldiers admired the spectacle. "There it goes," one of them said.

I didn't want to get into the truck. I thought, I've gone far enough, now they can shoot me. I dropped to my hands and rolled under the carriage. When I came out the other side, I scrambled to my feet and started running. There were no soldiers on that side and it was a moment before they even understood what had happened. I ran across the road and into a field, where there was a hedge of acacia shrubs. I made for these shrubs. I could hear shots fired, two or three, then a round of rapid fire, like a jackhammer, but I didn't stop running. The ground was uneven, but it was hard and dry. Of course I was in terror, expecting to be killed in the next mo-

ment, but after having been cooped up so long, it felt wonderful to be running in the cold, fresh air. I heard a shout from one of the women. "Run, Jelena," she said. I reached the hedge and ran on, straight beyond it, so that it protected me from sight. I could hear the men shouting, the engine starting up, but no more shots. These sounds grew distant. There was a forest at the edge of the field, that was my goal, and I felt it reaching out its branches to me, encouraging me. I rushed through the brush at the verge and in among the thick trunks of the trees. At last, out of breath, I slowed to a walk and looked back. Then I stopped. No one was chasing me. I had escaped.

But for how long? I thought. And into what? It had been clear from the way the soldiers were acting that something was going on in the war, that they had either been ordered or forced to move on. Perhaps my best option was to stay where I was and return to the restaurant in the morning. I was soon thirsty and hungry, shivering with cold and too tired to go far. I walked along the edge of the forest—I was afraid to go into it for fear of bears—keeping my eye on the field, which looked like a soft pale blanket flung out in the moonlight. I had no destination, I was just walking. I thought if I could find a stream I might follow it and it would lead me to a town, or at least a farmhouse. I walked and listened and walked a little more until I was exhausted and then I sat down near a tree and fell asleep. When I woke it was just dawn, the air was heavy and damp and a white fog had rolled in, as thick as potato soup. I could barely see a foot in front of my face. My teeth were chattering, my stomach groaned with hunger. I got up, took a few steps one way, then the other. It was hopeless; I couldn't see where I was going. I looked down at my feet. My shoes were thin and wet. I noticed that the grass against my left shoe was sparse, worn down. I took a step into the spot. Now the flattened area was in front of me. Another side step and it was rough again. I got down on my hands and knees and looked under the fog. It was a footpath, leading off into the *whiteness. Where it goes, I thought, that is where I am going. So, one step at a time, I followed the path. It went up an incline, it turned, widened. The fog began to lift so that I could see a few feet before and behind. It was eerily silent, but that was good; if anything moved I'd hear it. The forest thinned, the path broke out across a field rough with stubble. Clouds had rolled in and it began to rain. I stopped and drank the heavenly water from my cupped hands. Then I followed the path with my head down, committed to it now as if it was a line and I was a fish being steadily pulled out of the sea. Trees, rocks, bushes, time passed, and then I was standing on a grassy hill looking down over a terraced vineyard at the back of a farmhouse. Smoke poured from the chimney. The door stood open; there was no one in sight.*

If only I knew where I was, I thought, or if there was some way to know what people lived here, which side they were on. I wasn't sure any longer what country I was in. I understood that it didn't matter what I called it, because whatever I called it, it was a country at war. War is a country; that's what I learned, and it always looks the same. The citizens share a culture, which is the culture of trying to save their necks. The soldiers have another culture, the culture of creating havoc. Suspicion is the currency; the economics are despair. I hadn't grown up in this country; I wasn't used to it. I stood on the hill in the rain, afraid to move. The smoke from the chimney, the open door, tantalized me. It would be warm inside. There might be a kind old woman who would offer me food and dry clothes, or there might be a man with a gun sitting at a table ready to shoot me. Tears sprang to my eyes. It turned out that I wanted to live. This seemed enormously sad to me. I set off into the field—it wasn't very wide—keeping out of view of the door. I came up on the side of the house. It was an old stone cottage, small, with thick walls, a tile roof, and high casement windows. I couldn't see in. I crept around to the back, pressed close to the wall. The rain was pouring down in sheets, making water spouts from the corners of the roof. That was the only sound. I crouched down—why I don't know—and crept to the edge of the open door. From there I could see part of the kitchen: a sink, a counter with onions in a basket. Those onions made my mouth water. A sharp crack startled me and I flattened myself against the wall, but then I recognized the sound. It was wood sputtering in the stove. I stepped away from the wall and into the open doorway.

There was no one there. But someone had been there, and recently, because the stove was putting out a flood of heat, which drew me in like a welcoming word. It was a small kitchen with a table and three chairs, an ancient icebox, a few iron pots hanging from hooks in the beams, a sideboard for dishes. The dishes were everywhere, smashed to bits; the chairs were turned over. A lace curtain had been torn from the window and stomped underfoot. Broken bottles of cherry rajika stained the stone floor blood red. They came here and took the people away, I thought. I moved close to the stove and wrung out my skirt and my hair. The stove was closed and damped down. There was a good amount of split wood piled in the box. I could dry out and be warm all night, and there were the onions. Perhaps something more. Under the sink I discovered a basket of potatoes and in the icebox, with what joy I can hardly describe, I found a glass pitcher half full of fresh milk. I took it out at once and drank from the spout, praising cows from the bottom of my heart. What a feast I would have! I looked around the kitchen avidly and through the arched doorway that opened into the second room. I couldn't make out much through the gloom. The shutters must be closed in there, I thought. I set the pitcher on the counter and went closer, cautiously, because I suddenly had the sensation that I was not alone, that someone was watching me. I glanced back at the door, gauging whether I could get out before someone could catch me. "Is there anyone here?" I said.

More silence. I took another step, stretching out my neck but braced to run in the opposite direction, my senses all on the alert like a curious cat. Then I shouted and leaped back into the kitchen. There was a man sitting in a chair facing me, but slumped over, his chin touching his breastbone. I had, in that first moment, the impression that he was black. "Oh God," I said, putting my hands over my face. Why? To see if I was still there. My brain was sorting out what my eyes had dimly seen. Surely to be sitting like that without falling over, he was bound to the chair. Was he alive? Had I detected any motion? Part of me wanted to flee the house, run out the door into the forest, and take my chances with the bears. But another part always wants to know, doesn't it? Cautiously I peeked past the doorway and allowed my eyes to adjust to the dark. He was tied up; he wasn't moving, the blackness was dried blood. He was covered in it, on his clothes and on his exposed flesh. I confess that as I approached him, I hoped he was dead. I assumed I would be able to tell this by looking at his eyes, but this turned out to be impossible because his eyes were two black holes lined in gore. His lips and cheeks were bruised black, one of his teeth was in his lap. A few flies marched about, on his neck and around the shocking hole in his skull. It was this hole and the flies that made me certain he was dead. Soon they would be swarming. I backed away slowly, my hand holding my stomach, which was threatening to eject the milk I'd just drunk in this man's kitchen. A few more flies appeared from nowhere, alighting on his battered face. "It's too horrible," I said. I looked around the room. There was an iron bedstead neatly made up against the wall. I went to it and pulled off the quilted coverlet, brought it to the corpse, and draped it over him. I didn't have the nerve to touch him. Then I went back to the kitchen and tried to figure out what to do.

I decided it would be best to stay there through the night. Obviously this place had already been attacked. They wouldn't be likely to come back. I had food, heat, water; I could dry out, eat, sleep on the floor by the stove, and in the morning perhaps they would have moved farther away. None of this was coherent; I was simply exhausted and terrified and too confused to go on. Later the thought that I'd spent the night in that cottage with a dead man in the next room gave me a chill, especially because when I walked out in the morning, I found his wife lying facedown in the yard under her clothesline, her clean sheets dripping onto her crushed skull. It had stopped raining; the sun came out and bathed the saturated world with light. At the front of the house I found a road and followed it for several miles, past other cottages and outbuildings. Some had been set on fire and were still smoldering. Dead cows, horses, goats littered the yards. Not a living soul was in sight. I felt I had walked out of the land of the living, that I was the only person alive in a world of corpses. I came to a crossroads and there I saw what I took at first to be a mirage. It was a white tent staked out under an old oak, and next to it, two canvas-covered jeeps. A man in a green uniform and a blue helmet came out of the tent and waved to me. When I got closer, he called out in a language I didn't recognize. Later I found out it was Czech.

So it was UN troops.

Yes. The peacekeepers. Later Serbs killed them too.

And they took you out?

Eventually. At first they took me to one of their safe areas. That was a different kind of hell.

Another dinner party, the third in a month. Why is Brendan suddenly in demand? Is it pity or is it just easy to round out a dinner table with a single guest? Are widowers more fun? Could it be that his thoughtful and solicitous hosts like him better without his wife? So far he hasn't been subjected to the eligible female tablemate—it's too soon for that—but he senses that it's in the cards. He's healthy, not bad looking, tenured; he won't be allowed an indefinite period of mourning.

His colleagues don't talk about history much. They prefer college gossip, travelogues, or politics. Tonight the subject is the impending war, which will certainly begin very soon. No one at the table supports it, though Brendan has his doubts about Mel Barker, who punctuates the pauses in the cantata of outrage with the refrain that Saddam Hussein "really is a very bad guy."

"No one doubts that, Mel," David Bodley exclaims. "But the world is full of tyrants. When things get bad enough, their own people do them in. Look at Ceauşescu in Romania; they shot him on television. Mubarak is a bad guy, Africa is packed with them, Kim Jong Il is a lunatic and he's armed. There's no end of lunatics with power, so the question is, why this lunatic? It's not just because he's a very bad guy."

Then the theories are trotted out like thoroughbreds at the track, each with its own fans ready to lay bets. It's oil, it's arrogance, it's arrogance abetted by ignorance of the region, it's a personal vendetta, it's a distractionary tactic because they can't find Osama, it's designed to give Haliburton unlimited access to the United States treasury, it's a bid to consolidate all power in the executive branch—real CEOs don't do Congress, it's the necessity for an enemy, it's a religious crusade.

Brendan listens dully, in partial agreement with everything on offer. All this and more, he thinks, dipping his spoon beneath the oleaginous surface of the bouillabaisse, which disgorges a fragrance of tantalizing complexity. Mary Bodley, his hostess, is a marvelous cook, but it takes her forever to get her guests to the table. This irritated Chloe, who thought it was a strategy. "You can't tell if the food is really as good as it seems because by the time Mary serves it, everyone is starving," she complained. Sometimes, as a counterstrategy, she drank a glass of milk before dinner at the Bodleys'. This recollection makes him smile as he tastes the soup. Sublime. When there is a lull in the real-motive catalog, he says softly to his hostess, "Mary, this is delicious."

"Fantastic," Mel agrees and there is a chorus of superlatives around the table.

"I got the recipe from our landlady in Provence," Mary demurs. "She's just somebody's grandmother, but what a chef!"

The talk turns to Provence, where all agree they wish they were right now. The wood crackles in the fireplace, outside an icy rain falls like silver needles. It is affirmed that March is the worst month of the year.

In settings such as this, with a glass of good Italian wine at his fingertips, rare crustaceans commingling in the porcelain bowl before him, the hearty, earnest conversation of his hyper-educated colleagues flowing around him as freely as the wine, Brendan's apprehension of the privilege of his life can transmogrify into a feeling of alienation from his peers. Small things—the table arrangement of pink rosebuds and sprigs of lavender—stymie him. Roses in March, how is it possible? Like Chloe, Mary Bodley has a penchant for domestic arrangements; everything in her house is beautiful or functional, preferably both. Now that Chloe is gone, Brendan's been having trouble keeping up the standard. Yesterday he noticed a dark stain on the chintz upholstery of a living room chair. How did it get there? The wallpaper is peeling in the upstairs bath. What's to be done about it?

The talk has turned to children. "How is Toby?" Mary asks.

"He's fine," Brendan says. "He's in Trieste. He and his wife are staying with her mother." It sounds so uncomplicated, why say more?

"Trieste!" Amy Treadwell exclaims. "How wonderful. I haven't been there in years. I remember that amazing piazza on the sea. It's the biggest in Europe. And the Adriatic is quite fierce there, and the wind! They call it the *Bora*. We saw an iron table blow right into the waves. The locals hardly raised their eyebrows."

"Yes," Brendan agrees. "The wind is fierce."

Off they go. The Adriatic, and then the Veneto. Will Venice sink under the weight of Japanese tourists toting cameras? The trip to the Lido is really rather *triste*, isn't it. It's all so Thomas Mann, especially off-season.

Brendan swallows a spoonful of his soup. He's lost the thread of the conversation, but it doesn't matter; no one notices. A funny story about a gondolier and a suitcase provokes an eruption of laughter. He joins in, though he missed the punch line. Why is he laughing? Carefully he lays his spoon in the bowl and reaches for his wineglass. He feels odd, not well. Wine or water, which one will help? Mary Bodley is smiling at him, watching him make the choice. He decides on water, swallows half a glass. It isn't nausea, it's not his stomach. His stomach is fine. He picks up his spoon again.

No. It isn't nausea. It's something worse. He recognizes it; it is loathing. His head is swimming with it. He has to blink his eyes to chase impending tears away. He loathes his colleagues. Their conversation, so urbane and smug, repulses him. Oh, European travel! How delightful!

Yet why should he despise them? How many times has he

joined in these itinerary recaps, recalling a particularly pleasant meal, a view, or a work of art; exchanging exclamations, yes, the climb to Vallombrosa on a hot afternoon, it's exhausting, a shin-splinter, but then the inviting shade of the monastery grounds, the surprising chill in the air even on the hottest day in August. There's something magical about the place. How frigid it must be in the winter.

"Brendan?" Mary says. "Are you quite all right?"

To his own surprise, he shakes his head. No. He's not all right. "I'm awfully sorry," he says, pushing back his chair. "I'm afraid I'm not feeling very well."

A geyser of sympathy erupts from the company. In their effusions he reads the question, is he sick or is it grief? Mary rises from her chair. "Perhaps you should lie down in the guest bedroom. You do look pale."

"No," he says. "But I think I'd better go home."

"Should you be driving?" she says, but she leads him from the dining room toward the door. "That doesn't sound safe if you're feeling poorly. You know you're welcome to stay over. The weather is dreadful."

"It's just rain," Brendan says. "It's not freezing. It isn't very far."

"Why don't you let David drive you?"

He imagines being driven through the night by his cheerful, insensitive department chair. *How's the book going?* Yes, that would be his first question. He has arrived at the foyer, where the huddle of damp coats on the coat tree gives off the scent of wet sheep. Brendan confides in his hostess. "There's nothing really wrong with me," he says. "I'm just not fit for company. Some days are better than others."

"I understand," she says. "It's too soon."

"Yes. That's it."

Is this a lie? He isn't sure. He locates his coat and lifts it from the rack. Mary helps him into it, her anxiety evidently alleviated by his confession. "Make my excuses, will you?" he says, and she murmurs, "Of course, dear, of course." He can imagine the concern with which she will explain his behavior to her bemused guests, who have now spent several moments speculating about him. *Poor fellow. He's taking it very hard. It's touching, really.*

In the car he experiences relief, embarrassment, and frustration, in that order. The latter arrives with the thought of the bouillabaisse, which he hardly touched. What a waste. Now it's late, he has had no dinner, there's not much in the house, and he's in no mood for cooking. He looks up at the lights twinkling behind the curtains of the house, the sloping lawn which is largely clear of snow, though the drive is edged with a long, dirty wedge of it, left by the plow. The rain is a drizzle; the icy air clears his head. He turns on the engine and pulls away slowly, as if he doesn't want to be observed. My God, he is thinking, I just walked out of David Bodley's dinner party. Mary will clear his place—*Oh, too bad, he didn't finish his soup*—and then the talk will turn to something else.

"It doesn't matter," he says. He flips on the CD player and picks up on the Brahms quintet where he left off. Melancholy is routed by Triumph as he turns from the quiet residential street onto the state road. He recalls a line from an old film, Ingmar Bergman, wasn't it? A man is talking about his marriage: "There has to be an end to suffering," he says. Chloe loved Bergman, but Brendan found him humorless and tedious.

He doesn't want to go home to the empty house with his empty stomach. He takes the exit to the street behind the college and turns on to another lined with restaurants and bars. He'll go to The Briar, where everything will be familiar but no one will ask him how he's doing. It's a popular place, the food is good, and he can eat at the bar. He cheers up at the thought; after all, he's very hungry.

Inside it's crowded. A party of diners is perched on the edge of the stage near the door, sipping drinks and talking as they wait for a table. It's a small room with a stone floor that amplifies the noise and a high ceiling from which large wooden fans are strategically suspended. The artwork is eclectic: posters advertising beer, color photos of the local landscape featuring moony-eyed livestock, old black-and-white prints of stern elders in frock coats and laced-up bodices elaborately framed in ebony and gold. The theme is no theme, Chloe once observed. The waitress—he knows her, her name is Susan—floats toward him through the crowd, balancing, with marvelous aplomb, a tray full of drinks. "Dinner?" she says as she passes close by.

"Yes," Brendan says. "The bar is fine."

"There's a seat on the far end," she replies.

The bar runs the length of the room; high, wide, mirror-backed, and lined with padded leather stools. The bartender, Libby, is in constant motion, but she sees Brendan as he climbs into the empty seat and raises her eyebrows and her chin to acknowledge him. He studies the list of specials on the chalkboard; they have grouper tonight, Chloe's favorite. "Drink?" Libby says, pumping a silver shaker up and down with one hand while distributing olives across three glasses with the other.

"That looks good," he says. "I'll have a martini."

"Straight up," she says, but it's not a question. "No lemon."

"Right."

"Goose."

"Right," he says again. He returns his attention to the board. He doesn't want fish; he wants something substantial. The flank steak is the obvious choice. He looks around the room. Susan is laughing at her diners, who are all grinning back at her. At a corner table, a tall, elegant black woman holds her fork in the air, speaking intently to a dapper white-haired man twice her age who listens closely, his brow furrowed. Brendan doesn't recognize anyone, though the man at the other end of the bar knocking back a beer looks familiar. Psychology department? Maybe English. Libby appears with his martini. "You eating?" she says.

"I'll have the flank steak," he says. She lines up the flatware and napkin in front of him. "Coming right up," she says.

The drink is good, icy cold. Brendan feels better already. He was right to come here. The couple on one side of him are deep in conversation; the woman on the other is drinking something red and staring at the TV above the bar with a vacant expression, what Chloe called the "TV face." There are two screens here on either end of the bar. Sometimes they run sports events with the sound mercifully off. He takes another swallow of his drink and looks up at the screen.

It's a movie. A night scene, a city. A fifties-style high-rise in the foreground, frankly ugly, behind it a range of shadowy buildings, one of which is on fire. The flames leap and stretch into the sky, sending up flurries of sparks like fireflies swarming on a summer evening. As he watches, the sky above a palm tree on the right flushes a deep virulent red, throwing the spidery fronds into black relief. A plume of smoke issues from somewhere below the camera's frame, drifting lazily toward the palm. It's pretty. Brendan takes another sip of the martini. Is it Miami? At last he notices the crawl of illegible words across the bottom of the screen and it dawns on him that this is a newscast. He turns to the woman with the red drink, whose eyes are fixed on the screen, her mouth slightly ajar. "What is this?" he asks her.

"It's Baghdad," she says, without looking at him.

"Oh," he says. So it has begun.

The soundtrack is presumably sirens and explosions, but here it is laughter, glasses clinking, idle, amiable chatter. Most people are not looking at the screen, though Libby glances up at it as she washes out a few glasses and there's a couple at a table near the bar who gaze at it, chewing thoughtfully. It's like that dreadful club in the Mafia TV show, Brendan thinks, where men plot crimes while naked women pretend to have sex with poles right in front of them. An obscenity is taking place in the room, but the volume is down, and no one can be bothered to watch it.

They count on that, the ones who planned this, and they were right to count on it. Brendan's steak arrives. "How long has that been going on?" he asks Libby, who says, "What?" He points at the television.

"Shock and awe?" she says contemptuously. "About half an hour."

That's right. *Shock and awe*; the name they've dreamed up for this, which is the *means*, to be justified by the *end*. No omelette without breaking eggs, and we had no alternative, having exhausted diplomacy and set deadline after deadline. *Sic semper*

tyrannis, etc. Who can doubt that they are congratulating themselves, pouring out a little expensive scotch, except for the
president, who drinks Diet Coke, lifting their glasses to the
enterprise that they have had some difficulty bringing about,
what with those imbeciles at the UN and world opinion in
general, and the French in particular. They probably have a
big screen, volume way up, the phones ringing off the hook.
Here we go! Soon the president will have to go to bed—it's way
past his bedtime—where he will sleep the untroubled sleep of
the just.

As Baghdad goes up in flames, Brendan tries his steak. The
meat is delicious and he's hungry; he addresses it steadily, cutting
and chewing until it's all gone. Smoke fills the screen. For some
reason there are flashes of green light shooting through it. The
buildings are dark; obviously they blew out the power first.

No one ever thinks they will actually do it, though it's common knowledge that eventually they always do. He recalls reading of Serbian amazement when Belgrade was bombed. That
wasn't so long ago; Jelena's war, and Salome's, though she was
only a child. The war that separated them.

The thing to do is to take the long view of it; this is his profession, after all. What's really happening on that screen is
history-in-the-making, and not just recent history, but, should
the planet survive, ancient history. Our fate is ever to rush into
the past as if we thought it was the future. But we are in the history van, along with all the other curious, faded civilizations
that failed for reasons now obvious. Like the Etruscans, we will
be unearthed, rummaged. Perhaps people will find it amusing
to try to live, in a daily way, as we did, without benefit of, say,
time travel or space cars, or spare organs from the clone farm.

They might read about this event, the bombing of the ancient city of Baghdad—no, not read it, but experience it in some sensory-surround history booth, books having gone the way of the vinyl record—and have a clear idea of what it meant when it happened, how it figured in the graph of that curious country, once powerful, now forgotten.

But in that future world, Brendan feels confident, some things won't have changed. Technology advances, not much else. Scrapping over territory is just not going to let up, whether it's about real estate in this world or the imaginary landscape of the next. Given the certainty that negotiations will break down and new hostilities arise from the perception of betrayal and broken faith, the persistence of the recourse to alliances, whether political or cultural, appears to be a kind of invincible stupidity, but it will go on. The rise to power of wealthy and belligerent families is inevitable, and nothing, not class revolt, not anarchy, not democratic ideals or institutions, can stop it.

Case in point, Brendan concludes, lifting his glass to the exploding city before him.

"You are not," a voice says clearly, "proposing a toast to this crime."

He sets down his glass, confused. It's the woman with the red drink. She's frowning at him, a mighty, excessive frown, but in spite of it he notices that she is pretty. Not young, but well maintained; not someone who drinks alone in a bar every night.

"Not at all," he says. "I'm completely opposed to this."

"I should hope so," she replies coldly. Her eyes drift back to the screen.

A toast? Brendan thinks. Is she mad? Does she seriously

imagine that, apart from the planners and the war profiteers lining up in the halls of power, any sane person would propose a toast to the events on this television screen? He stares at the rude woman. Like-minded, but a bitch nonetheless. Then he catches Libby's eye and describes a check in the air with his index finger. The war show isn't going to end anytime soon, and he wants to go home and send a message to Toby.

Outside it's drizzling and black as pitch. He's not sensible of just how black until he leaves the campus area and turns onto the parkway. He has a moment of anxiety—is the road slippery, has he had too much to drink?—but it fades as he turns on his bright lights and hunches down behind the wheel. There's not another car in sight. His head feels clear; a quick test of the brakes assures him that he can stop without sliding. He accelerates carefully, flicking on the radio for company. He expects the airwaves to be clogged with war news, but it's the usual late-night jazz show playing an old Billie Holiday recording, a song he hasn't heard in years. *Hush now, don't explain*, she croons and he sings along, scanning the road ahead. *I'm glad, you're back. Don't explain*. She takes him all the way to the sign for his exit. Then the obnoxious announcer comes on, blathering about the greats of the past. Brendan hits the station button as he moves into the right lane. The voice of the president, oiled with fake gravitas, invades the car, setting his every nerve on edge. *Now that the conflict has come*, the voice informs him, *the only way to limit its duration . . .*

"Is for you to be put up in front of a firing squad," Brendan snaps. For one moment he shifts his eyes to his hand, silencing the commander in chief with a quick jab to the off button. Satisfied, he refocuses on the road ahead.

The deer is standing in his lane, its eyes gleaming like golden coins, so close he can see the ears twitching in the rain.

. He slams on the brakes with such force his left hip lifts from the seat. He can feel the tires bearing down, seeking purchase on the slick pavement, the shift in the rear as they begin to slide. He holds the steering wheel loosely in his hands, his senses so supremely attentive that he is omniscient. He knows many things at once—that the deer is moving off to the left, that there are no cars behind him so it doesn't matter if the skid carries the back of the car into the other lane, that rather than swerve his best option is to allow the front end to be pulled back by the natural rotation of the skid. It takes a long time; he gives each second its excruciating due, but at last the car comes to a stop. He is facing the wrong way in the passing lane and there are headlights rushing toward him. Where did that car come from? He leans on the horn, flashes his lights, afraid to move in any direction. "Jesus," he mutters, "don't hit me." The car moves to the right lane, and as it passes a man yells at him from the passenger window. Brendan can't hear him because his own window is closed, but he sees the beefy face contorted with outrage. It's moving fast, a fortress of a car, so top-heavy it leans perilously as the angry driver changes lanes again, throwing up a furrow of water like a plow in a dusty field. Then it's gone and all is perfectly dark and still. Brendan turns the car around, returning slowly to the right lane and onto the exit ramp. When he gets to the state road, he pulls into the break-down lane and stops. His legs are limp as kittens, his heart pounds against his ribs.

If the other car had been closer there would have been a collision, broadside, or even head-on, and he might have been killed. Toby, thus orphaned, would return from Trieste for another funeral. With the life insurance and the sale of the house, this orphan could live quite comfortably for some time, he and Salome and their baby. Like the illustrated edition of *Wuthering Heights*, a new biography of Frederick of Hohenstaufen would never see the light of print, and this would matter to no one. Brendan shakes his head at his bleak fantasy. His heart has calmed down. He puts the car in gear and drives with exaggerated caution the rest of the way home.

The house is dark. Mike, disgruntled and hungry, paces on the terrace. Brendan lets him in and dutifully fills the food bowl, refreshes the water. His brain replays the evening, the discomfiture at the dinner party, the exploding city on the television screen, the unpleasant woman drinking alone at the bar, the near death-by-deer in the rainy darkness. Quite a night. He pours himself a glass of port and wanders through the dark hall to his desk, where he flicks on the lamp and the computer. He opens his e-mail, contemplating the time difference; it's five A.M. in Trieste. Toby doesn't know that in his sleep his country has begun yet another of its wars.

There's a message from him in the in-box, sent in the afternoon. The subject line is all caps: *VILKA TALKS!* And there's an attachment. Brendan settles into his chair, his spirits lifting as he sees that the message is long and the attachment is two photos.

Toby begins without salutation: *And her first word is "gelato." I discovered that this poor child has spent eight years in Italy without ever trying it. Jelena doesn't eat it and doesn't have a freezer—a poor excuse, if you ask me. I brought her a cup of chocolate and pistachio about ten days ago and you should have seen her face when she tasted it. Her eyes just*

lit up and she almost smiled. So I started getting her a cup every night af-
ter dinner. We've been through all the flavors now and she is so hooked on
it that she waits by the door when I go out. I always say "I'm going to get
your gelato" when I leave. Tonight when I came in she put both arms up
in the air and said "gelato" clear as a bell. We almost fainted. She's much
improved in other ways too. She goes for days without any fits and she sits
on a chair at the table. Sometimes she even uses a spoon. Now I want to
take her down to the gelato bar. Then she can choose her own flavor—if
she can name it. That's my plan. Hope you're well. The girls send greet-
ings to our American father. Pictures attached. Love, Toby.

"Amazing," Brendan says, clicking on the first photo square.

It's a touching picture. Toby, Salome, and Vilka are sitting on
the floor eating gelato from paper cups. Salome is heavily pregnant now; she props the cup on her belly with one hand, brings
the spoon to her mouth with the other. She's gazing over Vilka's
head at Toby with an expression of proprietary confidence, as a
mother regards her child when he is clever and good. Toby has
finished his ice cream; the cup is near his knee. He looks down
thoughtfully at Vilka, who leans against his side licking the last
of the gelato from her cup. Her face is hidden by her hair, but
her posture suggests animal contentment. Her legs are sprawled
out before her and she holds the cup with both hands. In the
background the dining table, strewn with dishes, broken bits of
bread, and half-empty glasses, sports a new cloth.

Brendan opens the next photo, conscious of the wish that
Jelena will be in it. He gets his wish. She and Salome are sitting
on the couch; Vilka is on the floor in front of them. All three
are looking up at the camera. Doubtless they have been told to
smile. Salome's smile is wide and fake, her eyes glitter menac-
ingly; she's making a joke of it. Jelena's chin is raised; her eyes

dreamy and distant, she's there, but not entirely. Her mouth lifts slightly at the corners. She's wearing a bright blue sweater he doesn't recognize, a good color on her.

Vilka is trying hard to look at the camera, but she can't do it because it frightens her. Her brows are contracted and her eyes have a disconcerting inwardness. Her mouth is ajar. She has drawn her thin shoulders up tightly, almost to her ears. She has chocolate ice cream on her chin and her nose, a little dab on her cheekbone. The scar on her cheek is visible. Combined with the ice cream, it makes Brendan shudder. He recalls what Jelena told him when he asked her about the scar.

"It's a crescent moon," she said. "To show she's a Muslim."

"So it wasn't an accident?"

"Serbs did it," she said. "They killed her parents and her two sisters. They cut this moon on her father's buttocks and her mother's breast. The sisters were raped and strangled, probably in front of her. For some reason they didn't kill her. She was a baby, maybe three years old, no one knows. When they found her she had been locked up with her dead relatives a few days. She was covered in blood and excrement."

"My God," he said.

"These things always happen in wars," she said calmly. "It takes the lid off of everything. The ones who enjoy inflicting pain, the torturers who used to confine themselves to abusing animals or their wives can now excite themselves by finding out how it feels to gouge out an old man's eyes or slash a woman's breasts. They come out of the woodwork. Who guessed how many there were? And they all have the same credo: For my just cause the enemy must suffer. His cries of pain are my vindication."

Brendan, unable to speak, sat looking down at Vilka, who was chewing on the ear of her bear.

"This poor creature was somebody's enemy," Jelena concluded.

"How did you find her?"

"She wound up in the camp I was in. I asked about her and the administrator told me this story. No one wanted her, so when I got my passport, I took her with me. There are two women in this building who stay with her when I'm at work. One of them lost her own daughter in the war, so she won't let me pay her."

"Will she ever get better?"

"She's a lot better than she was. But I must tell you, my dear historian, she is strongly drawn to your son, more than she has been to anyone before. Maybe it's because he's an innocent, like she is."

"Toby is kindhearted."

"Yes, kindhearted. You must be proud of him."

"I am," Brendan said.

He clicks back to the first photo to have a closer look at Toby, this boy who has had his character sorely tested of late, though he doesn't seem to know it. He looks good; he's even put on a little weight. His hair is longer than he usually keeps it; this may be at Salome's suggestion. He's concentrated on Vilka, looking down over her hair; he can probably see her tongue licking out the last streaks of gelato. There's a quality of confidence about him. He has won the trust of a wounded creature and he has a plan to bring her out of suffering and darkness. It starts with gelato. "I'm proud of you," Brendan says to the screen.

He clicks back to the second photo. There she is. The blue sweater has some kind of trim at the neck, something glittery. It looks festive. The skirt is black, her legs are crossed. He can't see the shoes because Vilka is in front of them. Her hair is loose; it strays over her forehead and her cheek. She looks as if she's about to speak and Brendan very much wants to hear what she has to say.

As he sits back in his chair, his eyes dart to the framed engraving over his desk. It's new; he's not used to it yet and though he knows it's there, it still surprises him. A man digging up a grave while another, wrapped in a cloak, looks on. It's a windy night; the juniper, the prototype for which is in the field behind the studio, is bent by the force of the blast. The icy sky swirls overhead. The scene is framed by a window ledge, putting the viewer in the moral position of a voyeur. It's happening, this midnight grave robbing, over there. Brendan notices a hawk caught up in the turmoil of the night sky.

"These are brilliant," the publisher said when she came up to see the plates. "What a pity she didn't finish." The project would be reassigned, which was a considerable annoyance for the publisher, or so she implied. How inconvenient for an artist to drop dead before her work was done. The small advance would have to be returned. But there was no hurry, she assured Brendan.

Brilliant, he agrees. Also eerie, that Chloe's last work should so resolutely address the grave. He'd chosen this print for his study because it struck him that digging up the dead was his profession. Now he's thinking of something else, of the mass graves which, he read in Sunday's paper, are yet to be unearthed in Tulsa, Oklahoma, of all places, where elderly survivors of the race riots recall seeing bodies piled in wagons and stacked "like cordwood" along the streets of the black enclave called Greenwood, bodies that later disappeared.

The disinterment in Chloe's engraving exists outside history. That she was thinking about Heathcliff in the last days of her life, this interloper for whom even the grave was not sacred, strikes Brendan as poignant. He consoles himself with the now well-worn touchstone of his memory, that the last words he said to her on the phone from Trieste, where he had gone at her bidding, were "I love you."

He finishes his port, returning his attention to the bright photograph on the computer screen.

It's off season. If he goes to that site that sells last-minute tickets and he's not particular about which airport he flies out of, he can probably get a flight in the next week or so. Toby can reserve his grim little room in the shabby hotel. He'll have to ask Joan Chase to look after Mike, which she'll be happy to do as she so wants to be helpful and it will give her a chance to poke her nose into everything in the house. He clicks back to Toby's message and then to the reply icon. The new heading appears. In the subject line he types: *Coming over.*

❖ ❖

The camp was a miserable place, crowded and muddy. We slept in bunk beds lined up in a shed heated by a woodstove. The food was poor, but there was meat and cheese and bread. There didn't seem to be any vegetables left in the world. My fellow refugees were mostly peasants from the farms and villages nearby. They'd been driven from their houses with nothing but the clothes they were wearing. They sat around the stove telling one another the same horror stories over and over. Time stood still in that place.

I met an Italian woman, Ana Banchi, a kind person who worked for Caritas. When she brought us coats, I spoke to her in Italian and she asked me to go with her on her rounds and translate for her. She didn't like throwing piles of used clothes at people; she tried to make it personal, to find out what they needed. We became friends and she helped me in the camp and later when I came here. She found out through the Red Cross that Branko had been in a camp in Slovenia and that he and the children had gone directly from there to his relatives in America, just as he had always dreamed of doing.

So you knew they were alive.

Oh yes. Ana gave me Branko's address in America. In the south, what is that place?

Louisiana.

Yes, that's it. Ana thought I would write to him and go to America. I told her my husband and I had been estranged before the war. I didn't want to say more than that. I had no intention of trying to join them; I was just relieved to know they were safe. I thought I'd done them enough harm and they'd be better off believing I was dead. But in order to get a passport I needed a document, the Domovnica, to prove I was Croatian. I tried calling my father, but I couldn't find him. Later I learned he'd gone to Holland. He died there a few years ago. I felt sure that Branko had gathered the papers before he left: he would have needed them to get to Slovenia and he was careful about that sort of thing. I couldn't bring myself to write to him. I asked Ana to do it for me, just to say that I was alive and could he send the document so I could get a passport and go to Italy. She thought it very odd, but she agreed. He sent it right away, without a note of any kind. That was how I knew he didn't want to hear from me.

How cruel.

Not really. He left it to me. All these years he's known I could show up at any moment. It can't have been easy for him.

That's why he never married.

Yes. We're still married. Do you mind if I smoke?

No. Go ahead.

When I came here with Vilka I wanted to forget my former life in my former country; I swore off the past. I didn't want to hear any more about it, not about the war, about them, about us. I didn't want to hear my own language, though I hear it in my head and in my dreams. When I hear it on the street here, my heart races toward it like a horse to its barn—my own familiar hay. It's like a drug, I crave it, but it's killing me. I'm worse than an exile, because the place I came from doesn't exist anymore. Yugoslavia. It was real to me, I grew up there, but they've removed it from the map.

The night Salome knocked at the door it felt as if an old scarred-over wound was suddenly torn open. I couldn't speak for the pain. She gave me such a look; I can hardly describe it, and she said, "Mama, it's me," in a small voice. I put my arms around her and held her while she wept, but I didn't cry myself. I was in shock, I think. All the pain I'd caused her when I was alive and when she thought I was dead poured out of her in those tears. She forgave me everything in a moment. But for me it wasn't so easy. Holding her, it all came back to me, the war, and before that when we were happy, when she was born, my mother-in-law, Milan, and my little boy I loved so much who died because of me. I could weep for a thousand years and still not forgive myself, so I don't weep. I have no tears.

Did you tell Salome what happened to you during the war?

No. How could I? I made up a story about that night Josip was killed. I said the soldiers put me in jail and when I got out they told me they had killed the rest of the family. I said I was in a refugee camp a long time. I said I couldn't talk about the past, which is true, I can't bear thinking

about it, but since Salome's been here it's all boiled up again and I'm stew-
ing in it. She's very dear, but she wants me to be the person I was before,
the one who made her feel safe. She's not satisfied with me, and she's jeal-
ous of Vilka. I don't think it's good for her to be here, especially with the
baby coming. I think she should go back to America with Toby.

Wouldn't you miss her?

I miss my whole life. But it's not my life anymore. I live here now.

Toby prefers the big covered market to the small shops on their
street, but it's a long walk and he has to cross two perilously
busy streets to get there. The return trip offers the additional
challenge of being uphill. When he arrives at last at the apartment, laden with bags of produce, meat, and eggs, there are
four flights of stairs to finish him off. He is stalwart, not pausing until he's at the door, where he lowers his bounty to the
floor and digs in his pocket for the key. Before he retrieves it,
to his surprise, the door opens and Salome looks out at him
expectantly.

"You're back early," he says.

She comes out to help him. "We only had to wait an hour."

"Take this one," Toby says. "That one's heavy." He follows
her inside, pulling the door closed behind him, and hoists the
bags onto the kitchen table. This room, the front room as opposed to the back room, is windowless, so the overhead light is
on. The building, like so much of Trieste, has seen better days,
but the high ceilings and wood floors remain. There's even a
plaster cornice edging the walls. The kitchen is tucked into a
corner, the table seats two. They took this place because the

furniture was not falling apart. The mattress is, in fact, good, and the old iron bedstead is solid.

"This lettuce looks pretty tired," Salome says, unpacking bags.

"It's the best they had. What did the doctor say?"

"Nothing. He says I'm a fine healthy girl. I don't like him. I don't like that clinic."

"Do you want to try someplace else? There must be other clinics."

"I don't like these Italian doctors. They examine you alone in a room, without a nurse; it gives me the creeps. Then when we go out, Mother has to translate for me and she never asks any questions. If I ask her to translate a question, she looks at me like she thinks I'm a big baby."

"I'm sure she doesn't think that."

"It's all very old-world. No one questions authority. You do what the man in the uniform tells you to do."

"Well, darling, it *is* the old world."

"These carrots are filthy."

"Put them in the sink."

Salome takes the carrots, drops them in the sink, and turns on the water. She stands rubbing them clean while Toby folds the bags, watching her. From behind he can hardly detect that she's pregnant. The only clue is her stance, which is a little wider than normal; that and the fact that her arms are extended because she has to reach beyond her stomach. She turns off the water and, drying her hands on the dish towel, faces her husband. "I don't like Trieste," she says.

"It's not so bad," Toby says.

"And I don't like this apartment."

"It isn't very nice."

"Nothing works. The oven has one temperature, six hundred degrees, there's not enough hot water, and the refrigerator is either iced up completely or pouring water all over the floor."

"I'm getting the feeling you're unhappy about something."

"Well, do *you* like it here?"

"There are things I like about it. But if you want to go back to the States . . ."

"I'd feel guilty about leaving my mother."

"Don't you think she'd understand?"

"Maybe she won't even care that much. She's not very excited about the baby."

"Your mother isn't excited about anything."

"She's excited about you. All she talked about at the doctor's was you and Vilka."

"Vilka's coming along. You should have seen her this morning. She really wanted to swing with the other children."

"Yes, I know all about it. You're a genius."

"Are you annoyed that your mother likes me?"

"Only if she likes you more than she likes me, which is what I think sometimes."

"Mothers and daughters are always at odds, aren't they?"

"How could you possibly know anything about that?" She has finished washing the carrots, which she spreads out on the drain board to dry. One rolls off to the floor and she curses as she bends awkwardly over her stomach to retrieve it.

"You're grouchy, darling," Toby observes. "Did something happen at the doctor's that you haven't told me?"

"No. I'm just not happy here. I don't want to have the baby in Trieste. I realized that today at the clinic. I want to go back."

"Then we'll go back."

"But where will we go? How will we live?"

"The same way we live here. We'll find an apartment, I'll get a job."

"I was thinking it might be a good idea if we live in your father's house."

"With my father? I don't think you'd like that."

"Why not? There's plenty of room."

"That's true." The house appears before him, vast, minus his mother. "It just didn't occur to me."

"I like that house." Salome pulls a chair out from the table and eases into it. "My poor feet hurt," she says.

"I didn't think you liked it."

"No? Well, I do. Who wouldn't?"

Toby makes no reply. She's right; who wouldn't like his father's house? And that's because it's his mother's house. She spent twenty-five years making it comfortable and inviting. He recollects her straight back at her sewing machine, her fingers pulling the yards of fabric for the living room drapes steadily past the ratcheting needle. The tic-tic of the machine, the material, printed with a pattern of birds climbing among blue branches, billowing into folds on the floor, the buttery sheen of the pine boards in the afternoon light; it all comes to him, vivid and serene. How old was he when she made those drapes? Ten? Eleven? He was eating a cookie he'd taken from the jar in the kitchen as he passed through. She sensed him there behind her. She lifted her foot from the pedal and, as the machine flagged to a halt, she turned to him. "Hello, darling," she said. "How was school?"

Salome points out that it will be much better for the baby if they live in the country. "If we live in the city," she says, "he'll be like those babies in their strollers who are all blue from carbon monoxide because they're at the same level as the exhaust pipes."

The air is better, Toby agrees, but he's distracted, and his reply doesn't satisfy her. "What are you thinking about?" she says.

"My mother," he admits.

Salome frowns. She hadn't pretended that his mother's death caused her deep sadness; she'd hardly known Chloe and they hadn't exactly hit it off, but she was shocked, they both were, and she was sympathetic. After all, she knew what it was to lose a mother. "Are you sad?" she asks. She pulls herself up to put the eggs into the undersized refrigerator.

"I had a happy childhood," he says. "I was so secure, I didn't even think about it. Mom was always willing to talk to me, even when she was working. She would stop what she was doing to talk to me."

"Do you miss her?"

"She said such terrible things to me that day, when we told her about the baby. I was so angry with her, I couldn't forgive her. And then she died."

"What things did she say?"

"It doesn't matter. I just couldn't forgive her."

"But she said things about me."

His brain reruns the tape for him—What do you know about her? Is she even a citizen? Is she after a green card? She's trying to trap you? She's more interested in this house than she is in you? How do you know this baby is yours? You're being played for a fool. She'll ruin your life. How could you do this; how could you be so stupid?

"It doesn't matter," he says again.

"She wanted to poison you against me."

Toby gives Salome his attention. She is standing before him, her hands on her hips, her feet planted apart, stolid and sullen. Her big stomach stretches the weave of her oversized sweater, her hair curls out in all directions, her eyes are hot. She looks just like the drawing Chloe made of her: *the hornet-headed girl.* What was the rest of it? *Run for your life.* "She just didn't know anything about you," he says. "And she loved me."

"If she loved you, she would have trusted you."

"Well, she didn't put me in charge of the family finances when I was fifteen or something, that's true," he says testily. "She indulged me, she cared for me. Was that such a crime? Why does my mother have to be the villain of this piece?"

"She didn't give us a chance."

"You didn't give her a chance."

"You still take her side against me?"

"She's dead, Salome. Her side is dead. She was my mother, she loved me, let her rest."

But Salome won't let his mother rest. "I'm sure she loved you when you were a child," she persists. "I'm not contesting that. But she didn't want you to be an adult. She had no respect for you, and she hated me, though I never did a thing to her. She thought you needed to be protected from me."

Toby grimaces. "Jesus, will you stop with that. I'm beginning to think she was right."

She narrows her eyes. "Oh, really," she says. "Well, that's just great. That's just exactly what I needed to hear today."

"And let me just point out that your mother isn't exactly a paragon," he suggests.

"How can you talk to me like this?" She goes back to the table and drops into the chair again.

Toby regards her gloomily. She rests her cheek in one hand and works her shoes off with the other. She looks like a weary child. We're too young for this, he thinks, but he's not sure what *this* is. "What time are you going to meet your father?" she asks.

"At six," Toby says.

❖ ❖

For a change, the weather is decent. The wind has died down; the clouds are thin streaks in the startling blue of the sky. The sun bathes the pale facades of the building in a limpid golden light. Brendan has left his coat in the hotel, though he wears a sweater and his scarf is tied in the approved fashion to keep his neck warm. He's made a stop at the Slovenian pastry shop to purchase an almond cake, the only sweet Jelena likes. His day is laid out: lunch with Jelena at her apartment, a walk with her through the old quarter to the house of her British employer, then a self-guided tour of the churches on the Canal Grande, a meeting with Toby at the café on the Piazza Unitá, and finally dinner with Jelena and Salome at the seafood restaurant near the fish market.

Though his day is planned, his sense of his own possibilities is so expanded as to be vertiginous. He has a routine; everything feels familiar now except himself. He eats well, sleeps well, drinks perhaps too much in the evenings, but he wakes clearheaded, eager to be up and about. He showers in his miserable bathroom and goes straight to the café. The barista is used to him now; he waves him to a table when he comes in the door. While writing steadily in his notebook—which is rapidly filling, he'll buy a new one today—he drinks an espresso and eats a cornetto. His notebook is divided into three sections: his impressions of Trieste, notes for an essay on writing history, and a detailed reconstruction of the stories Jelena has told him. He has no idea what he will do with any of this writing, nor does he care. It feels good to sit there, with a pen and notebook instead of a screen, working away at sentences one at a time.

As he arrives at the apartment building, he catches his own reflection in the shop window next door, a lean man, his thinning hair mussed by the breeze, carrying a fussily wrapped package of cake. That could be anyone, he thinks, and presses the familiar bell. The buzzer screeches, the door clicks, and he steps inside. At the end of the long climb he finds Jelena in the open doorway, fixing him with a skeptical eye. "Are you trying to make me fat with this cake?" she says.

"You're not fat," he says. "And you like it. Why shouldn't you eat it?"

"There's no arguing with Americans, I find," she replies, stepping aside to usher him in. Vilka is lying on the floor coloring in a book Toby brought her. She covers each page with fierce slashes of red and orange. When she looks up at Brendan he notes something like curiosity in her eyes; it's almost the expression of a normal child. He exchanges cheek kisses with Jelena and hands over the cake. "It's a gorgeous day," he says.

"Yes, a real spring day," she agrees. "I opened the window for the first time this year."

The table is laid with dishes: cold ham, the sheep's milk cheese he likes, a dish of boiled chard and potatoes, peppers, tomatoes, bread, and the jar of pickled vegetables that never seems to run out. "Shall we sit?" Jelena says. Vilka gets up and approaches the table.

"Did she go out again this morning?" he asks.

"She did, yes. Toby has worked a miracle." Jelena brings a bowl of cottage cheese to the table. "This is for you," she says to Vilka. "Come and sit with us."

"Where did you go?"

"Toby found a little travesty of a park just around the corner. I never walk that way, so I didn't know it was there. There's a swing set and a few children were swinging. She was fascinated by that, but, of course, she wouldn't go too close. She's so undersized the children took her to be their age and two of them came over to speak to her. That frightened her, so Toby picked her up and then she was calm."

Vilka climbs into the empty chair, her expression resolute, as if she has made up her mind to take an enormous risk. "Here's your cheese," Jelena says. "Toby tells me I must talk to her more." The child takes up the spoon and begins eating, her eyes fixed on the bowl.

"And she must go out every day," Jelena continues. "He's very firm about that. Will you open the water?"

"Did Salome come with Toby?"

"No. She had a doctor's appointment. I met her at the clinic. She was in a bad humor because she likes to sleep late and she doesn't like the doctor. Have some of this ham."

Brendan spears a slice and flops it onto his plate. "What did the doctor say?"

"What is there to say? She's fine. She's pregnant. It's not an illness."

"Toby worries about her."

"Yes, well, that's why she has nothing to worry about. She has everyone spinning around her. Toby adores her."

"He does. He told me once he wants to know everything about her."

"I don't think she's so hard to know."

"He says it's his mission."

"His mission." She smiles, shakes a cigarette from the ever-present pack. "And what's your mission, I wonder."

"Me?"

"You're an American; you must have a mission."

"You're right. Well, I think it must be to make you stop smoking."

"You Americans. You taught the world to smoke. Humphrey Bogart, all those movies. Now no one can smoke. Well, I'm sorry to disappoint you, but your mission is doomed to failure." She brings the cigarette to her lips.

Brendan lights a match and holds the quivering flame out to her. "Your life is like this flame and those cigarettes are extinguishing it."

"That's some kind of dreadful metaphor. You'll never make it work."

"Probably not. So you won't quit."

"No. I don't think so."

Vilka has finished her cheese. She drops the spoon into the bowl and slips out of the chair, rubbing her eyes with both fists.

"Nap time," Brendan observes. The child makes sliding steps to the couch and curls up on the cushions, pulling the blanket over her legs.

"Eat some of this," Jelena says, passing the plate of chard and potatoes to him.

"I will," he says. "I like the way you fix it."

"My mother made it this way."

"You haven't told me much about your mother."

"Oh, my poor mother. Well, she was my father's slave. That's all there is to that story. Haven't you heard enough about my miserable history? I think you must be like Toby; you want to know everything."

"I've been writing it down."

"Oh, no. Why would you do that?"

"I don't want to forget any of it. You can't deny it's quite a story."

"It's a horrible story, but no worse than many I could tell about other people. I don't know why I told you any of it."

"Well, because I asked."

"That must be it." She puffs at the cigarette. Though it is hardly diminished, she stubs it out in the ashtray. "You ask so many questions. I never met such a man."

"I have one more, but I'm not sure how to put it."

She takes a deep draught from her water glass. "This sounds very serious," she says. "What is it?"

"Well, it's this. I wondered if, after what happened to you in the war, you could feel anything but revulsion for . . ."

"The opposite sex," she offers. "And all that comes with it."

"Yes," he says. He slices a bit of potato, puts it in his mouth, and swallows without chewing, unable to meet her eyes though he can feel her watching him, amused by his embarrassment.

"Well, my dear historian," she says. "I'm not immune to ordinary human feeling. At least not yet."

Carefully he crosses his knife and fork in his plate and pushes it aside. With a sense of reaching a great distance, he lays his hand across hers on the table. "Jelena," he says earnestly. "Would you please just call me Brendan? Could you do that?"

Her eyes rest on their hands, a smile of surprising diffidence plays around her mouth. "Yes," she says, "I could do that."

"Then do it."

"My dear Brendan," she says.

❦❦

First a marine draped an American flag over Saddam's head, but the Iraqis didn't like that at all, so they substituted an old Iraqi flag. They tied a rope around Saddam's neck, hooked it up to a cable, and attached it to a tank recovery vehicle. Somebody removed the Iraqi flag, the marines started up the vehicle, and after two tries the statue began to tilt. When it hit the pavement, the jubilant Iraqis threw their shoes at it and danced in the dust. "This is a moment of enormous, enormous symbolism, breathtaking," said the BBC correspondent.

Brendan folds the paper and weighs it down with his saucer. British commentators have gotten as bad as Americans; they gush like schoolgirls. Still, it's always good news when a statue of a dictator is pulled down, though what follows can be alarming. The Romans, ever frugal, recycled their statues, changing the nameplates when one tyrant fell from favor and another rose to take his place. This statue of Saddam, described as four times human scale, was put up by himself to himself on the occasion of his sixty-fifth birthday. A great mass of metal, doubtless hollow, but heavy nonetheless; to what junkyard of history did they haul it?

Brendan finishes his coffee, examining his feelings about this news. He finds them decidedly mixed. He wouldn't mind being proved wrong, and he doesn't doubt that the majority of the people in that country are euphoric at the downfall of this brutal dictator. If it all works out well, the world will happily swallow the notion that the end justifies the means and proceed to business as usual, business being the operative word. And if it doesn't, if Brendan is proved right, then this place will become another hell on earth. Therefore he can't, in any conscience, wish to be right. So be it, he thinks. In this case, I'd rather be wrong than vindicated. Let me be wrong.

The scene around him is placid and charming; the wide paving stones that end at the sea, the cheerful pedestrians strolling along the quay, luxuriating in the sun and the fragrance of the salty air. One among them separates and turns toward the café. It's Toby, coming to meet him. He hasn't yet spotted his father. For a few moments Brendan enjoys observing his son unobserved, a point of view rarely available to the indulgent parent. Toby has a long stride, a purposeful manner, but it strikes Brendan that his shoulders are bowed a little, that, amidst the cheerful *Triestini*, he appears slightly downcast. He's lost his mother, he's about to become a father, he's very young. He scans the tables, recognizes his father, and lifts his hand in a mock salute. Brendan raises his forearm, paddling his fingers in the air. When his son arrives there is no further greeting; after all, they see each other every day. Toby pulls out a chair and sits down. "So how were the churches?" he asks.

"Dark, heavily vaulted."

"I haven't done much in the way of tourism. I never seem to have time. And the weather's been so bad."

"It has," Brendan agrees. "But perhaps spring is here at last."

"Yes," Toby says. "It's great today."

The waiter appears, offering a studied paradigm of indifference to their orders and disappearing at once. "We never come to this place," Toby observes. "It's strictly turista, the prices are ridiculous."

"I know," Brendan says. "But you pay for the view and on a day like this, it's worth it."

Toby takes in the recommended view, relaxing now that his opinion has been duly registered. "You're right about that," he says.

"So how is Salome?"

"She's OK."

"Jelena told me you took Vilka to the park this morning."

"She did really well."

"She said you've worked a miracle with her."

"It wasn't a miracle. I just paid attention to her."

Brendan considers this gruff dismissal of praise, which sounds more like pique than modesty. "Do you think Jelena has neglected her?"

Toby adjusts his chair so that he's facing his father. "Frankly, Dad, yes, I do."

"In what way?"

"Not criminally, obviously. She takes care of her physically. But have you noticed that she hardly ever talks to her? Sometimes weeks go by and she doesn't take her out of that apartment."

"It's been pretty cold."

"Sure. There are always good excuses not to make an effort."

"Well, thanks to you, she's making an effort now. You've made her see what's possible for Vilka, and you know she's very grateful. She thinks the world of you."

"That's great, but I feel like I'm trying to teach her how to be a mother, and it makes me wonder what she was like when Salome was little."

"I thought you liked Jelena."

"I do. When I first got here, I was crazy about her. I thought she was so sophisticated and independent. She gets by on almost nothing and she never complains. She took us in and tried to help us without ever being pushy about anything. And I know she took Vilka when no one else wanted her, in the camp. She saved her life. But . . . I don't know. Sometimes I think she's just not that interested in any of us. Salome thinks so too; it hurts her a lot."

"Jelena thinks Salome is jealous of Vilka."

"Does she? Did she tell you that?"

"Yes."

"Is she upset about it?"

"No. It's perfectly natural."

"I hadn't thought about it, but maybe she's right. Whenever I talk about Vilka, Salome changes the subject."

The waiter reappears with the coffee and prosecco. Brendan and Toby grin at each other as he carefully sets them down in reverse order. He takes up Brendan's empty cup and, in ponderous silence, secures the flimsy cash register receipt beneath his water glass. When he turns away, Toby passes the wine to his father and takes the coffee cup in return. "He had a fifty-fifty chance," Brendan observes, lifting his glass. Toby sucks the foam off his coffee, then sets the cup down decisively. "Salome wants to go back to the States," he announces. "She doesn't want to have the baby here."

"And how do you feel about that?"

"I think it's really up to her. I just want her to be happy."

"Yes. I can see how you might want that."

"When are you going back?"

"I'm not sure. I'm not in a hurry. I like it here."

"You must be sick of that hotel."

"I hardly notice it. I've started writing something. I'm not sure what it is yet, but it interests me."

"That's good." Toby drains his cup and glances over his shoulder at a trio of giddy teenage girls passing by, their arms linked, two of them shouting into cell phones. "Actually," he continues, returning his attention to his father, "I think it's time for us to go back. We're wasting our time here."

Brendan pulls his wallet from his pocket and consults the receipt. "What will you do?"

"I guess I'll look for some kind of job. I can't go back to school until fall."

Anchoring a bill with two heavy coins, Brendan finishes the wine and pushes his chair back from the table. "We should talk about that," he says.

Toby does a quick addition of the cash. "Highway robbery," he says.

"Shall we take a walk on the audacious *molo*?" Brendan suggests. "We won't get a better day for it."

"Sure," Toby agrees.

"We'll take a strollo on the *molo*," Brendan quips.

Toby winces. "That's awful," he says.

"I know," Brendan says. Once they leave the shade of the umbrella, they are caught up in the languid *passeggiata* on the quay. Brendan gives his son a long look as they turn onto the *molo audace*, the wide stone jetty that ends in the sea. The filigreed iron lampposts dangling their white glass globes contrast fancifully with the stubby black mushrooms of the moorings; it's like a floating ballroom. The name comes from a ship, but Brendan thinks it might as well refer to the daring of anyone who attempts to walk on it when the wind is high. "When will you leave?" he asks his son.

"We'll stay until the end of the month. The rent is paid until then."

This introduces the subject of money and they are momentarily silenced by it. Brendan takes it up manfully. "I'm thinking of selling the house," he says.

Toby is startled. "Why would you do that?" he says. "Do you need the money?"

"No. But I don't need such a big place and you and Salome will need help. If I sell it, it's worth a lot now. You could buy something small in Brooklyn or maybe the Lower East Side."

"And where would you live?"

"I thought I'd rent something near the college. I'm going to stay on half-time for the next few years, so I'll only teach in the fall."

"Can you do that?"

"I'll be taking leave without pay; they never object to that."

"Can you live on half your salary?"

"I think so. I'll be retiring in a few years and I've got a good pension. And your mother had put quite a bit away in her retirement plan. I was surprised at how much it amounted to. She was always good with money."

"Dad, I don't think you should sell the house."

"I don't see the point of keeping it if I'm only there four months of the year."

"Where will you be the rest of the time?"

"I'll be here."

Toby takes this information in slowly, mulling it over until they reach the end of the jetty. "What will you do here?" he says.

"Well, since you're leaving, I think I'll take over your apartment at first. I'll be glad to get out of the hotel and it's a lot cheaper. Then Jelena and I can take our time finding something larger for both of us." Brendan chuckles as drop-jawed amazement sits upon his son. So satisfying, shocking the young.

"Whoa," Toby says, frankly staggering.

"Don't fall in the sea," Brendan warns him.

"Are you going to marry Jelena?"

"It's too soon to think about that. And anyway, it depends on whether Branko is willing to divorce her."

"This is just incredible."

"Is it?"

"I don't want to hurt your feelings, but Mom hasn't been gone that long."

"I don't think ten minutes pass that I don't think about your mother," Brendan says. He taps his temple. "She's in my head. But this decision has nothing to do with her."

"Salome isn't going to like this."

"She'd prefer her mother to struggle on alone to the grave. I can understand that."

"Don't be sarcastic, Dad. This is serious."

"I am serious. You'll have to forgive me if Salome's opinion isn't as important to me as it is to you."

"She thinks her parents might get back together."

"Has she spoken to her father?"

"Not yet. But she plans to call him when we go back. She's forgiven him for not trying to find her mother. She thinks there's blame on both sides and once they accept it, they'll be reconciled."

"There's something you should know about that."

"About what?"

"Branko knew Jelena was alive. She contacted him before she came to Italy."

"How do you know this?"

"She told me."

"Jesus," Toby exclaims. "This is too much."

"It's a lot at once, I agree."

"I thought we were going to have a conversation about our going home. I was going to ask you if we could live in the house with you until we figure out what to do next."

"You want to live in the house?"

"Well, we did, until you told me you're going to sell it."

"I was going to sell it for you. But if you two want to live in it, it's yours. I assumed you'd want to live in the city."

"Salome thinks the city isn't a great place for a baby. My plan was to find some work until fall and then arrange a three-day schedule at school and commute down there on the train. If I do an independent study this summer, I could graduate in January."

"Really. This is an excellent plan. We'll use your mother's money to pay your tuition, that's exactly what she'd want to do with it. In the fall when I'm there, I'll live in her studio; then I won't have to get an apartment and I won't have to empty out the house, which frankly, I was really dreading."

"You don't have to live in the studio, Dad."

"No. It will suit me just fine. I'd rather not be in the house with a baby."

"Right. I didn't think about that. They cry a lot, don't they?"

"Just at first," Brendan says.

"So we can go home at the end of the month and you'll come to us in the fall."

"It's settled," Brendan agrees. A fishing boat, idly trawling the waves, lumbers past the *molo* in the fading light. They watch it go by, companionable again. "So you're in love with Jelena," Toby says, testing the notion.

"We like being together. I'm surprised you haven't noticed."

"No, I didn't. I guess she has been more cheerful lately. Will she come to America with you?"

"I don't think so. She'd be miserable there."

"I feel sorry for Branko. When Salome finds out he knew Jelena was here all this time, she's going to have a fit."

"Don't tell her then."

"I can't keep secrets from her."

"It's up to her parents to tell her; it's between them. Why should you get into it?"

"I guess you're right. It's hard to know what to do. Will they tell her, do you think?"

"I don't know."

"Poor Salome. She really wanted to fix it all, you know, her family. She wanted it to be like it was before the war. She thought her mother would love her so much that whatever happened could just be erased."

"A lot happened."

"Do you know about it?"

"I do."

"Did Jelena have an affair? That's what Salome thinks."

"She did."

Toby puts his hand over his eyes. "Don't tell me any more."

"You're right. It's better if you don't know."

The fishing boat revs its engine and chugs off toward the horizon. As they watch, the wake spreads soundlessly, smacks against the jetty wall, and washes over the stones at their feet. "Marriage is so complicated," Toby observes. "I thought it would be simpler."

"It's a minefield, actually," Brendan says. "You just have to pick your way through it and hope you don't get blown to bits."

"That's a pretty grim analogy, Dad."

"OK. So maybe it's more like boating. When the weather's good, as it is today, you sail along blissfully, but when a storm comes up, and they do without warning, it takes all your strength just to stay afloat."

"That's not much better," Toby says, but he studies the water as if there might be a lesson in it.

"And then there are the whales and the sharks to watch out for," Brendan adds.

Toby laughs.

"And the icebergs." Brendan consults his watch. "We'd better head over to the restaurant," he says. "We don't want to keep them waiting."

Toby nods, giving one last look at the unquiet sea. "And other people's shipwrecks," he concludes.

The American father and his son cease their contemplation of the deep and turn back across the quay to the old city, where they will join the foreign woman and her daughter.

Acknowledgments

In my effort to comprehend the events that resulted in the collapse of the former Yugoslavia and the brutal war that followed, I found the fiction and essays of Slavenka Drakulić and Dubravka Ugrešić particularly helpful, and I am grateful to them both for their clear, unsentimental rendering of a world gone mad. Brian Hall's brisk travelogue *The Impossible Country* gave me a sense of how this breakup looked to an outsider bent on making friends and not getting killed in the process.

My thanks are due to many people who helped and encouraged me in the preparation of this novel, most notably my agent, Nikki Smith, and my editors, Nan Talese and Alan Samson. Thanks also to Lorna Owen for her careful reading and close attention to all things Croatian.

I am especially indebted to Barry Moser, who kindly offered me a tour of his studio and his classroom, entertained me with terrific stories at dinner, and sent me off with a corrected proof of his book on wood engraving, *Thin White Lines*, which proved interesting, informative, and, like its author, utterly charming.

No day passes when I am not grateful for the ongoing conversation and inspiration provided by my companion, John Cullen, and my daughter, Adrienne Martin.

Valerie Martin is the author of three collections of short fiction, most recently *The Unfinished Novel and Other Stories*, and seven novels, including *Italian Fever*; *The Great Divorce*; *Mary Reilly*, the Dr. Jekyll and Mr. Hyde story told from the viewpoint of a housemaid, which was filmed with Julia Roberts and John Malkovich; and the 2003 Orange Prize-winning *Property*. She is also the author of a nonfiction work about St. Francis of Assisi: *Salvation: Scenes from the Life of St. Francis*.

A NOTE ABOUT THE TYPE

This book has been typeset in Monotype Garamond, a version of the original Garamond first introduced in 1541. This beautiful, classic font has been a standard among book designers and printers for more than four hundred years. While opinion varies as to the role that type-cutter Claude Garamond played in the development of the typeface that bears his name, there is no doubt that this font had great influence on the evolution of other typefaces from the sixteenth century to the present.

Trespass

Reading Notes

In Brief

According to her son, his new girlfriend is 'different' and 'very serious'. Chloe sees lots of dark hair, dark eyes, and sharp features as she moves across the room towards her. She has arranged to meet Toby and the new girl – Salome – in a nice restaurant she knows Toby likes but it isn't long before Chloe is wishing her son had chosen someone like the bright-eyed waitress for his girlfriend rather than Salome.

When Chloe tells her husband Brendan about the meal later, she can't bear to talk of Salome for too long. She just gives him the important bits – Salome is a Croat and daughter of Louisiana's 'Oyster King'. She's also abrupt, and made Chloe feel 'creepy'. Not the most auspicious start, Brendan feels.

Chloe is an illustrator and has to take the rough with the smooth. The last job was tedious in the extreme, but the next will be exciting and she is longing to immerse herself in the new engravings, but first – kettle on. As she settles into her reading chair, she is jolted by the sound of a rifle shot. The report was very close – on her land – in her wood. As she rises her thoughts turn to the doe she had spooked on the way to the studio. Damn the trespassing hunter!

Brendan is jolted from the Fifth Crusade by the shots. He'd only just got going as well. Thoughts of his wife and his son had occupied his morning so far. This Salome at least

sounded different, but he knows that no one would ever be good enough for Chloe's only child — storm clouds gather on the horizon.

It's the Marxist Macalister that is troubling Toby. Is he a threat? The way that Salome is whispering to him, resting her hand on his arm. This is a new one for Toby; he has never faced rejection before. Is he just imagining something?

The first thing Chloe meets after crashing from the porch is a not very attractive dog. Mind you, he's not unfriendly and comes trotting up. The same cannot be said of the dog's owner when he appears through the undergrowth. In a heavy foreign accent he apologises for trespassing, but points out that he needs the rabbits he hunts for food — she doesn't. Chloe's legs tremble as she walks away.

Toby and Salome are coming for the weekend. They have something they want to discuss apparently. As they show Salome round, they discover a rabbit's head by the studio. It seems the storm clouds have rolled closer and it's getting darker in Chloe's world.

About the Author

Valerie Martin was born in Missouri in 1948, and raised in New Orleans. She lived in Italy for three years, and now lives in upstate New York.

She is the author of eight novels including *Italian Fever, Property* (which won the Orange prize) and *Mary Reilly* and three short story collections, the most recent of which is *The Unfinished Novel and Other Stories*. She has also written a non-fiction study of St Francis of Assisi – *Salvation: Scenes from the Life of St Francis*. Her novel *Mary Reilly* was filmed by Stephen Frears and starred Julia Roberts and John Malkovich.

The Story Behind Trespass

It was 2004 and, for some mysterious reason, I was thinking about war. I'd finished my novel *Property*, set in the 19th century, and I wanted to leave the past behind and try my hand at something contemporary, something that wouldn't require so much research. I knew I didn't want to write about terrorists, but I was interested in how Americans responded to terrorism, which is very different from the way Europeans respond. Expressions like 'the war on Terror', bandied about in the press, struck me as peculiarly American and made my hair stand on end. It seemed, apart from our freedoms, language itself was under attack.

At that time I lived in an old farmhouse in upstate New York with seven acres of neglected woods behind it. When I bought the house these woods seemed inviting – I pictured myself walking around communing with trees, building a writing studio where I would have no phone or even electricity. Before long I understood that these things would not happen. I couldn't afford to build the studio and walking in the woods was unpleasant because of the underbrush. In the fall of our first year, the property was invaded by a darker tenant than the deer and the occasional sound of gunfire disrupted our serenity. We heard it at odd, dim hours, 5 am, or just before dark. We had a poacher.

For a while I tried to ignore it — but one day as I was standing in the yard, I heard gunfire very near. *That does it!* I thought and charged into the woods where, in short order, I came upon first the dog and then the man himself. He wasn't a very threatening-looking fellow and I spoke to him politely at first, informing him that our land was posted. His reply was something not quite English and his action was to slink away. I turned back thinking two things at once: first, that he could shoot me if he felt like it, and second, that I couldn't identify his accent. I had also made up my mind that I wanted him off my land.

Until I owned a wood thoughts like these had never crossed my mind. Who does this guy think he is, shooting rabbits on my land? Those are my rabbits! What if he shoots the cat! And so on. Listening to myself gave me a headache. Was it possible that owning land I didn't use put me in a morally compromising position, one that left me puffed up with anger and self-righteousness?

This was the first experience that led to my novel. The second came to me indirectly, through a chance remark. A friend and I were talking about New Orleans food, and he said that the oyster fishermen down the river in Plaquemines parish were mostly Croatians. Croats in Louisiana? How did they get there? A little research revealed that the first wave of Croatians arrived on those marshy shores in the early part of the 20th century, just

before the Great War, and that they had maintained their connection to the motherland, receiving another wave of refugees in the early 90s, when the former Yugoslavia began to fall apart.

I wondered about this refugee community in Louisiana, and whether the people there held onto their language and national identity. So on a visit to my home town of New Orleans, I persuaded a friend to go on a little research trip down the river. On a cool, gray, November day, we set out to explore the hamlets of Pointe à la Hache (which I had always been curious about as it was the town where my maternal grandmother grew up), Bohemia, Empire, and, if we got that far, Venice. I hardly need to tell you that these towns are simply gone now. At that time they weren't exactly thriving. Pointe à la Hache was a burnt-out court house and a dozen houses, Bohemia was a closed-up country store, but Empire was a real town, with a charming neat white church on the lawn of which Our Lady of Medjugorje stood contemplating her own patiently folded hands. This was it. We were in the land of Yugos.

We had been told that there was a marina outside of Empire where the oysterman unloaded the bounty of the Gulf of Mexico. It didn't take long to find it and we pulled into the shell-strewn parking lot. We went out and stood near a truck, discussing whether we should go to the dock and try to strike up a conversation. But before we arrived at

a strategy, a very large man carrying a canvas sack came sauntering towards us. He eyed us closely as he approached, clearly curious as to what two older ladies were doing in such a place – we hadn't seen another woman since leaving Empire. As he threw the bag into the truck he gave a shrug that could have been a greeting.

'Excuse me,' my friend said, pointing toward a barge-like fortress of a boat pulled up at the dock. 'Is that an oyster lugger?'

'Yah,' he said. 'That's a lugger.' He had an accent as thick as a board. 'Do you like oysters?'

'Oh, yes,' she said. 'We're from New Orleans.'

He pulled a small knife with a curved blade from somewhere near his waist and cut the heavy string on the canvas bag. 'You will try these, fresh from water.'

And so began an amazing conversation during which I asked questions and our informant answered, all the while opening shell after shell and pouring the slimy contents down my dear friend's throat. Louisiana oysters are big, and she smiled and swallowed and encouraged him to open yet another. She told me later she'd never tasted anything like them; they were cold from the water and tasted of brine. Meanwhile I learned that our oysterman's name was Josef Major, not, you might think, a Croatian name, but it turned out it was spelled m-a-g-y-a-r, the name of the fierce nomadic tribes that swept down upon medieval Europe

from the Eurasian plains. At one point I asked, 'Are you Croatian?' and he replied, somewhat taken aback, 'How do you know this?' He told us all about the oyster business, the leases he held where the oysters were 'seeded' until they were ready to be harvested, and he waved his big paw toward the water just as a cattle rancher might indicate his bellowing herds; there were his underwater pastures, where the oysters roamed and the shrimp and the pompano played. He also told me he had a daughter in college in Dubrovnik.

'She tells me, Papa, why are you there in Louisiana, you should come back to your country, but I say, I must stay here and make money to pay for your college.' He was touchingly proud of his daughter.

We thanked him heartily and stumbled to the car. 'He's the one,' I said. 'He's the Oyster King.'

A complex history began to unspool in my imagination, a history of refugees and solid American citizens, of a recent war and an impending one, of a bright world in which the threat of the unknown, of the foreigner, the stranger, forever lurks in the shadows, threatening the fragile security of those fortunate enough to live in the realms of light.

Valerie Martin

For Discussion

- In the very first paragraph of the novel, the author prepares us for Salome. How does she do this?

- Why 'Salome'?

- 'Well, perhaps since she doesn't have a mother, she wants to be one.' Do you think Brendon is right? Or does it tell us more of Brendon than Salome?

- 'He has arrived at the source of her foreignness.' How is the theme of foreignness explored in the novel?

- 'Living near the forest doesn't mean we must go exploring there.' Is this how Brendon lives his life? Is it also a wider observation?

- 'She is now and always has been innocent.' Is this true of Chloe?

- How does the author view Europe?

- 'Like so many men, he wanted to have a secret life.' Is this true do you think?

- 'Your mother wants to buy me a new axe, but I never see one I like better than this one.' What does this tell us of Brendan and Chloe?

- 'How clear moral choices are to the young.' Why?

- What is the significance of birds in the novel?

- How many sorts of trespassing are there in the novel?

Suggested Further Reading

The Gravedigger's Daughter by Joyce Carol Oates

Croatia: A Nation Forged in War by Marcus Tanner

Away by Amy Bloom

They Would Never Hurt a Fly by Slavenka Drakulić

The Road Home by Rose Tremain